se who prey

tho

WIT

JENNIFER MOFFETT

those

who

prey

 Atheneum New York London Toronto Sydney New Delhi

An imprint of Simon & Schuster Children's Publishing Division

1230 Avenue of the Americas, New York, New York 10020

Atheneum logo is a trademark of Simon & Schuster, Inc.

For information about special discounts for bulk purchases, please contact Simon & Schuster Special Sales at 1-866-506-1949 or business@simonandschuster.com.

The Simon & Schuster Speakers Bureau can bring authors to your live event. For more information or to book an event, contact the Simon & Schuster Speakers Bureau at 1-866-248-3049 or visit our website at www.simonspeakers.com.

Book design by Irene Metaxatos

The text for this book was set in Aldine 401 BT Std.

Manufactured in the United States of America

First Edition

10 9 8 7 6 5 4 3 2 1

Library of Congress Cataloging-in-Publication Data

Names: Moffett, Jennifer, author.

Title: Those who prey / Jennifer Moffett.

Description: First edition. | New York : Atheneum Books for Young Readers, [2020] | Audience: Ages 14 up. | Audience: Grades 10-12. | Summary: "College freshman Emily is seduced into joining a cult with deadly results"— Provided by publisher.

Identifiers: LCCN 2019046022 | ISBN 9781534450967 (hardcover) | ISBN 9781534450981 (eBook)

Subjects: CYAC: Cults—Fiction. | Universities and colleges—Fiction.

Classification: LCC PZ7.1.M6377 Tho 2020 | DDC [Fic]—dc23

LC record available at https://lccn.loc.gov/2019046022

To Jeffrey

Italy, July 1994

I wake up outside under scattered stars.

I try to move, but nothing happens. I'm too heavy, too numb. A breeze brushes across my face, stirring the smell of dirt under my hair.

My hand is clenched around gravel. I remember the sound of rapid crunching underfoot. The pain when I fell. A voice in my head. *Get up. Run.*

A hand strokes my hair. I hear my mother's voice. *Sweet girl,* she says.

I'm frozen with panic. "Did I die?"

Shhhhhhhh. She's stroking my hair and humming.

A breeze rustles against my ear. I try to scream, but my mouth tastes like it's full of metal. My tongue is heavy and thick. Something is crawling on my arm. No, under my skin. Spiders. Ants. Millions of microscopic bugs. Every pore on my body is taut, covered with goose bumps. My palms burn with scratches. I clench the gravel in my hand as the stars begin to gyrate into a pattern, like headlights moving along invisible interstates in the sky.

A raw terror overrides my discomfort. The humming stops.

Mama? I squeeze my eyes shut. They open again to the same sky, the stars now a jangled blur. I'm alone.

My memories are out of reach, careening ahead of my questions in scrambled clips. *Running. Running away—where is—oh my God.*

My first coherent thought is like a shot of adrenaline: No one can save us.

EMILY X-

A journey into the world's fastest-growing religious cult with the freshman girl next door.

By Julia O. James

AT FIRST GLANCE, her backpack is just like so many others on campus: dark nylon with multiple pockets and zippers. Inside, there are keys and a Walkman, cassette tapes and textbooks—from art history to natural science—and an array of corresponding notebooks with her name at the top of each one.

Tucked inside an outer pocket is a pamphlet.

According to the university's spokesperson, at least four thousand other students received the exact same pamphlet this year. "And that's just an estimate from this campus alone."

The title is printed in bold above a photo showing attractive young students smiling at one another in a sunlit quad:

7 Steps to Multiplying Ministries: A Student's Guide.

• • •

INTERVIEWS FOR EMILY X—

Article by Julia O. James

DR. LUCY CRANSTON, *Emily's Art History Professor (Boston):*
Emily was such a bright student. She was always on time
and prepared for class. She did seem a bit distracted
toward the end of the semester, but this is very alarming
to hear.

SUMMER, *Emily's Childhood Friend (Oceanview, Mississippi):*
I should have called more or sent letters. We talked about
me flying up there, but my schedule got crazy and I never
had enough time off work to visit her.

SADIE, *Emily's Former Dorm Roommate:*
Emily was a sweet soul. I probably gave her a hard time,
and I regret that now. I was going through some serious
personal shit. I honestly don't think she realized I was
using, like, all the time.

EMILY'S DAD, *(Oceanview, Mississippi):*
I do not have a comment at this time.

TAMARA, *Emily's Stepsister (Oceanview, Mississippi):*
I told her not to go to school in Boston, but Emily never
listens to me. That's all I can say, since I really wasn't
supposed to say anything in the first place.

DEBORAH KLEIN, *Emily's Godmother (Zurich, Switzerland):*
This is completely off the record. I don't want you

portraying her as some sort of flighty girl in your— Wait. Would you confirm that for me?

Emily is a seeker, a deep thinker, a brilliant girl, and I think she was trying to get closer to her mother. It makes sense, considering the circumstances. Unfortunately, for her father especially, I believe she ultimately succeeded.

PART ONE

Boston, Spring Semester 1994

"Truth, like light, blinds. Falsehood, on the contrary,
is a beautiful twilight that enhances every object.
—ALBERT CAMUS

Rituals

I'm nose-deep into Henry James when Christina Livingston storms through the common room. Her stale eye makeup and disheveled hair signal her apparent mental state. She frantically searches every corner of the room, even crouching down on the floor to look under chairs and tables.

Trying not to laugh, I imagine my former roommate, Sadie, mock-singing the first thought in my head: *Driving that train. High on cocaine.* It was Sadie's theme song for Christina, but Sadie had other lyric snippets on file just for me, like the chorus to "Here Comes Your Man" when random guys she deemed undesirable walked by.

I turn the page of my book and pretend to read, hoping Christina will go away. She's the type who procrastinates until she has to stay up all night snorting Ritalin through a cut-up plastic straw to cram for a test. She actually used to do this in my room with Sadie when they thought I was asleep.

Christina snaps her fingers twice in quick succession. *"Hey."*

I look up.

"Where's my notebook?" she asks. The animated bears on her T-shirt gleefully kick their way into a tie-dyed vortex as if mocking me. Christina's eyebrows lift into an expression that's both confrontational and patient. As in: I have all morning to calmly harass you until you help me find it.

"I have no idea," I say.

She tilts her head and edges closer. "Well, it was here a few minutes ago, and now it's gone. You're the only person here, so what do you *think* happened to it?"

"I honestly don't know, Christina. I just got here." It's hard to sound nice when it comes to Christina. Why would anyone want her notes for anything other than as entertaining drivel set to the sound effect of a cracked egg sizzling in a pan? *This is your brain on drugs.*

Christina scratches up and down her forearm as she paces. "You know I really don't need this shit from you, *narc.*"

The nickname makes me flinch. It's been inescapable since the morning I finally had to tell someone about Sadie. There was no other choice—her skin was too pale, her pulse erratic. Even when I shook her as hard as I could, she wouldn't wake up, and I had no idea what she'd taken. I panicked.

"Sadie hated you, you know," Christina hisses. My hands begin shaking. I know better than to tell her Sadie thanked me in the ER, where I never left her side, even though Sadie's other "friends" never checked on her once. Before Sadie's abrupt departure, I thought they were my friends too, but I guess the word holds a looser definition your freshman year of college. It took moving up here to realize just how far 1,485 miles (I counted) was to be away from your best friend. Summer stayed back home to work at a restaurant while taking art classes at the community college. It still hurts to remember how Summer rushed me off the phone the last few times I had tried to call her, either running to class or going to hang out with the other friends I left behind. I finally wised up and just stopped trying.

I turn to see Sadie's other so-called friends approach the doorway looking for Christina. *Shit.* I don't feel like dealing with them right now. I clutch my book and barrel out of the room. "Good luck with her," I say as I pass, hoping for a sympathetic reaction, but they stare through me with silent hostility. I rush down the corridor, where each metal door flaunts personalized magnets and colorful Post-it notes with friendly messages. I resist the urge to tear them down to make them match mine: a dull, gray slate.

Blinking back tears, I slam my door and lock it. Silence overcomes me. "Home sweet home," I say sarcastically to

Sadie's blank side of the room, where pinholes in the wall are the only evidence that she was ever here at all. This has pretty much been my life all second semester—in my dorm, alone.

At times like this, I have two choices: curl up in bed and let myself cry, or perform the ritual that keeps me here even when I want to leave.

My eyes flick to the bed before I get myself together and walk up to my phone and pick up the receiver. The dial tone blares into my ear as I think about what I would actually say to the person who answers. Dad would say: *I told you it was a bad idea. Just come home.* Even when he's worried, his voice is laced with a condescension that says I was too young to move so far away. Part of the ritual is never allowing myself to press the numbers when I'm this upset. The dial tone is like an extended wrong-answer buzz—*nope, try again.* Sometimes I even picture a ridiculously annoying cheerleader: *Just give college life one more chance!*

Before, Christina's misdirected vitriol over her stupid notebook was something Sadie and I would have laughed at, easily brushed off, but now it's just one more reminder that I don't belong here. That I never did. With white knuckles, I hang up the phone. *I will not let them be right about me.* I grab my backpack, already running through my checklist of reading assignments as I shrug it over my shoulder before running out the door. The slam echoes as I hurry off, taking me even farther away from home.

As I step out of my dorm and into the early spring sun, I nearly run into a group of girls who are too busy laughing at something one of them said to notice anyone else around them. One sounds so much like Summer that my heart constricts. She's probably in her pottery class at the community college right now, or drawing on her deck under her mom's noisy wind chimes. I miss her, but I was the one who pored over stacks of glossy brochures featuring glittering cities far from home, and students smiling at professors who seemed happy and enlightened. (*"So* staged," my older stepsister, Tamara, had said, rolling her eyes.)

And maybe Tamara was right. Maybe I couldn't see past the idea of new possibilities. Dad even offered to let me take a year off first, since I was barely seventeen at graduation. They'd bumped me up a grade in middle school so I could "stay challenged." Dad had second thoughts about that decision when it was time for me to move away, but I was more than ready for a new beginning.

The sidewalks in the college brochure photos became uncharted paths through flawless green quads. I pictured them blanketed with layers of jewel-toned leaves that would morph into dark gray mazes carved through powdery snow, and then sprinkled with pink cherry blossoms this time of year—far away from all the things back home that never seem to change.

So I chose Boston, even after Dad was reluctant to let me move so far away. Unless I could change my name, nearby colleges would have been a nightmare. Dad's trials had started to attract publicity—it turns out challenging profitable industries, and the wealthiest people at the top, also attracted pretty big enemies. And then there's Tamara's notorious reputation (for very different reasons). I just wanted the chance to start adulthood with the space to stand on my own, without people waiting to watch me fall. I'd already started preferring my locked bedroom to high school activities and social events. And I'm pretty sure Dad noticed, or at least he started staring at me with that glassy-eyed expression, the one that makes me wonder if he's worried I'm turning into the person we never can bring ourselves to talk about: my mother.

On my own. I asked for it. It's what I thought I wanted. But it's hard to see people so happy where they belong when my "uncharted paths" turned out to be regular sidewalks where other people's eyes rarely meet mine.

So now, here I am, every day, walking across bridges that span interstates, drifting through the rectangular shadows wedged between tall buildings, in and out of elevators, and up and down steel escalators. And I've learned that if I refuse to turn around, I stay just far enough away from the possibility of giving up and going home.

My secret study spot is a nearby coffee shop where my favorite chair waits against a fractured brick wall and people congregate behind stacks of books without any expectation to socialize. It's where the outside motion of pedestrians and traffic creates a peripheral energy that allows me to fall deep into faraway worlds that exist only between pages.

Henry James and I have always had issues, the main one being that I cannot get past two pages of his long-winded sentences without my eyes glazing over. But when the story finally does take off, I can actually hear the layered muslin skirts pass by (*a hundred frills and flounces, and knots of pale-colored ribbon*). Gentlemen click by with their canes. And then everyone around me is sipping tea from dainty cups. At the very moment Mr. Winterbourne is pondering Daisy's level of virtue (*Some people had told him that, after all, American girls were exceedingly innocent; and others had told him that, after all, they were not.*), a male voice speaks.

"Do you actually like that kind of stuff, or is it for a class?"

Glancing up, I blink as the world around me sharpens back into focus.

A guy with dark, wavy hair looks at me expectantly from the chair next to mine before asking again, "I was just wondering what you think of your book."

He leans toward me and pushes his hair off his forehead in a casual sweep. The other details of him register simultaneously: navy T-shirt, worn jeans, hiking boots. He's tall with a lean muscular build, the kind you wouldn't really notice unless he gave you a hug. Pretty much the kind of guy most girls would gladly dive into a murky pool of trouble for.

"Oh, um," I stutter, dropping my eyes back down to my

book. It's been so long since someone approached me like this. First semester was full of getting-to-know-you activities and parties—now it seems like everyone has settled into closed-off groups, leaving me stranded on a social island with nothing but textbooks.

"It's for a class," I say finally. "I guess it's good if you like long, complicated sentences."

He smiles. "I prefer Hemingway myself," he says.

I roll my eyes. "*Every* guy likes Hemingway." He laughs, and I begin to relax. "Are you an English major?"

"Yep," the mystery guy answers. "You?"

"Undecided." English is one of the many majors I'm still considering. I fell in love with literature in high school, and Dad says majoring in English would be good preparation for law school, but I've never wanted to follow his path. He just doesn't know that yet.

"So, would you read it for fun?" he prods.

"Eh, I don't know. I'm not sure if I should admit this, but it's my third attempt. Henry James is, like, the king of semicolons."

He laughs. "Well, there's nothin' worse than a mess of semicolons," he says, this time revealing the hint of a familiar accent.

I scoot forward in my chair. "Where are you from?" I ask.

"Louisiana."

"*Really?*" Not many Gulf Coast grads choose to make the move up north, if only for the preference of sun over snow.

"Yes, ma'am. But don't tell anyone." He whispers the last part.

This time, I recognize the smooth drawl, the blurred syllables most people up here pronounce differently.

"I take it you aren't from here either."

"Wow. How'd you know?" I'm sarcastic. I learned to hide my Southern accent at school by talking fast—or not at all—to avoid the mocking that inevitably followed, but sometimes, like now, I can't stop it from loosening into its natural rhythm.

"Okay. Let me guess where." He squints at me. "Alabama."

"Nope."

His eyebrows shoot up. "No? Well, I guess you'll have to give me a hint, then."

I think for a second. "Our states are connected."

"So, we're connected, huh?" His eyes light up with intrigue.

Something flutters inside my chest and dissipates into a slight dizziness.

"Arkansas?" he guesses.

I shake my head no, my lips sealed into a smile.

He leans in closer and narrows his eyes. "I know." He looks around as if making sure no one else can hear us. "Say 'y'all,'" he whispers.

I laugh and look straight into his pale green eyes, the edges crinkled in amusement. "Y'all," I whisper like a secret, laying the accent on thick.

He holds me with his stare. "Well, I can't wait to get to know you better, Emily, so I can hear all about Mississippi." He extends his hand. "I'm Josh," he says.

I reach out to shake it then pause. "Wait. How'd you know my name?"

He nods down at the table where my name is Sharpied in all caps on the front of my notebook. He grins at me. "You think I'm psychic or something?"

Releasing his hand, I try not to seem embarrassed.

His face contorts into an odd expression like he just thought of something else. "A few of my friends are meeting here tomorrow. Want to join us around seven thirty?"

"Oh, yeah, sure." I'm too surprised to say anything else.

Josh picks up his book and stands. "Great. I look forward to seeing you then, Emily." And then he's gone as abruptly as he appeared.

I look around the room disoriented, as if waking from a dream. A guy in gray sweatpants is snoring on the tattered couch beside me. A coffee grinder punctuates the faint sounds of jazz. Two girls with backpacks open the door, letting in the rushing sound of traffic. I catch myself staring at the window for signs of Josh. There's nothing except the constant passage of cars, but I can still hear his parting words: *I look forward to seeing you.*

Smiling into my anthology, I flip back to Henry James. I don't even notice the semicolons this time as the scenes rattle back to life.

Pollock Knows Best

A rt Appreciation is my favorite class, but today I can't stop staring at the bits of paint and plaster stuck to my desk. They sharpen in and out of focus as I trace the bumpy patterns with my finger.

Dr. Cranston is lecturing, yet her words don't register. She's pacing in front of us, her hair sticking out at messy angles. When she clicks the slide projector, I snap to attention. A Jackson Pollock painting appears on the giant screen. "Aesthetics," she says. "Remember that word we learned in our first day of class? What is our personal response to art? How do we attempt to *define* it?" She turns her back to the screen and waves her arm toward the image. "Can you define this?"

I stare into the curved lines of splattered paint where the stringy sweeps of white seem to dance in front of the darkness behind them. The classroom is quiet. Dr. Cranston grabs the cat-eye glasses hanging from a chain around her neck and places them over her eyes. She tilts her head at us, squinting through that moment when professors expect more than we're capable of giving. Sometimes I wonder if they forget we're all just teenagers waiting to receive prepaid knowledge.

"Nothing?" she asks.

A male voice behind me says, "Random splatter." Someone laughs.

She glances at the back of the room with controlled irritation. "I don't mean in the literal sense. Anyone else?"

"Chaos," a girl with braided hair in the front row answers—a drama major, no doubt, judging by her breathy enunciation of the word.

"Chaos. Hmm. I like that. Maybe." Dr. Cranston rubs her chin with cautious optimism. The projector reflects a white light onto her glasses until she turns to tap the screen. "But what if *defining* it isn't the point? Maybe the point is to experience it as a field of energy—and as, in the words of your textbook, 'moving remnants illuminating the act of creation.'"

While everyone else shifts forward to write it down, I picture the words—"energy," "remnants," "creation"—and stare into the dust-speckled light of the projector.

Dr. Cranston clicks to the next slide, a quote from Jackson Pollock. She reads it out loud: "'When I am in my painting, I'm not aware of what I'm doing.' Have you ever felt this way about anything you do?" She scans the room.

I think about exploring museums—a place where I feel the least alone. Circling the same statue or gazing at the same painting has a way of connecting people, even if it's just for a few moments. I also love volunteering at a nearby soup kitchen. It started with a mandatory freshmen volunteer day when Sadie and I signed up to visit with elderly guests for a meal. Although Sadie never showed up, I enjoyed chatting with a nice eighty-year-old lady named Helen. Ever since Sadie left, Helen is sometimes my only human contact.

Dr. Cranston paces again, catching my attention. "Here's a tip. If something makes you feel that way, it's probably what you're meant to be doing with your life."

I stare at my paint-splattered desk and try to imagine the place I'll spend every weekday after college. I wish I could picture it, but I just can't. This is why I'm here. And it's why I stay.

I spot Josh first. I'd been nervously excited to hang out with him—I could barely concentrate during *any* of my classes today, not just Art Appreciation, and spent an embarrassingly long amount of time choosing my outfit, only to end up in the same thing I'd been wearing all day.

Josh sits on a couch in the back corner with two other

students: an attractive well-dressed guy and redheaded girl. They seem relaxed, just happy to be hanging out together. I hesitate at the door, suddenly unsure how to approach their familiar dynamic. Then I lock eyes with Josh, and my apprehension softens.

He stands up to greet me. "Hey, I'm so glad you came. I want you to meet my friends," he says, guiding me toward them.

The girl with red hair is even more striking up close. She's staring at me in an inquisitive way, yet still friendly— the exact opposite of Sadie's friends.

"This is Emily," Josh says. His hand is warm on my back. I can smell the clean scent of soap radiating from his skin.

"I'm Heather," she says. Her eyes are wide and watery and slightly tilted in kittenlike contours, with minimal if any makeup. Her mouth is pursed to the side as if she's amused.

"Nice to meet you," I say.

I look over to the other couch where the preppy guy with floppy brown hair keeps tucking it behind his ears like it's a habit. "Hi," he says. "I'm Andrew." He stands up and shakes my hand. His hands are soft with long, slender fingers, the kind you'd want to tangle into your own during a movie. He's incredibly good looking, but his smile seems forced. And he keeps glancing at the others as if he's distracted.

"Want some coffee?" Josh asks me.

"Sure." I stand there awkwardly as he walks away.

Andrew sits back down and pats the empty spot on the couch. "Have a seat."

Josh is already standing under a giant blackboard crammed with chalk-scribbled options, so I sit beside Andrew.

Heather bends forward to put her bag on the floor. When she sits back up, her hair springs with her. Her curls are loose in a Julia Roberts sort of way, and Heather radiates that same magnetic energy. I've always wondered what it would be like to draw the attention of an entire room. "Josh said you're from the South," she says. "I have good friends from Nashville. They're the nicest people I've ever met in my life. They're like my family."

"Yeah. I guess we Southerners are known for our hospitality," I say. Heather offers me a genuine smile.

Andrew shifts to face my direction and crosses his leg, exposing a blue Polo logo on his tan sock. "You know, you really don't have a thick accent. Not like *that* guy, at least." Andrew points to Josh, who is casually propped against the brick wall, still waiting for my coffee. Heather laughs at Andrew like it's some sort of inside joke.

"Yeah, just ask Dr. Davidson," Heather says. Andrew bursts out laughing.

"Who is Dr. Davidson?" I ask.

"You'll have to ask Josh about that," Andrew says. "It's hilarious."

"Ask me what?" Josh hands me my coffee and sits down next to Heather.

"Dr. Davidson," Heather says with a smirk. She leans over and elbows his arm.

"No." Josh sinks back into the couch and smiles at me. "It's too embarrassing."

"You should tell her," Andrew says. "She'll totally understand."

I take a sip of my coffee and watch expectantly.

Josh exhales a dramatic sigh. "I said 'yes, ma'am' to my psych professor. In class. By the way, don't say 'ma'am' to a female professor—or any female north of Nashville."

Heather and Andrew burst out laughing.

A sudden heat spreads across my face. I actually made this exact same mistake my first week of school. Luckily, it happened in the privacy of the professor's office, but it did not go over well. I'm still too humiliated by the look of horror on my professor's face to share this with anyone.

"What did she do?" I ask Josh.

"Well, she called me 'sweetheart' and suggested we reintroduce ourselves."

Heather cringes dramatically. "And . . . ," she says, hitting Josh's arm as if prompting him to finish the story.

Josh looks up at the ceiling with an amused embarrassment. He shrugs but doesn't elaborate. "And now she picks on him," Andrew chimes in. "Trust me. I'm in there. She calls Josh 'Mr. Ma'am' in class." Heather and Andrew start laughing again.

Heather pulls her feet up under her thighs as if making herself at home. She smiles at Josh again. "I promise. We aren't making fun of you." She tries to hold in her laughter, but can't stop another outburst.

I notice Josh is laughing with them, as if resigned to the humiliation.

"Isn't that the most hilarious thing?" Heather asks me.

"Pretty funny," I agree. Josh's laidback attitude is refreshing. I was so horrified when I made the same mistake that I almost dropped the class.

"So, Emily." Heather shifts her attention to me. "Are you in a sorority?"

I let out an abrupt laugh. "Um, no."

I immediately regret my judging tone. Greek life was never something I wanted to be a part of like a lot of girls I grew up with. "Oh, Em. It's such a good way to meet people," Tamara always said. She was just as quick to judge the other sororities though. "Full of QRs," she'd say, then add in a conspiratorial whisper, "You know. *Questionable. Reputation.*" (Irony wasn't Tamara's specialty.)

"Sorry—are you in a sorority?" I ask Heather. I could easily see her as the girl at the front of the group photo, draped over a giant Omega or X or triangle—a prime recruit.

"Oh, no," Heather dismisses with a flip of her hand. "I'm on full scholarship, so there's no time for that. Also, I like to focus on . . . deeper things," she says. "There are way more important things in this world than watching *90210* with fifty other girls in a common room or getting so wasted that you can't even remember what you've done."

"Amen to that," Andrew says, raising his coffee cup as if to toast.

I sip my coffee through a smile. Where were these people last semester?

"I don't think I've seen you around, Emily," Heather says. "What dorm are you in?"

"The Towers," I answer.

"Oh, nice! Do you like your roommate?" Heather asks.

"Oh. Uh. I don't have one," I stumble. "Sadie, um . . ." I pause. "She moved back home over the break. I guess she missed the California sunshine." I realize the irony in this statement, as Sadie pretty much holed up in our blacked-out dorm room all day and stayed out all night only to do it all over again for weeks on end.

"Ugh, I'm so jealous," Heather says. "My roommate gets on my last nerve. She never shuts up. Thank goodness she's taking eighteen hours this semester and is always in the library, or I swear I would've killed her with my bare hands by now."

I laugh politely. Sadie was likable on her good days, and I actually miss our "camaraderie of opposite upbringings" (as she called it). With her gone, I would welcome an overly chatty roommate.

I shake off the encroaching loneliness and add, "Well, if it makes you feel better, it's never quiet in the Towers, even without a roommate."

"So that's why you study *here*," Josh says. He turns to

Heather. "I met Emily here reading Henry James for the . . . What was it? Third time?" He turns back to me and gives a small wink. I blush.

Heather cups her coffee in both hands just under her chin, her eyes wide with interest. "Oh, tell me about your class!"

"Yeah, it's just a survey class, but I'm really enjoying it." Heather, Josh, and Andrew all look at me, urging me to continue. My words dry up and I shift nervously with the awareness of the attention directed at me from every angle.

Andrew must notice my discomfort and thankfully cuts in. "I adored my survey class. The classics and all. Of course, I'd already read them in prep school," Andrew says.

"Where are you from?" I ask Andrew.

"The Midwest," he says vaguely, straightening his posture. He tucks his hair behind his ears again. "But I was pretty much raised by boarding school headmasters." He leans forward to pick up his coffee and glances at his watch. "Guys, we'd better get going soon or we'll be late," he says to Heather.

Heather looks at her watch. "Oh my goodness, where did the time go?"

My mood suddenly deflates as I helplessly watch them gather their things.

"Sorry, we have a symposium tonight," Josh explains to me, slinging his backpack over his shoulder.

"Oh, no problem," I insist, adding a casual, dismissive flip of my hand to hide my disappointment. "Are you all taking the same class?"

"It's also a Bible study," Heather says matter-of-factly.

I glance at Josh, surprised. He doesn't seem the least bit embarrassed. "I would have asked you to come, but—"

"It's invitation only," Heather interjects, sounding simultaneously apologetic and condescending. She loops her bag over her shoulder and stands. "The reading assignments have to be completed in advance, like your lit class."

"Sometimes we get together just to hang out, though," Josh says quickly. "Maybe you'd like to join us? We could meet here again."

"Sure," I say, still a bit stunned by the abrupt end to our evening.

Josh lingers behind as Heather and Andrew make their way to the door, watching until they're a certain distance away before saying in a mock-serious tone, "Well, I guess I'm going to need your phone number, then." He digs into his backpack and hands me a pen and piece of paper.

I write down my number, trying to suppress the smile on my face, and hand it to him. "Have fun," I say.

He leans down to whisper as he walks past, "Yes, ma'am."

mystical manipulation: when things seem coincidental, but in reality, they are carefully planned and orchestrated

Primary Research

straighten things when I'm anxious.

The photos on my desk are a welcome distraction as I wait for Josh's call. My dad under a tailgate tent, his arm around the freckled shoulder of my stepmom, Patti, in a ruffled top. Me with Summer in her dad's boat, Summer's tongue rolled out in homage to the Rolling Stones logo on her shirt. Tamara's party pics featuring tipsy smiles hovering over red Solo cups. Patti mails so many of these that I've never had to ask why Tamara doesn't call me . . . like, ever. The reasons are printed under the Greek symbols labeling each one: *Woodstock. Sadie Hawkins. Spring Fling.* "Wish you were here." *Yeah, right.*

Then there's the other one, the photo Dad snuck into my

suitcase before I left for Boston: a black-and-white candid shot of my mother. It's slightly blurry, and her expression is distant, like she's lost in a complicated thought sitting under a tree on the campus where she met my dad. Looking at her photo is like staring at an empty blank on a test when you can't remember the answer, and even when you try and try, nothing comes except the blinding frustration that you'll never get it right.

I sigh and put the photo down. My attention moves to my window. Thousands of lights blink and shift outside, like a jittery constellation that echoes my sense of restlessness. When the phone finally rings, my heart leaps as I answer.

"So did you have fun?" Josh asks.

"Did *you*?" I still feel a tinge of resentment over being abandoned for their exclusive meeting.

"I did, actually. Both at the coffee shop and at the symposium."

I pause. "So. You're religious?"

"Are you not? Being from the God-fearing depths of the Bible Belt where there are more churches than restaurants?"

"Well, I guess. I mean—"

"I'm joking with you. The symposiums aren't anything like those churches back home, more like hanging out with friends." He pauses. "But just out of curiosity, which religion are you?"

"Episcopalian," I say. "Of the part-time variety," I add in a faux-dignified Southern drawl.

"Hello, my name is lapsed Roman Catholic. Nice to meet you."

We laugh as I pick up the phone and stretch the cord over to my bed. Talking to Josh is the most relaxed I've been with anyone since I moved to Boston.

"Anything else you want to know?" Josh asks.

I want to know everything about him. I settle for: "Hmmm. Favorite food?"

"What? That's a boring question, but okay. Hmmm. Pizza," he says.

"Ha! That's a boring answer. You don't miss Southern food?"

"Okay. I'll admit it. I'd trade a thousand lobster rolls for one extra spicy crawfish boil any day."

"Same. Here."

A longer pause expands. I rush to fill it. "So what do you hate about Boston?"

"Nothing. I absolutely love it here."

"Really? There has to be something."

"No. I really do. I've made some of the best friends I've ever had."

I'm stumped. I'd always been good at making friends until I moved here, where I somehow managed to drive them all away in one fell swoop.

"I take it from your silence you haven't had that same experience," he says.

I sigh. "Not so much."

"Well, it sounds like you haven't been looking in the right places. Do you want to know what I think?"

"What?"

"I think you should hang out with us again. Heather and Andrew really liked you. Heather wouldn't stop asking questions about you." He pauses. "I, for one, am still not quite sure about you, though."

I laugh. "And why is that?"

"I don't know yet. I think it's going to require some research."

"Research, huh? Microfilm? Microfiche? Card catalog?"

Josh laughs. "I'm thinking primary research."

"And what does that entail?"

"It means I think I need to spend more time with you to figure it out. Why don't you meet up with us again tomorrow? You'll get to meet my roommate this time."

A twinge of anxiety creeps into my voice. "And what if your roommate doesn't like me?" *Ugh*. What was supposed to be a joke makes me sound pathetic and desperate instead.

Josh pauses. "Well, Ben typically likes the same people I like."

"I thought you said you weren't sure about me," I joke.

He pauses. "Maybe I lied."

When I arrive back at the coffee shop the next day, Heather is sitting by herself on the same couch as before, arranging a neat stack of note pads and tiny pencils on the sofa table.

"What's all this?" I ask. I recognize the Pictionary board before she answers.

"Emily!" she says, a genuine smile breaking across her face. "Do you know how to play Pictionary?"

"Um, yeah. I've played it before." I sit across from her. "So who all's coming?" I try to sound casual, but my high-pitched voice betrays me.

If Heather noticed, she doesn't react. "Ben, Josh's roommate, but Josh probably already told you that. And Andrew. And, of course, Josh." Heather smirks before dumping a tiny Ziploc of colorful cubes onto the game board. She glances at the door and suddenly waves at someone behind me. My heart races as I turn to see who walked in.

Josh smiles as they come toward us. A shorter and stockier, maybe older guy is next to him, and I think I see Andrew trailing a little behind. "Hello, boys," Heather says confidently.

The shorter guy extends his hand. "Hi, Emily. I'm Ben."

"Nice to meet you." I shake his hand and smile. He doesn't smile back, but it seems more like an indication of a focused personality than rudeness.

Andrew gives me a half smile, and I'm struck by how different he looks. His hair is cut very short, and a little uneven. It looks like someone attempted a haircut after a drunken night out.

"Nice hair," I offer, sensing he might be a little self-conscious about his new look.

Andrew reaches to tuck away strands that are no longer there. "Thanks," he says flatly.

Josh moves to sit down beside me until Ben gestures for him to sit next to Heather instead. I try to hide my disappointment by turning back to Andrew. Andrew's eyes dart around the circle as he scoots forward. "Are you a good artist? I hope so because it looks like we're going to be partners."

Heather clears her throat. "Should we go ahead and get started, then?" She shifts a handful of curls from one side of her face to the other.

I nervously wipe my hands on my jeans. The last time we met was so easy, just talking and getting to know one another. A board game feels forced—pressured.

"Now, who wants to roll first?" Heather asks.

Ben leans back in the wooden chair between the two couches and crosses his ankle over his knee. "Well, I'm just observing today since we have an odd number." He cuts his eyes at Heather as if it's her fault.

"I invited Shannon," Heather says. "She canceled at the last minute, though." She shoots Ben a frustrated look.

"You can be the scorekeeper," Josh says to Ben, as if smoothing things over. "We don't trust Andrew with that job—competitive prep-school boy that he is."

"I don't like to lose," Andrew whispers to me with a conspiratorial look.

"Great!" Heather glances at Josh as she hands Ben a notepad. She seems grateful, but for what, I'm not sure.

It doesn't take long to break the ice. By my second coffee, we're laughing, scribbling, and guessing words. Even Ben cracks a smile when Josh draws a boat, prompting Heather to guess "Row, row, row your boat" over and over. Josh sketches stick figures flinging themselves into a mass of water, and Heather growls in frustration as the sand drains through the hourglass. Her eyes suddenly widen. "*Life* boat!"

Heather high-fives Josh for breaking the tied score, as several familiar patrons glare at us over their study materials. Being part of the annoyingly loud group—a part of any group—is a welcome change for me. I can't help but smile. How have I been so oblivious that I never even noticed Josh and his friends hanging out here before now?

Ben interrupts my thoughts. "It's Emily's turn."

I snap to attention and pick up the dice. Rolling a five lands me on a tan square with an *A* in the middle of it. "The category is . . . action," Andrew says.

The energy suddenly changes when everyone gets quiet. The suctioning scream of an espresso machine fills the room. Heather stares at Andrew with a pointed intensity as he draws a card and studies it carefully. He gives me an anxious glance before drawing a stick figure with *X*'s for eyes. He adds a squiggly mouth with a tongue sticking out.

"Uh . . . Sick. Food poisoning," I say.

Andrew shakes his head. He draws a tombstone over the stick figure's head.

"Death? Die?"

He sketches a group of circles. They become more stick figures standing over the dead one.

"Um . . . funeral. Bury!"

Andrew shakes his head and draws more circles. He creates another stick figure with a tear in its eye then manically taps his pencil on the group of figures, leaving ugly marks on all of their faces.

"Distraught?" I guess again.

He nods again, signaling me with hand gestures to keep going. I glance at Heather who is fixated on the white sand streaming into the bottom half of the hourglass. "Upset! Mourn?"

More enthusiastic nodding. Andrew draws long straight lines going north to south then east to west. He carefully connects the ends.

"A cross!" Finally, something I recognize.

As he's drawing another stick figure on the cross, Heather makes a loud buzzer sound. "Time's up!"

I give Andrew an apologetic shrug. "What was the word?" I ask him.

"Sacrifice," he says in frustration. I lift my hands to my face and apologize, as he tosses the pad onto the board. "And we don't have time to catch up," he says with a sigh.

Ben checks his watch. "You're right. We've got to run."

Heather leans back against the couch as the guys gather their things. "Aw," she says. "I guess we'll have to stay here all by ourselves. I hope we can survive!" She rolls her eyes at me as we wave bye to them. "They're going to a men's study group. No girls allowed and all that." Heather turns to me. "I wanted to talk to you anyway."

I tilt my head. "Oh?"

"I need a new study partner."

"But we don't have any classes together . . ."

"Not for school, for the symposium! If you want to join, that is." She pauses to take a sip of her coffee. "It requires a *lot* of work—both on your own and with me."

The idea of committing to extra homework makes me pause. My grades are good—they're the one thing I've managed to master up here—but I don't want to sabotage my routine. "Oh, um, my classes take up a lot of—"

Heather cuts me off: "Oh, don't worry. I'll work with you closely every step of the way, and of course Josh and the others will be there for you. And this way you can hang out with us all the time so we won't get interrupted like yesterday."

Spending more time with them, even at church events, which have never much appealed to me, would definitely be preferable to my life as an accidental hermit.

"Listen," she continues, "the group leaders are *extremely* picky about offering invitations, which is why I'm asking first to be sure you're interested. They take commitment very seriously, but I assured them you're incredibly bright—someone who wouldn't back down from a challenge." Heather tilts her head with a knowing grin. "I can just tell that about you."

"Wow, that's really nice of you to say." Her kind words trigger a rush of affirmation I haven't felt in months.

"I don't want you to feel pressured, though," she adds nonchalantly. "I could always tell them to give your spot to an alternate—"

"No," I say, surprising myself when I touch her arm in a reflexive motion. "I'd love to."

STEP 3: Show how life's answers can be found in our official study guides. An exclusive invitation to the Kingdom Symposium is only for the brightest disciples.

L.Y.L.A.S.

My alarm begins its steady beeping at 6:00 a.m.

Just as I start to drift back to sleep, something slides under my door. I get up to see who is out there, but no one's in the hallway. My name is written in giant calligraphy across the envelope on the floor. I turn it over and lift the embossed sticker. A formal invitation is inside:

You are cordially invited to the Kingdom Symposium.

It's at a place called The Castle this Thursday night. There's an address and a folded piece of paper with a hand-written note attached:

Complete the enclosed form with
your Bible.
(Both required for entrance.)

L.Y.L.A.S. (Love Ya Like a Sister),
Heather

The enclosed paper is a chart filled with empty squares and blanks, labeled with abbreviations like *BTs* and *QTs* footnoted with Heather's handwritten explanations. *BT— Bible Talk: partner-guided studies with selected scriptures. QT— Quiet Time: a guided period of personal reflection.* At the end, there's a double line where you total the numbers. Squinting in concentration, I read the instructions to process my first challenge. It reminds me of the balance sheets from high school accounting class that came with sealed packets filled with mock bills and invoices and a green-lined sheet with two choices: debit or credit. I remember my sense of accomplishment when all the seemingly unrelated numbers added up to the same total on both sides. I took the assignment as seriously as someone starting her own business, even though nothing was really at stake beyond a minor grade. My dad always teased me by saying my greatest gift ("and *curse*," he would add) is never being able to do anything halfway.

Scanning the tasks again, I'm confident I can ace this. Then, in a panic, I realize I need an actual Bible. So I gather my things, check my watch, and race out the door.

\|||/

The hushed energy of the library is a reminder of why it's one of my favorite places. I love the electric hum of the fluorescent lights. The challenge of pulling out a card catalog drawer to find an exact book. The tangible satisfaction of writing the letter-number combination on a scrap of paper with a tiny four-inch pencil, just like the ones jammed into the backs of church pews back home.

Past the Dewy Decimal *B*'s, I find the colorful cloth spines of Ancient Greece. I touch them with my fingertips, a habit I've never outgrown, as I glide through a sea of philosophy and a long glossy stretch of newly purchased self-help. Then I see them: Holy Bibles. I pull a black textured leather spine with a cursive font and sit on the floor. The pages fall open to a random chapter, and I scan for interesting words: "moneychangers," "den of thieves," "Bethany," "the fig tree withered away." I've never actually read the Bible—I mean, *really* read it. I open it again, this time to the back where the bright-colored maps with dark brown veins fan across ancient lands, reaching all the way to the Dead Sea. I close it and rub my hand across the front cover to flatten the pages. The leather smells like a relic, triggering a sense of nostalgia I can't quite pinpoint. A tinge of cautious hope prompts me to stand with determination. *I could start right now.*

I walk past the building for my next class knowing I'm going to skip it for the first time. Slowing my pace, I savor the tree-flanked sidewalks sprinkled with pink cherry blossoms, as if a procession of careless flower girls had just passed ahead of me. *This* is how I imagined Boston would be—the picturesque photos just like in the college brochures. The city must have bloomed overnight because the last time I even noticed the trees, they were still bare. I stop to pick a flower and place the stem above my ear, smiling as I cross the street to hop on the T. Once in the Common, I unpack my worksheets under a willow beside the glistening pond.

Looking up the required Bible verses outlined on my sheet, I carefully fill out the chart, including how many verses I read and the amount of time I spent studying each one. The task is surprisingly satisfying—QTs are a lot like my literature homework, and BTs like an independent study, so I decide to go ahead and complete it myself instead of waiting for my study partner like the instructions suggest.

The last thing on the checklist is to say a prayer, but there's no instruction. Praying is something I've never really tried unscripted. Growing up, we were taught a specific prayer for every occasion. Besides, how would anyone even know if I prayed by myself or not? My eyes scan down to the last question on my sheet: *Describe how it felt to say the prayer out loud.*

I sigh, deciding to take a shot at the silent impromptu method. After a few seconds, my thoughts race in multiple directions until my mind freezes up. I shut my eyes and focus on the blankness behind my eyelids.

Dear God . . . No. That sounds like Dad dictating a letter.

Okay. Try again. *God?* Ugh. What? Am I waiting for an actual answer?

The problem is, I don't know what I'm supposed to pray for. All *A*'s? World peace? I open my eyes again with a sigh. *Maybe I can fudge this part. . . .*

I scan the Common, looking for inspiration. When I spot a group of girls in matching shirts (no doubt off to some mandatory event), clarity hits me. My eyes flutter shut as I pray: *God . . . Help me feel less . . . alone.* Just asking brings enormous relief. A comforting presence overwhelms me, as I breathe in deeply and listen to the water lapping against the bank. My eyes open to see willow branches stirring circles into the pond's surface like I've been pulled into a scene straight from Shakespeare: *Willow, willow, willow—a willow grows aslant a brook.* I study and pray until dusk falls, and I swear I can hear the sound of cicadas rising and falling, like something otherworldly calling me home.

I sit there for so long—mesmerized, calm, completely at peace—that I lose track of time. The cafeteria is preparing to close when I dash in to grab my usual dinner to-go before heading back to my dorm. I open the door to my room to find a red number three blinking into the darkness. I turn on the lights and press play on my answering machine with a loud beep. *You have three messages.* The first is Patti. *Skip. Beep.* The second an annoying guy from a math study group I signed up for and apparently totally forgot about. *Next.* I take a deep breath before listening to the third. *Please be him.*

"Hi, it's Josh. Call me." I scribble his number onto my art history notes. My heart races as I dial. He answers immediately. "Hi," I say too quickly. "It's Emily. I'm just . . . calling you . . . back." I sound ridiculous. Why am I so bad at this?

"So what'd you think about my friends?" he says. His casual tone immediately puts me at ease.

"I think you're going to a *lot* of trouble to set me up with Andrew," I joke.

His outburst of laughter makes me smile. "Not the case at all," he says. "We just thought you'd make a better Pictionary team."

"Uh-huh. *You* just wanted to win," I tease. "So, after you left, Heather asked me to be her study partner. I'm still not completely sure I know what that means exactly."

"Really? Wow." He sounds surprised. Heather definitely made it sound like a huge honor to get a spot, but I didn't expect Josh to be so impressed. "Well," he says. "One thing it means is we'll be seeing a lot more of you. Is it just me, or does it seem like we have to leave too soon every time I'm with you?"

"It isn't just you," I say, smiling into the phone. "I can understand, though. It's cool you have friends with the same interests." It suddenly occurs to me that Heather is the type of person who probably actually enjoys volunteering and would maybe like coming to the senior home with me. "I've had a hard time with that. I mean, in Boston."

"Hmm . . . It sounds to me like you're homesick."

"Maybe." An image of my hometown beach with my friends around a bonfire flashes through my mind. "I miss the water."

"I guess you haven't looked out your window yet." He's sarcastic.

The other dorm rooms across from my tower are a grid of lights against the night. My view so often makes me feel small and insignificant, like I'm lost in a sea of windows. Despondency seeps into my voice: "Yeah, but it isn't the same."

"I know what you mean," he says gently.

As our conversation shifts to home, I can picture us talking like this while driving down a wide-open interstate, through lush green mountains until they flatten into a sun-pierced, pine-columned homestretch. Over the rivers and bayous that wind through golden mazes of marsh grass, and into the open Gulf. *Home.*

"You sound sleepy," he finally says in a soft voice.

I sigh, trying to keep my eyes open.

"Listen," he says. "Before I let you go. Don't say anything to Heather about me calling you. It's kind of a rule that I give you distance at this point." I hear someone through the other line say something in the background. "I've gotta go. Talk soon," Josh whispers. He hangs up before I can even say good-bye.

My heart sinks. *Give me distance? And he wants to keep us a secret from Heather?* Suddenly wide-awake, I try not to get too worked up. I pull my covers up and focus on the part before things got weird: If he can't stop thinking about me, then he'll explain.

Better yet, maybe he can explain it in person.

STEP 4: Memorize the Salvation Formula:
DISCIPLE=CHRISTIAN=SAVED.

The Castle

Lights flicker behind the glass of the rounded wooden door, where the friendly sounds of socializing echo from the other side. I've walked by the Castle dozens of times, but I've never been inside. I always thought it was only for weddings and alumni functions. A flash of insecurity makes me pause. Thankfully, when I walk in, Heather is the first person I see in the entryway.

"Emily! You came!" She rushes to give me a hug. "I'll take those for you." She pulls the invitation and completed checklist from my hand. "Listen, I'm about to speak. We'll meet up right after, though," she says before racing into the crowd.

The room is packed with mingling female students. A

woman in a formal black dress plays a grand piano under the enormous Gothic-arched window. My head is thrumming with an eager excitement, similar to orientation week when everyone bonded together through a shared new experience. The same optimism I felt then rushes through me now, except this time no one is making jokes about being forced to be here. We were chosen to be part of this, and not because it's on the same checklist of every other freshman.

I'd almost forgotten what it's like to feel wanted.

Heather approaches a podium in front of the intricately carved staircase. She adjusts the microphone and clears her throat. "Welcome to our symposium on discipling partnerships," she says. Everyone turns, eager to listen. "First, I would like to thank Kingdom on Campus for hosting this event." Heather leads a round of applause. "Without their tireless efforts, these symposiums simply would not be possible. And this incredible turnout is a testimony to their success." More clapping.

As she talks, I can't help but become distracted by this room: the dark paneled walls, stone fireplace, and wood-beamed ceiling. It all seems from another century. The stained-glass lantern above looks like it should be flickering onto a crowd of floor-length velvet dresses. Loud applause pulls me back to reality just as an attractive blond lady wearing a silk fuchsia dress takes the microphone from Heather. She seems more like my stepmom than any professor I've seen around Boston.

"Thank you so much," the lady says in a surprising Southern accent. She puts her hand on her chest as if grateful, and moves it to Heather's back in a gesture of pride. Heather beams at her approval. "As the sector leader for our campus missions, I'm *so* proud of Heather's dedication to spreading our message on the importance of discipleship. And as our top volunteer, Heather made the highly successful Boston Needs project a bigger success than ever. Thanks to the generous outpouring of special donations from students like you, nearly seven hundred poor and needy families were served. With your help, we hope to *double* that amount next time!"

As everyone applauds, a surge of curiosity about the focus on charity work prompts me to make a mental note to ask more about Boston Needs. "Now for the part you've been waiting for. Members, it's time to find your guests and tables." The adjacent room is full of small, round tables topped with place cards. "We'll spend the rest of the symposium getting to know each other and determining your discipleship needs in this beautiful venue. Our goal is to help *you*, wherever you may be on your journey. This is the reason we're all here, so go! Go, go, go!"

The ascending rumble of people searching for one another amplifies the room. I start to move with the crowd, but Heather comes up from behind me and snags my arm. "Oh, no, we're VIP," she says.

Her hand still on my arm, Heather leads me up a mahogany staircase. The din of voices quiets as we climb past an enormous castlelike window where the car lights flash and glow on the other side of night. Heather leads us into an empty room and sets my Bible Talk worksheet on the table. "Sit, sit, sit," she instructs. I pull out a chair as Heather takes a pen from her bag and begins studying my answers. She makes a *tsk*ing sound. "Okay. Now, see? This is why it's better to wait and study together as partners for the BTs," she says.

Soon the worksheet I spent hours completing is covered in accusing blue ink. Maybe I should have followed the instructions and waited to complete the BTs *with* Heather, even though I thought I understood the interpretations.

"I'm so sorry for working ahead. I was trying to . . ." I trail off, desperate to fill the silence with something other than the critical swipes of Heather's pen, but not wanting to say the wrong thing. "Could we maybe discuss what I did wrong? Talking it out really helps me remember later on—"

"Where's your Bible?" Heather interrupts, looking up from my worksheet.

"Oh, uh, here." I dig through my backpack and put it on the table.

"Emily!" Her tone is the one used for puppies that do something bad and cute at the same time. "Your Bible has a due date!"

I laugh. Then I realize she's serious as she waits for me to elaborate.

"I didn't have one, so I got it from the library."

Heather blinks at me. I fidget under her stare.

"How do you not own a Bible?" Her voice is strained, her mouth a tight straight line.

"I guess I left it back home? But I can get another one. I mean, buy one."

Heather picks up my King James Version, scrutinizes the cover, and sets it back down. "Well, don't buy this one. Be sure to get the NIV translation. It's easier to follow the study guides accurately with the more modern version."

"I kind of like all the 'ye's' and 'thine's.'"

She smiles, once again kind (if not a little amused). "Well, think of the study guides as the *Cliff's Notes,* then. They'll save you tons of time with interpretation."

"Knock knock." The lady who was speaking earlier walks into the room. Heather stealthily slips my library Bible under the table and pushes hers between us to share before introducing me to Meredith.

"Well hello, Miss Emily. I'm so glad to meet you." She's even prettier up close. She carries herself like she's famous, as if she knows everyone is looking at her.

We shake hands as I respond, "Nice to meet you, too."

"Now, don't mind me," Meredith says. "I'm just going to hang out over here in case you have any questions." She settles into the other chair at our table as Heather continues reading.

I smile, but Heather seems more self-conscious now as she looks over my worksheet. Her eyebrows furrow in concentration, like it's an assignment she has to ace for a grade.

"I heard you talking about your Boston Needs program. I'd love to learn more," I say to Meredith, filling the silence in the room. "I've been volunteering for and donating to Senior Meals all semester."

Meredith's eyes light up with interest. "That's wonderful!" she says.

"Maybe we could even team up with them? I could put you in touch with the director."

Meredith shifts in her chair, but her small smile never leaves her face. "Well, we typically keep our community work separate from other organizations, so the Kingdom can spread the donations where they're needed without any outside conflicts, and to be sure all the money actually goes to the causes."

"Oh. Of course," I say. I have no idea how that side of a nonprofit actually works, so I don't question it. "Well, I'd still love to be involved with your community project."

"That's great, Emily. We collect special donations for Boston Needs at our Boston Garden services. I'd love to see you there so we can talk more and get you plugged in."

Heather abruptly pushes my marked-up worksheet back to me with a solemn look. "I think we should study together next time." She sounds worried and glances at Meredith.

My face grows hot with embarrassment. Meredith politely clears her throat. She takes my place card from the table and writes something under my name. "Here," she says, handing it to me. She cuts her eyes at Heather and taps the back of her pen against the table to close it decisively. "It's crazy how simple it is. You don't even need a Bible for this. It's all you need to know."

The card reads: *DISCIPLE=CHRISTIAN=SAVED*.

"With Emily, I think we can just get down to the important part," Meredith continues. Heather doesn't seem to notice Meredith's chiding tone directed at her. "Emily doesn't need as much guidance as some others, but she looks like she could use a prayer."

They both take my hands as if it's the most normal thing in the world. I hesitate, unsure of what I'm supposed to do. Though unexpected, the gesture is surprisingly reassuring. I follow their cues when they bow their heads and close their eyes.

"Dear God. Thank you for your wisdom and protection. Thank you for Emily, for her spirit of generosity and for guiding her to people who *truly* care about her." Her voice is composed yet affectionate, not ostentatious like the annoying preachers on television, but also not mechanical like the recitations I grew up saying. It's like she's talking to a well-respected friend. "Please protect her from pain and from stress and from sadness. And guide her through this journey." She squeezes my hand just before saying amen and letting go.

When I open my eyes, they're smiling. Meredith looks

at her watch and stands. Except for her blond hair, I realize she's not at all like my stepmom up close. Meredith seems effortlessly understated, and more striking as a result, like a model in a magazine. Maybe focusing on inner things radiates outward over time. Patti loves to primp, yet there's always something "off" in the end, like a too-bright lip color, or clumpy eyelashes from absentminded swipes of mascara. People used to say Patti was the opposite of my mother— never to me, of course, but I heard things. Since I lost my mom when I was so young it's hard for me to remember much about her myself, so I filed those things away like notations for a scrapbook.

"Well," Meredith says. "It was a pleasure to meet you, Emily." Her hand gently pats my shoulder. "I hope to see you again very soon. Until then, my biggest hope is that you'll continue praying on your own. The secret of prayer is that it actually works, sometimes in the most unimaginable ways."

"Wow," Heather says, looking out my dorm-room window. After the symposium, she was unusually quiet, so I suggested we come back here to hang out.

"Yeah," I say. "It's a crazy view."

"Well, forget the view," Heather says, casually pointing to my neck. "I couldn't stop staring at that amazing necklace at the symposium. It's absolutely beautiful. I've never seen anything like it."

"Thanks." I touch the irregular bumps of my mother's charms hanging around my neck. My hand hovers there instinctively, as if protecting the single thing that's most valuable to me.

Before moving to Boston, I wore it to my high school Senior Day. I'd had it forever, but never had an occasion where it felt appropriate to wear. When Dad noticed it, he struggled to swallow as his eyes glazed over into a faraway stare. I knew why. *She isn't here to see me graduate.* What he didn't understand is that wearing it somehow made me feel like part of her *was* with me. So I brought it to college, where I could wear it freely. The thought of being without it outweighed the possibility of losing it. When Sadie and Christina started getting high a lot, I never took it off—even slept in it—for fear that one of them would swipe it to sell for drug money in a moment of desperation.

As I watch Heather cheerfully exploring my room, I can't even fathom her doing something like that. She stops at my desk, picking up photos and putting them back down. She lifts the picture of Dad and Patti. "Awww. Are you close to your parents?"

"I guess," I say. I don't love talking about my family, especially with new people, but I'm relieved things feel normal with Heather, especially since it got a little awkward after our time with Meredith at the Castle. Meredith took my marked-up study guide with her on her way out and I could tell this bothered Heather a little.

"You must really miss them, being so far away," Heather says.

I think about Dad. Even though I was little, I could tell he'd changed the day we lost my mother. It's as if, in that moment, who he was had been completely swept away. Suddenly his life was full of new things—work, clubs, community events, boards of directors—things that would take up time but never pierce deep enough to get through the wall protecting his heart. I always suspected no one would ever know the weight of what he had lost. Not even me. Then once he married Patti a year and a half later, everyone said what I already knew: He became a brand-new man.

"Yeah," I say to Heather. "I mean, I guess. My dad stays busy, even when I'm at home, so I'm kind of used to not seeing him very much."

Heather gives me a sympathetic smile as if she understands. Her eyes fall back to the photo. "Your mom is gorgeous," she says. "What's she like?"

Shocked by her question, I notice with relief she's still holding the same photo. "Oh. That's Patti, my stepmom. I have no idea what my mom was like."

Heather looks at it again in confusion. Her expression softens as an awkward silence expands between us.

"My mother died when I was little," I explain without even thinking. It's surreal to say it. Everyone at home already knew, so there was never a need to say it out loud. I suddenly feel exposed.

Heather leans forward and gently places her hand on my arm. Her eyes are glossed with concern. "Emily, I'm *so* sorry. I had no idea."

I can tell she actually means it, but an unfamiliar anxiety creeps up my throat.

"Do you want to talk about it?"

I look down, and I'm surprised when a tear drops on the carpet below me. I've never talked about my mom, not really. Not even with Summer. It's not like I avoided it, it just never needed to be said. I was the girl with no mom. What else was there to say? Now the prospect of talking about her with a practical stranger—with *anyone*—overwhelms me. "I mean, I don't, I can't remember . . ." *Why can't I remember?* My throat tightens.

"Em." Heather squeezes my arm and I look up at her earnest expression. "She's in heaven. And it's a real thing, just like prayer. You know that, right?" Her smile beams with the confidence of a person who truly believes it—who actually cares enough to want *me* to believe it.

"You'll get to see her again," she says.

Her words hit me with a physical ache: I've never wanted anything more than this promise.

My Mother Is a Fish

They say I was too young to remember my mother's death, but the truth is, I remember exactly what happened that day.

People believe what's most convenient when they're trying to cope with a tragedy themselves. When you're little, the adults try to sugarcoat anything too horrible to explain. They'll even make it up as they go along with an eager smile that's meant to be reassuring. Once I was able to register the conflicting expression as pity, I knew I would always be known as the girl who lost her mother.

Back then, no one wanted to talk about what happened. But specific details have haunted me all these years, like clips from a movie, those peaceful flashes of mundane imagery to throw off viewers before the unthinkable happens. A fishing boat sliding behind the sharp rocky jetty. The tall concrete building behind us, towels draped over railings. A flock of brown pelicans. The shore littered with boogie boards and colorful beach toys.

We were at Orange Beach, all the way over near the Pass. We used to go there every summer. My mother would always swim in the ocean, just behind the breaking waves— the kind that surprise you with their force in the shallows, then recede so fast you have to wait it out before trudging back to dry sand. I still remember the thrill of being knocked down by the wall of water. The stinging blur of the saltwater in my eyes after each assault.

Back at the shore, battered and out of breath, I turned back to wave at my mother. She smiled and waved back. I watched her vanish into a swell. She resurfaced farther out each time until she finally became a distant bobbing dot in the vast ocean. Daddy was reading a book under a blue umbrella. His eyes crinkled into a smile, first at me and then periodically at the distant horizon where my mother was still swimming.

I worked to create the most elaborate mermaid dress ever made. My fingers dredged the outline of a mermaid tail, and then I began filling it in with the shells in my orange bucket, only pausing for rushed collection missions to the clear-foamed edge of the tide.

I didn't even realize anything was wrong until I heard strangers yelling toward the shore. Daddy stood up so fast he bumped his head on the umbrella. The young surfers charged out with their boards to help. Even under the clipped roar of the Coast Guard helicopter, I just sat there methodically arranging seashells on my mermaid dress because I knew good and well that my mama was sitting right beside me, her wet hair spilling down her tan shoulders like seaweed stuck to her arms, her usual smile telling me it was all fine because she was right there and nothing else going on around me was real. The charm necklace she always wore glistened against her clavicle. She was humming "You Are My Sunshine" when she touched my face. "My sweet girl," she said. And I knew with all certainty that she was okay because we finished that mermaid dress together—her big hand crossing over my little hand again and again until every shell was pressed into place.

Even as I sat under the sterile lights of the hospital waiting room, I insisted that she must be okay because we finished our mermaid. (*I was holding a seashell! I had proof!*) I still remember a tall stranger in the waiting room, an elderly man, staring at me as if both mesmerized and helpless, tears rolling down his wrinkled face. That's when a terrifying sludge of fear slid into my consciousness, smothering my breath. In a flash, I saw the mermaid was washed out, her face a gaping hollowed-out crater of sand, the shells scattered by the rising tide and sucked back into the churning ocean. I felt the icy panic spread through my entire body as a horrible sound forced its way out of my mouth. I'll never forget how that elderly man stared at me in horror, how he clutched his hands under his crossed arms, how he finally had to turn away.

And then my entire life as I knew it faded to black.

But my understanding of what happened didn't last long. She was my mom—she couldn't be gone. So I made up another less-traumatic version: My mother had become a mermaid. I would say this to anyone who would listen.

I drew pictures of my mermaid mom at school, and told everyone stories about her life under the sea. When this started, my teacher sent me to the nice lady in the office near the principal to draw more pictures for her and "just chat about things." I would tell Mrs. Sanderson how Mom shows me her slimy tail, just like a fish, and how it sparkles in every color imaginable. *It's so real.* She smiles and kisses my forehead, then swims off to be with her other mermaid friends. She says she can always watch over me this way, but I hear her only in my mind because she's already swimming away. Her voice sounds like Glinda the Good Witch, from my favorite movie.

One day, Mrs. Sanderson took both of my hands into her own. We stood there beside a giant window projecting a Technicolor world with rays of sunshine gleaming through giant oak limbs and lemon-yellow flowers lining the sidewalks underneath. She tightened her lips and squeezed my hands so hard it almost hurt, and then she told me the one thing that everyone else seemed to agree on when it came to explaining the death of my mother.

"Sweetheart," Mrs. Sanderson said. I remember her smoothing my hair behind my ears and gently putting her hands on my shoulders as if to keep me from floating away. "Your mother went on to be with the Lord."

It was like the whole world outside her window darkened and faded, and even now I sometimes find myself waiting for it to brighten back to the Before. But there's no getting back to the Before when you're trapped in the After.

And that day at school was the last time I ever drew a mermaid or spoke of my mother.

Girl Before Mirror

The next week, Heather sifts through the clothes in my closet, where each rejected hanger screeches with rhythmic shoves to the left.

"Why don't you ever wear any of this?" she asks.

Heather decided we must find the perfect outfits before my first church service on Sunday. "It's important to look as sharp as possible. Our appearance directly reflects our spiritual commitment. And, to be honest"—she lifts a pair of frayed blue jeans off the floor—"you could really use some help in that department."

"Hey," I protest from my bed littered with notebooks, where I'm studying for an art exam. "I've been busy."

"Don't you want Josh to notice?" Heather can't bring up

Josh's name without using that suggestive tone or adding a smirk. I ignore the bait. She still doesn't know he calls me, and I'm afraid of giving her a reaction to interpret. I haven't actually seen Josh since the Pictionary game, but his calls are the bright spots in my day. Somehow, he always manages to catch me when Heather isn't around, which is rare these days. After our conversation about my mom, Heather quickly became more than just a Bible study partner; we are friends, and to Heather that means spending almost every free moment together.

I study the Picassos from my list. The first one is a colorful abstract image of two figures facing each other. The female on the left pushes one hand against a thick vertical barrier; her other arm reaches through it to grasp a distorted version of herself. *This is* Girl Before Mirror. *The barrier is the mirror. Check.*

"A little birdie told me Josh has been talking about you to his Discipling Partner. What do you think about that?" She arches an eyebrow, and turns back to sifting through clothes again.

I pause to wrap my head around this new piece of information. "Who. Ben?"

"Yes. Josh doesn't do *anything* without Ben's approval, and Ben can be very . . . well, let's just say, opinionated."

I remember how Ben's presence at the Pictionary game sparked a sense of edginess. It was so contrary to my first encounter with just Josh, Heather, and Andrew. An uneasiness seeps into my thoughts.

Heather inhales a sharp gasp. "Oooo, Em. This is cute. Can I borrow it?" She pulls out a forest green skirt and matching beaded top.

"You can have it," I say.

"Wait. They still have the tags on them," Heather says, frowning. "Are you sure?"

"It's okay. I don't care."

I've never liked the clothes my stepmother Patti bought for me, but I don't have the heart to tell her. Throughout high school she tried so hard to bond with me in the only ways she knew how, shopping being the primary one. So when I first broke the news to Patti and Dad about going to Boston for college, she spent months scouring catalogs to acquire a cold-weather wardrobe for me, something I'd never needed on the Gulf Coast. The problem is she's never quite processed the fact that I don't dress like my stepsister, Tamara. Patti would literally faint if she knew I wore the same 501s and faded sweatshirt four days in a row without washing them.

I look back down at the list of art left to memorize. A twinge of anxiety darts through my mind. I've only checked off three things. It's the first time I've ever allowed myself to get behind in art history—in any of my classes—and my exam is tomorrow morning. I haven't even been to the coffee shop to study since we played Pictionary.

Although the Quiet Time and Bible Talks have been cutting into my studies, I really look forward to them. My

QTs, the solitary periods of reflection and prayer, leave me centered in a way I've never experienced before, and I like the challenge of the BTs, the study guides staggered with blanks, and the slippery sound the onionskin pages make as we search for the answers. When a verse interpretation confuses me, Heather guides me to its true meaning.

Heather practically lives in my dorm room now. We've even started meeting up at lunch, sometimes ditching the cafeteria for the food stalls at Quincy Market, trying something new each time. Since I met Heather, Boston has become an exciting city I enjoy exploring, but it also feels more like *home*—something I never expected to feel.

I look up the next image as Heather struggles with the zipper of the suede skirt. I smile at the goofy way she's contorting herself to get it to zip. I've never met anyone with more determination than Heather.

"Just wait until you hear him speak," she says, as she closes the stubborn gap with a quick *zip*.

"Who?" I'm looking at my notes again, suddenly overwhelmed by the stress of having to memorize more than one hundred images in my art history book, which is open to a full-page reprint of Botticelli's *The Birth of Venus*.

"Um. Earth to Emily?" Heather turns around to shoot me a disapproving look. "The *Leader*," she answers. She pulls the top over her head, and then frees her hair from its neckline. Maybe it's my fatigue, or the utter desperation to cram for this exam, but in that moment, Heather's reflection

looks eerily similar to Botticelli's redhead perched atop the
half-shell in my textbook. Only a nineties version, clad in
Ralph Lauren.

I smile as I look back down at my list and write:
Heather = Venus, then place a check mark beside the word
Botticelli with a small wave of relief.

Heather begins digging through my closet again. She
pulls out a green and pink floral-print Laura Ashley outfit,
the kind with a Peter Pan collar and balloon-shaped pants.
"Nooo, no, no," I say, remembering the day I got the outfit
in the mail. The note said, "I thought this would look so
cute on you. Love, Patti." I also remember how Sadie had
walked into our dorm room just as I was trying it on, and
then proceeded to laugh at me periodically for the rest of
the day.

"Oh, this will match the green in my outfit perfectly,
though," Heather says. She hangs it on my closet door and
stands beside it. *"See?"* she pleads.

I picture my stepmother watching this unfold with a
tight-lipped smile, her eyes sparkling approval. *Oh, Emil-
eeeeee*, she'd say. *It just makes me so happy that you liked it.*
Maybe I'll mail Patti a picture of Heather and me together
to appease her two nagging concerns: bad fashion choices
and lack of friends. "All right. Fine," I say, determined to get
back to my notes.

I have exactly two hours to finish studying if I want to
get a decent night's sleep and wake up in time for my QT

before the exam. I try to block out my other assignments and the packed calendar of looming deadlines.

"It's settled, then," Heather says. She peels off the skirt, pulls her jeans on, and looks down at her watch. "Oh! We almost forgot about our BT!"

My face turns numb with panic. "Heather. I've *got* to study for art. I'm scared I'm going to fail this test."

"I have an idea," she says, grabbing an index card off my desk. "We can have a shorter BT . . . without Bibles." Her eyes flicker defiantly.

I sigh. "Okay, as long you *promise* it will be quick." I sit up and re-clip my hair—still hesitant but grateful for her concession. Heather hands me an index card and leads me to my desk chair.

"Okay. Close your eyes." I do as she says and breathe in. "Think about your frustrations. Think about specific things. Like a list. What frustrates you more than anything? It could be people, places, situations, anything. Just think about it, and then write it all down on this card."

I open my eyes and scoot my chair up to the desk. My mind begins spewing frustrations faster than I can write. Exhaustion. This dorm. Noise. Deadlines. Papers. Exams. Not enough time to roam museums. Sadie. Sadie's friends staring through me. ANGER. (*Why am I so angry?*) My mother will never see me graduate from college. Or get married. My mother will never know me at all. I will never know her. Dad.

Rage creeps into my hand as I write. Then a wave of sadness overlaps the anger.

"Are you done?" Heather is smiling at the success of this activity, but her tone changes when she notices my expression. "Trust me, you'll feel better in a sec."

As I look at my card jam-packed with scribbled words, I feel gutted and exposed. "Are you going to read this?" I ask.

"Of course not. This is just between you and God. Fold it in half if you want."

I fold the card over and press the edge back and forth.

"Just focus on one thing: your life without *any* of these frustrations. How would it feel? Kneel on the floor and close your eyes, and then hold your card in your hand."

I follow her instructions.

Heather moves around as she talks. "Think about your life free of every single item on this card as you rip it up."

I tear it slowly. It's a satisfying sound. I stack the halves and tear through them again. And then I rip it into over and over. I look down at the shredded mess.

Heather goes to my window and yanks it as far as it will open. The traffic noise drifts inside as the wind gusts into the room. I inhale the cool breeze as she looks at me expectantly. "Now pick up those pieces and let them go."

Gathering the paper fragments, I approach my window. In the distance, the surface of the river reflects a glittery patch of buildings. Down below, people stroll in every direction. I fling the pieces out the window, where they disappear into the night like secret confetti. As the fragments of words fall toward the sidewalk, I imagine one falling into an unsuspecting passerby's bag filled with mundane necessities, carried too far away to ever be recovered. It feels like the words on that list don't even belong to me anymore.

Heather slams the window shut. "All gone," she says with a wide smile. "See how easy?"

I stare out the window into the blinking night. A sense of peace overcomes me. I can't remember ever feeling this *free*. For years I've been carrying burdens that no one ever noticed or bothered to care about—until now. People I've only known for a few weeks have shown me more kindness and care than people I've known for my entire life. I look to Heather, a comforting and supportive smile on her face, and I can't help but believe that maybe this really is the way.

love bombing: the use of attention and affection to influence an individual; induces a social high and instills a deep trust; can lead to physical attraction

A Place You Miss the Most

The first one is delicately perched on my Art Appreciation desk.

I haven't seen an origami animal since elementary school when a classmate's mother showed my class how to make them. We were given squares of thin, bright paper and a list of instructions for folding it in specific directions. I still remember the mess I made of my attempt that day, but this one is a perfect swan with an elongated neck made of notebook paper. It sits on my desk like an elaborate question mark.

I slide into my seat and glance at the guy beside me. His face is buried into his arm. I turn around. The girl behind me is scanning her notes.

"Excuse me. Do you know who left this?" I hold up the swan.

"No," she says, glancing at me for a mere second before looking back at her textbook. She tugs at the French braid draped over her shoulder and squeezes her eyes shut as she mouths answers to the possible questions Dr. Cranston may throw at us.

I probably should be cramming too, but now I'm way too distracted. I've been sitting in the same spot since the first week of class—this had to be for me, right? I pick up the swan and see the red ink on the undersides of the folded paper, my name written in a tiny masculine scrawl along the other side of its neck. *Open me*, it says.

I carefully pull its tail until Dr. Cranston's voice interrupts.

"Put your books and notes away, everyone. Time for your exam."

I slip the swan into my backpack and try to focus on what I memorized the night before.

The moment the test is over, I rush out of the classroom. Students stream around me as they crown themselves with headphones, their Walkmans hissing a cacophony of lo-fi music from wherever they clicked stop before class. I pull the swan out of my backpack and lean against the wall to tug at its folds, struggling to get to the message inside:

The next one lies
in a pond
on the back of a swan.
Today at one.

I try to imagine Josh writing these lines or even folding this piece of paper. It just doesn't seem like him based on the little I know. But who else would it be? I wander through the glass doors and into the sunlight. As I'm crossing Commonwealth, a bus glides by a little too closely. It honks a warning just as I figure it out. *The Swan Boats.*

By the time I get to the Common, there's a line of tourists. The Swan Boats always seemed like the equivalent of a carousel ride at the mall, yet today I'm eager to board. I scan the benches on the boat. Nothing. The back row is empty, so I slide across just as the young boat driver settles into a metal tractorlike seat behind a large carved rendering of a swan.

As we take off, I try to relax. A sense of freedom hits me as the boat disconnects from land, but I can't stop searching the grassy banks for Josh. The breeze makes me smile. Trees hover politely along the curved bank, the wall of buildings creating a solid fortress behind them. And, for a moment, I forget why I'm here.

"Are you Emily?" a voice behind me asks.

I spin around to see the boat driver pulling something out of his shirt pocket. He's smiling when he hands me an origami fish.

"Do you know who left this?" I ask.

"A tall guy," he says. "Like maybe a student or something." I realize by his constant movement that he's actually pedaling our boat. He looks over me as if focusing on our route. I turn around to open the fish:

Come find me in
A place you miss the most
Near countless boats
Glass walls inside
Where fish can hide but there's no tide.

My mind spins. Glass walls inside. Where fish can hide.

The moment the Swan Boat docks, I rush to the T and check the wall map to find the aquarium stop. When I get there, I push through the metal doors and maneuver around the crush of people. The smell of saltwater fills the air. A bold sense of adventure consumes me as I hold the origami fish. I'm almost positive I'm looking for Josh. A tinge of insecurity seeps in as I imagine him going to all of this trouble. I never received this much attention before; even my high school boyfriend wasn't this thoughtful. It's enough to make me giddy.

I look around again to see thick crowds of families with kids, tourists with maps, guides corralling people onto a ferry. Just as I begin to doubt my understanding of the riddle, someone taps my shoulder. Josh's smile is mischievous.

I swat his arm reflexively. "Seriously?" I hold up the origami.

"What? Did you make that for me?" He smirks.

I swat his arm again, my adrenaline high still strong.

"Hey now." He wraps his arm around my shoulder as we
walk together. "Just come with me." He hands me a ticket
as we walk past the line snaking around the corded guides. I
steady myself against him, fighting the light-headed effects
of our surprise first . . . Wait. Is this a date?

My nerves begin to calm as Josh leads me up the spiral landing surrounding the cylindrical tank that runs all the
way up to the ceiling. The eerie glow of the room adds a
sense of intrigue, like we're on some kind of mission. I laugh
at this thought, and he gives me a mock-offended look.

"Why are we here?" I ask him.

"Isn't this what you said you miss?" he asks.

"Fish tanks?" I joke.

"No, silly. The water."

"I know," I say with a side glance. I can't believe he
planned all this for me. My smile won't leave my face. We
keep walking along the glass walls spiraling upward, as if
mesmerized, swept up in the same momentum as the fish.
"It's amazing to me how they crammed the entire ocean into
this tiny place," he says.

A bright yellow fish darts along the window as we circle
upward. I try to follow it, but it swims into the middle, out
of view. I turn to him. "Are your friends here?"

"Nope."

"Wow. So we're actually alone?" I mock gasp. "What would Ben and Heather say?"

Josh doesn't answer. He suddenly seems uncomfortable, looking down at his feet instead of the fish. "Sorry, I was just joking . . . ," I say, kicking myself for bringing it up and ruining the moment.

He looks at me. "I know you must think this is all kind of strange. And I guess it is." He turns his back to lean against the glass wall. When he looks at me again, I focus on a giant mountain of coral to avoid eye contact so he won't see that yes, I think it's a little strange that the Kingdom is having such a positive impact on my life, but the random stipulations are becoming extremely frustrating. "I just wanted to find a way to see you again, without anyone else around," he continues.

"You mean, Andrew isn't around the corner waiting for me to disappoint him in Pictionary again?"

Josh laughs, but his expression is still pensive. He looks like he's struggling with an explanation, yet can't figure out how to start.

"Listen. I'm happy you did this," I say, sensing enough of the upper hand to be assertive. "I mean, no one has ever made origami for me before." I smile up at him. "It's just . . . I don't understand why you didn't just call me to ask me out. I can go ahead and tell you the answer is yes." I push at his chest playfully. He still looks serious.

"But I couldn't say yes. I mean, not yet, so we have to be careful."

I quietly trace my finger along the aquarium glass. A large fish glides by out of nowhere, startling me before swimming away. My emotions are shifting so quickly that it's difficult to pinpoint anything beyond confusion. "Okay. I don't understand."

"It . . . it's complicated. There are rules I should be following, and you should too, until you're saved." He exhales as if relieved to have finally said it.

I run my finger along my mother's charm necklace out of habit. "What do you mean by saved?"

"Saved means baptized. And Heather can make the road to that step very intense. Look. I want to hang out with you. Why do you think I'm taking this chance?" His eyes seem genuinely conflicted, and I let myself look into them a few seconds too long under the dim glow of the aquarium lights.

"I've been studying with Heather every day. I'm even going to church with her soon."

Josh runs his hand through his hair. "There's more to it than that. I mean, there's more to learn in the BTs, and when you're baptized, it's probably a little different than what you're thinking. You have to be dunked all the way underwater."

"That's no big deal. Half my friends back home were baptized that way."

"But . . ." He fidgets with his shirt before looking into

my eyes; his expression is earnest, almost vulnerable. "It's so much more than a technicality," Josh says.

"What is it, then?" I ask. I narrow my eyes in concentration, eager to understand, yet also hoping it won't be something like believing we're all secretly inhabited by aliens from another planet. A mother with a stroller moves toward us to get a closer look at the glass. Josh and I step to the side, making room for them.

"Okay," he continues. He nudges my arm and we step into another empty spot by the glass for privacy. He's almost whispering. "Just imagine the worst things that ever have happened to you. Or the worst decisions you ever made. Everything in your life you've ever regretted." His eyes gleam with a sincerity so rare with guys my age. "Have you ever wanted to feel free of those things for good? To know there's no way they can ever come back to haunt you?"

"Yes," I say without hesitation. I stare at the fish again, pretend to watch them swim, but Josh's words are stirring something in a long-hidden corner of my heart. It's hard to remember a time when I haven't been generally depressed on good days and with acute heart-wrenching pain on the bad ones.

"Here's what I know," he continues, breaking me out of my own thoughts. "Those negative things can be completely erased. All of it. Everything in your future can be freed from your past. I wish I could describe the feeling I had at my baptism. It was basically pure . . . relief." His expression turns sheepish, like he's a little embarrassed to have revealed something so personal.

"It sounds amazing," I say, eager to dispel any awkwardness. "I mean, sign me up for the zero-negativity life." I lift my hand to mock-volunteer. Joking closes the door to the protected part of my heart that was stirring just moments ago.

As Josh laughs, I can see relief replace his unease from before. Then he leans into me and brushes his fingertip along my cheek. "You're amazing. Do you know that?"

My head feels like it's swimming sideways, even though I'm trying everything within my power to stay composed. "So," I say, my protective defenses still up. "Important question. Once I'm dunked, do we still have to hide back here with these stingrays?"

Josh lets out a laugh. "Only if you want to." He gives me an amused side glance—a there's-more-to-you-than-I-expected look—before casually taking my hand. As I twine my fingers into his, something hits me: Maybe it's finally possible to be the real me here in Boston. Or an even better me. The confident almost-adult me living in a big city holding hands with a nice guy I could be really into.

We stroll to another window and stop where the view appears so different that it seems like a completely separate world. A few elementary kids in school uniforms crowd to our window. They squeal and jump back as an enormous stingray glides up against it, revealing its stark underbelly. Josh gently pulls me away to walk through every corner of the entire aquarium, not saying much beyond pointing out cool fish, our hands still connected, until we finally have no other option than to spiral back down and exit the building.

His hand lets go of mine when he opens the door, and my disappointment catches me off-guard. The brightness outside is blinding, maybe too bright to hold hands out in the open. We stand awkwardly, exposed in the afternoon sun after being in the dim aquarium, not knowing what to do next.

"So . . . ," I say like an open-ended question.

He looks around as if scanning the crowd before looking back at me with a strained expression. "So, can you promise me something?"

I lift my chin, curious. "What?"

"Listen. I know I already said not to mention our phone calls to Heather, but do you think we could keep today just between us? I feel terrible asking because she's your friend. She may not understand, though. . . ."

I exhale a defiant sigh. "Understand what? We're just . . . hanging out. I really don't get why it's such a big deal." I glance away, annoyed by his mixed signals. Why would he kill the mood like this?

Josh opens his mouth to say something, and then closes it. He lowers his voice and looks into my eyes. "It's kind of a rule that I can't quote-unquote officially hang out with you until you finish all the steps. No one wants you to feel pressured. And I really want to . . . hang out with you." He smiles. Butterflies whirl through my body, dissipating some of my aggravation.

While the secretiveness is annoying and I don't like the idea of keeping things from my only friend in Boston, the Kingdom is clearly important to Josh. And if he's willing to break the rules for me, the least I can do is keep quiet.

Desperate to drag this day out as long as possible, I scan the Long Wharf harbor, past the flurry of people and tents. The toothpick masts of distant sailboats levitate above the water. A water horn blares off the triangular huddle of old brick buildings. My eye catches a ferry sitting restlessly in its dock. "Well, I don't actually see Heather anywhere around here. Do you?"

"Nope," he says.

"I think I know how we can hang out just a little bit longer today," I say.

This time, I take his hand and lead him to the dock.

"You're *late*." Heather tilts her head back and peers down her nose at me.

I'm also sweaty and trying to catch my breath. After the ferry, I realized the time and rushed back to my dorm, but I wasn't fast enough. Heather was already waiting for me at my door.

"I'm so sorry. I lost track of time. . . ." I trail off, not wanting to say too much.

She makes a disgusted face as I walk past her into the room. "Why do you smell like fish?"

"I was walking." I fidget with my shirt. "By the river."

"Oh." She sounds surprised I wasn't out doing something to warrant a lecture. "Well, call me next time so I can go with you. Meredith has been on my case about exercising. I need to lose at least fifteen pounds to meet my goals."

I let out a relieved breath. "I promise."

"Listen, I have to go set up for our meeting, and you stink. Please take a shower before you come. Your appearance directly affects my ability to lead—"

"I'll be ready," I interrupt, already pulling clothes out of my closet.

Her eyes narrow at my curtness. "Don't be late," Heather orders on her way out, closing the door with more force than necessary.

The moment she's gone, my eyes burn with tears. Her burst of negativity was unexpected. And it hurts knowing that Josh is probably right—she wouldn't understand why we're breaking the rules. Every time I start to feel like things are actually going well, obstacles stack themselves in front of me all over again. They stretch out in my mind as far as I can imagine: meetings, studies, classes, QTs, BTs, answering to Heather, knowing the right answers. I want to experience that sensation of our ferry boat detaching from land again, to feel Josh wrap his arm around my shoulder.

Even though I'm grateful for the Kingdom community,

the extra pressure of so many mandatory tasks is like being on a roller coaster that never slows down. And her rudeness just now was totally uncalled for.

The urge to talk to my dad suddenly overpowers my ability to talk myself out of it. Maybe it will make us both feel better. I pick up the phone before I can reconsider it. My heart beats faster as I press the numbers. My dad's paralegal, Jean, picks up on the other end.

"Hey, it's me, Em. Is my dad there?"

Jean makes an apologetic moan on the other end of the line. "Oh, honey. You just missed them! They went up to Oxford. Didn't he tell you?"

He hadn't. Then again, I couldn't actually remember the last time we'd spoken directly. Patti and Jean have always fielded his updates when he's busy with a trial. The heavy weight of regret settles in the pit of my stomach.

"You could try him at the condo but there's no telling where they are right now. He's supposed to call for his messages, though. Do you want me to give him one?"

"Just tell him I'm finally going to The Garden this weekend." A rogue tear streams down my face. Jean doesn't seem to notice my shift in tone.

She laughs. "Ooooh! He'll love that."

"Yeah," I say. "Thanks, Ms. Jean."

I'm staring at the Charles River but seeing the winding marsh behind our house where Dad grills steaks, tilts back Heinekens, and used to play with our old dog, Sasha. The dull ache of homesickness creeps into my chest. I shut it down with the end-click of my phone.

All those times I didn't call because I didn't want to worry him, it never occurred to me he wouldn't have been there anyway.

Cheap Imitation

've never imagined the Boston Garden in this context.

Jam-packed Celtics game? *Yes*. Sold-out Grateful Dead concert? *Yes*. But a church service with eight thousand people in attendance is not something I expected to see in such a famous venue. The crowd rumbles in collective anticipation, like music fans right before a concert they've waited months to see.

My dad once told me all about the parquet floor at "The Garden." This was when he'd finally absorbed the fact that I was going to school up here. Dad was sharing trivial facts about a random subject (his way of bonding) when he told me the basketball court—made up of 247 wooden panels, to be exact—was notorious for "dead spots," or places where the variation in wood affected the way the ball bounced. Only the home team knew exactly where the dead spots were hidden so they could use it to their advantage.

I follow Heather in search of two adjacent empty seats in a sea of occupied rows that stretch down the curve facing the coliseum stage. A few college guys beside the aisle turn to check out Heather as I trail behind, embarrassed by the Laura Ashley outfit she'd picked out for me. We're running late because she insisted on fixing my hair right before we left, which resulted in forty-five minutes of making spiral ringlets with a tiny curling iron. She carefully ran her fingers through the springy curls, turning them into soft waves, just like hers, as she reminded me to bring my donation for the Boston Needs program. "They pass around a donation plate during the service, so it's better to have it ready before we get there."

Today, the air is charged with excitement. The crowd is boisterous and happy and diverse—far more than the churches back home. Rows of folding chairs line the floor facing the large stage, which is anchored by stacks of speakers and glossy-green plants. Small children are sprawled out drawing on their bulletins in front of the first row. When music starts playing, everyone rises to clap and dance, forming a chain with each person's hands linked to the next person's back. One song is familiar:

People all over the world

Join hands
Start a love train, love train

In between songs, I hear rapid-fire French behind me. There are couples with babies, older people, and young people (*lots* of young people) from all over the world. I've never seen so much enthusiasm during a religious ceremony, or so many different people coming together under the same roof of a church. Back home, churches always felt like an exclusive validation of preexisting social circles full of people who were already alike. This is the opposite. It's like a multicultural Benetton ad for God—a place where everyone is not just welcomed, but also *celebrated*. I can't stop looking around in awe. Heather flashes a knowing smile, like she knew I'd love this.

I crane my neck, seeing if I can spot Josh in the crowd. Heather said all the college students attend the Boston Garden service. Then I remember the outfit she talked me into wearing, and I'm grateful to blend into the vast crowd of people.

The singing stops abruptly and a palpable anticipation blankets the audience. It's a Larry-Bird-shooting-a-free-throw-in-overtime kind of hush. All eyes are focused on the stage. Rows and rows of faces reveal the same eager expression. Then everyone around me, including Heather, begins pulling out little notebooks and pens.

"Should I take notes?" I whisper to Heather.

"It's better if I take them for you at this point," she whispers back. Then the Leader takes command of the stage. We're too far away to see him clearly, but his face is projected onto the enormous JumboTron screen. He looks like a normal person around my dad's age, maybe younger, with clean-cut blond hair and an expensive suit. He reminds me of the young trial lawyers Dad has over for dinner. I recognize the same confidence and swagger, that effortless ability to captivate any given audience. It's his voice that draws me in. It has the assured instinct of knowing when to soothe and when to demand everyone's attention.

I settle into my seat and listen to the flow of words, the wave of laughter at his jokes, the occasional "amen" or "that's right" from the crowd. Even though it's so different from the tiny church where I grew up, the big crowd is exhilarating, like an affirmation we're all on the same side, rooting for a worthy cause. It's as if he's placing a warm hand on our shoulders all at the same time, reassuring us he's the chosen man who took the lead—the one who'll bring us all home.

"Today we've set a record! *Eight. Thousand.*" Wild cheering undulates through the crowd. I scoot to the edge of my seat and look around. A girl to my right unleashes an outburst of joy. The Leader lifts his hand to silence us. "Eight thousand disciples are here to celebrate our victory. *God's* victory. What do you think about that?" I jump up, even before Heather, to cheer with everyone else. Swept away by the momentum of the crowd, my eyes are glued to the stage to see what happens next.

"How many of you are good at math?" he asks. More cheering, with a few jeers from students, including Heather. I laugh as the Leader chuckles on stage. "Don't worry. I struggled with it too, but I wrote it down beforehand. Here. See if you can follow this. A small group of Hebrews—just under a hundred—went into Egypt and came out four hundred years later two million strong. Less than twenty years ago, we started this very church in Boston with just thirty disciples of Jesus. Just look around you now! That's nearly *thirty* times in growth. Now let's multiply some more, because that's what we do." He smiles. "We have plantings in Europe. In Australia. In Africa. In the South Pacific. And we have plans for every nation in this world. Now, it doesn't take a math genius to figure out that it won't take us four hundred years to reach our goal."

I picture this crowd multiplied in so many places, consumed by the same excitement of this service. It's amazing, the number of people we could help around the world. The Leader pauses in the middle of the stage and pumps his fists. "We are going to reach one million by the year 2000, because a million followers can change the entire world!" Heather and I stand to cheer again. The crowd is frenzied. I'm mesmerized by the rows of captivated expressions, all focused on the Leader as he strides back and forth like a caged lion.

"Now, here's the hard part. For some, more than others, maybe," he accuses the camera. "The good word says in our spiritual walk that we learn by imitation. That's not coming from me. That's coming from Paul, and he got it straight from the Lord. *Imitation*." He pauses, leans into the audience, and lowers his voice as if disciplining a child. "And let me tell you this. If you are not following wholeheartedly, and I mean *one hundred percent*"—he pauses again—"then you are just a *cheap imitation*." He says the last two words as if referring to something dirty and disgusting.

I turn to Heather, who writes this down and underlines the words twice. The Leader stops talking for so long it makes me slightly anxious. Everyone waits in silence for him to continue, like at a concert when the band is trying to decide what to play next. A few church members finally call out their requests. *Tell it! Go on!* I lean forward just as he stops pacing. "True imitation leads to salvation. And we all know there is a heaven. Amen?"

"Amen." I say it out loud with Heather this time.

"But don't forget that means there's also a hell. And, people, there *will* be a judgment."

The moment the service ends, Heather slices through the crowd like a boat hull cutting water. I follow her toward a hallway that appears to lead backstage. Suddenly nervous, I wonder if we're supposed to be back here. As if sensing my reluctance, Heather turns to wave me forward before pushing through a door. Inside, Meredith is greeting a circle of people surrounding her, like a celebrity fielding autograph requests. An enormous cake decorated as a scaled atlas is displayed on a skirted table. Tall candles pierce the nations where the Kingdom already has churches.

"Hey," someone says over my shoulder. I turn to see Andrew smiling. He leans into me and pats my back in a distanced hug.

"I didn't realize you're interested in an internship," he says to me. Before I can ask what he's talking about, Heather yanks my arm to keep us moving, too focused on keeping our spot in line to even say hi to Andrew. I shrug at him apologetically. Andrew gives a pretend grimace to the back of Heather's head to offer me his sympathy. I try not to laugh as he walks away to talk to Ben on the other side of the room.

When we finally get closer, Meredith's eyes glint in recognition at Heather. "Hey, sweetie," she says, but her eyes shift intermittently to see who is behind her.

I step up next to Heather.

"Well, hello, Emily. How are you?" Meredith says, beaming.

"Great," I say, still giddy from the energy of the crowd.

"Look at your adorable outfit," Meredith says to me. "My daughter Rachel has one similar. Did you know she just turned sixteen? I cannot be-*lieve* my baby girl is all grown up." Her gaze shifts back to Heather, who fidgets with her hair and clothes under Meredith's gaze. "Heather, honey. What in the world are you wearing?" Meredith asks with a small laugh.

Heather's disappointment overshadows her smile. "Oh," Heather looks down at her outfit, smoothing the fabric with her palms. "Uh—it's—"

Meredith narrows her eyes at Heather, her smile never leaving her lips. "Don't you think that skirt's a little tight?"

Heather's cheeks immediately flame. I duck my head, as if looking at my shoes will make me less of a witness to Heather's embarrassment.

"Have you been praying and fasting like we talked about?" Meredith asks Heather while scanning the people behind us again.

"Yes, of course, I—"

A random girl shoves past us. Meredith hugs her and shifts her attention away from us for a moment. Another girl cutting the cake hands me a large piece and tries to give one to Heather, who quickly puts her hand up to pass.

Meredith turns back to us as the girl who shoved me walks away. "Listen. I hope y'all stick around for the meeting. There's something very exciting I want to share with both of you." She's looking directly at me.

"Sure," Heather says, her cheeks still blazing.

Meredith tilts her head at Heather. "I really like the way you pulled your hair up." Heather smiles. Her hair is twisted in the back and clipped so that a controlled mess of curls spills over just so. I notice Meredith's hair is pulled up in a similar way but without the curls. "You too, Emily. Why, you and Heather could almost be sisters. What a perfect way to illustrate the idea of imitation," she says, beaming with delight. "So creative!"

I touch my curls that took so long to create. "She insisted." I nudge Heather.

"Well, I think you should wear it like that every single day," Meredith says before turning to another student waiting for her.

Even with the hair compliment, I can tell Heather is still upset about Meredith's skirt remark by the way she pulls at its hem as we push through the clot of people blocking a cluster of chairs.

We sit in silence as Heather continues to fuss with her clothes. "For what it's worth," I offer, "I think you look great."

Heather stops fidgeting and turns icy. "Meredith is the Leader's sister. And *my* DP. She's just holding me to the highest standards." Heather's eyes are proud and distant, taking on the exact aloofness Meredith had cut her with just moments ago. We sit down, and I stab my fork into the yellow fragment of Central America before taking a bite of cake. Just as I dig into the blue icing of the ocean, Josh walks up. My heart skips, and I try desperately to keep my reaction neutral with Heather right next to me.

"Hi, Heather," Josh says.

"Josh," she responds.

He turns to me. "It's good to see you, Emily. I haven't talked to you in ages." He's almost laughing. "How've you been?"

"Great," I choke. Heather watches me closely, but it's so hard not to smirk back at him. Josh's eyes glint with mischief, and we share a knowing look: *She didn't find out.* Suddenly, the loud screech of feedback startles everyone to attention. Meredith makes her way into the middle of the room, adjusting the microphone clipped to her dress, as students settle into empty chairs. Josh winks before walking off to lean against the wall beside Ben and Andrew.

"I'm sure you're all wondering why we're celebrating with the largest cake we've ever ordered. Well, we're here to talk about my husband." She pauses and looks around the room. "As you probably noticed, he was too sick to be here today, but that's okay because this isn't just about our dear Will. *This* is about the most important mission of our lifetime that he's been chosen to lead—the expansion of the Kingdom. We're in the process of scoping out possibilities for churches in every single nation in the world. And we're looking for young people just like you to serve as interns. I'm talking about exciting places like England, India, France, Italy."

Heather shifts in her chair. "*Voglio andare in Italia*," she says slowly to herself. "I've prayed and prayed for this," she whispers to me, grasping my forearm for emphasis.

Heather's sense of urgency permeates her grip. I've never been out of the country, and I imagine myself in Italy, the place where all the paintings and sculptures in my art history book come to life. I glance at Josh and my stomach flips as I picture him there with me, leading me through romantic piazzas. Am I even far enough through the steps to be eligible for an overseas internship? As Meredith describes far-away places where the Kingdom is making a difference, I listen, barely blinking, taking in every single detail until she extends her arms to accentuate her closing remarks: "As individuals, we can accomplish a lot. But as a Kingdom, we can accomplish *anything*."

As the meeting wraps up, Josh finds me again, leaning in close as he passes. "Talk to you tonight," he whispers. I smile and instinctively check to make sure Heather didn't hear. Luckily, she's busy chatting with another girl, her back to us. The excited chatter from potential interns swells around us, yet it feels like Josh and I are the only ones in the room. He briefly touches my hand before walking away.

breaking session: a confrontation-induced breakdown that occurs after confessing one's secrets; often viewed as a spiritual awakening with the promise of acceptance and forgiveness; can cause a radical shift in identity

Sins to Burn

et us pray have become Heather's three favorite words.

And her favorite way to end each prayer is exactly the same each time: "Forgive us our sins. Amen."

My sins were always an abstract idea, until Heather asked me to bring a list to our next meeting. We were finishing a BT when she sat there smirking like she had a huge secret to tell me and couldn't wait any longer. "Your next step is the final step before baptism. And I told Meredith you'd be ready by the next house meeting. This is the most important step because it leads to *total* spiritual freedom." She made a muffled squealing sound, but I couldn't get past the words "sin" and "list" as the title of a task. "As in write them all down?" I kept asking.

Heather assured me Josh wouldn't be there; it was a previously planned girls-only house study. Well, except for Will, whom I am very curious to finally meet in person. Even then, Heather promised she would be the only one to see my list. And while I didn't love the idea of Heather knowing all my sins, I pushed past that to focus on the after-baptism perks: Spiritual freedom. A support system in Boston. And, of course, more time with Josh. (Out in the open. *As a couple!*) Just thinking about this made me giddy enough to swallow my fears and break out the pen and paper.

By the time I arrive at Meredith and Will's house on the day of my baptism, my list reads:

1. Alcohol. (Heather said to include this.)
2. Marijuana. (I tried it twice but didn't get high.)
3. Physical relationship with one high school boyfriend.
4. Notebook of fairly explicit poetry from my creative writing class.
5. A *B* in high school chemistry (my only *B* ever).

My "Sin List" doesn't look so bad to me, especially considering my upbringing. I can't imagine what my high school friends' lists would look like, or, even worse, Tamara's. She spent an entire month at an oceanfront rehab facility in California the summer after her sophomore year of college. My dad said they could have saved tens of thousands of dollars by sending her out to one of the barrier islands with some food and a tent until she simply decided not to drink so much. Patti didn't tell him about the various pills she found rattling around in Tamara's purse.

I've always been the good girl, the levelheaded one who drives everyone home. Yet here I sit across from Heather, staring at the lavender walls of Meredith's teen daughter's bedroom. I'm nervous about handing over my list, my heart pounding so hard I'm scared if I look down, I'll actually see it pumping against my chest.

"This is it," Heather says with a strained smile, the same kind a teacher uses when she isn't sure whether a student will succeed or fail. "Your final step to salvation."

My eyes keep flicking toward the door, longing for an escape, as Heather opens my list. I focus on items in Rachel's room as a distraction—a ruffled pillow, a jam box, a poster of Amy Grant bending mid-snap in an animal-print blazer. The plastic eyes of stuffed animals stare at me blankly from the bowl-shaped cushion of a papasan chair. I jump at the sound of a door down the hall slamming and look to make sure our door is shut all the way.

"I know this is scary, Em," Heather reassures me, placing her hand on mine with a warm smile. "But I have to know your exact sins in order to help determine your spiritual weaknesses. It's my job to help you find your way on the path to righteousness." She looks back down at my list with a serious expression.

Josh told me this would be intense, though I had no idea *how* intense until now. *This will be over soon. How bad can it be?* I sit quietly rubbing the sweat from my palms onto my jeans. Heather's eyebrows furrow as she reads. When she finally looks up, she isn't happy.

"Emily? You are going to have to be *completely* honest with me here. I have to know *specifically* what you've struggled with so you can come to grips with your sins. It's the only way to become closer to God."

"Okay," I say warily. Did I leave something out? How would she even know?

"Do you trust me?" she asks. It almost sounds like an accusation.

I blink. "Of course."

A brief smile crosses her face before she homes in on my list. "On number three, for example, what exactly does 'physical relationship' mean?"

"Um . . ." I trail off, knowing I'd been vague. I never felt comfortable discussing anything sexual, even in front of friends. Dad and I never had "the talk" when I was younger, though Patti told me to ask her anything I wanted to know. She did say she might need a glass of wine first. I never ended up asking questions. Instead, I silently gleaned everything I needed to know from girlfriends at school, and more often, Tamara.

"Look," Heather says, putting my list aside. "As your DP, anything you tell me is completely confidential. In order to help you, I have to know *everything*. If you can't even make the leap to trust *me*, how are you ever going to fully trust in God?"

"This is just . . . difficult," I stammer. "It's weird talking about things like this."

She heaves a dramatic sigh. "Okay. I can make this a little bit easier, but you have to *promise* to answer every single question honestly."

"Okay." *This will be over soon. This will be over soon. This will be over soon.*

"Have you only been quote-unquote physical with this one particular boyfriend from high school?" She uses her fingers to emphasize the quotations.

"Yes."

"Did you actually have sexual intercourse with him?"

"Yes." I mumble it quickly.

"How many times?"

"Once." I try to block the awkward memory. *Eric Bolton.* It was something I'd rather not remember. At the time, I wasn't sure whether I felt disappointed because it was such an unpleasant mistake, or relieved that the big ordeal was finally over.

"Did you ever have oral sex with him?"

I pick at my nails while staring at them intently. "Yes," I admit.

"Who performed it, you or him?"

"Both," I whisper. My face is on fire. I look down at

a polka-dotted hair scrunchie peeking out from under the dresser and cringe as I hear Heather scribbling something onto my list.

"Anal sex?"

"No."

"Are you sure? Lots of people do it that way because they think it technically won't count as their first time."

"I'm pretty sure I would remember that." I laugh nervously.

Her eyes flare as she leans forward. "This is not a *joke*, Emily," she hisses. "We are *at war* with the temptations lurking in this world. This is your *soul* we are talking about here. If you don't feel broken by the cross of Jesus, then you should just go back to your dorm without me."

Her earnestness catches me short. My eyes burn with tears.

Heather sits up and composes herself. "Are you still in contact with this guy?"

"What do you mean?" I swipe my trembling finger across my eye and dry it on my jeans.

"Do you see him when you go home? Has he been up here to visit?"

"No and no," I say. I broke up with Eric way before I left for college, and I still feel guilty about it because he really liked me. Eric was the type of person I *thought* I was supposed to be with, yet I honestly didn't like him that much. Plus, I'd already realized my happiness would be contingent on leaving home, and I wasn't going to let anyone get in my way.

"Do you miss him?" Heather asks. She tilts her head as if concerned for me.

I pause, wondering what she wants me to say. I don't want Heather to think I'm cold-hearted or slutty, or anything, but I'm relieved we live in different states. Eric seemed needy afterward. Tamara, who, of course, found out about it, explained how the significance of your first time is a huge myth, and how the act itself is just a trial run. I found myself embarrassed by him afterwards, by things like his hair growing a little too long in the back, or the fact that his truck always smelled vaguely of fishing and sports equipment. It surprised me how little I cared when Eric started seeing Rebecca Randall, a popular girl on the dance team. It was actually a relief.

"No, I wouldn't say that I miss him," I finally say to Heather.

She eyes me suspiciously.

"Anyway, he has a serious girlfriend now," I add.

Heather sighs with relief. "Good. That will speed up the process, because any relationship like that would have to be completely cut off before you could be baptized."

At least Josh is already saved.

"Have you ever been sexually abused by a family member or another adult?"

"*What?*"

"Emily, it's okay to tell me. It's part of letting God heal your past so that you can move forward. I have to know absolutely everything."

"No, I've never been abused."

"Raped?"

"No."

"What about girlfriends? Have you ever experimented, like kissed or touched another girl?"

"No." I'm staring at the floor.

"Not even the girl in the photo in your room? The one where you're both wearing bikinis in a boat?"

"No! Heather, are we done yet? I messed around with *one* guy. What else do you want me to say?"

"Okay, fine." Heather throws her hands up in frustration. "There is no need to be so defensive and prideful with *me*. These are *your* mistakes, Emily. And as your DP, I am personally responsible for allowing you to admit them so we can ask God to take care of the rest. If you don't feel like doing that, then God help you on Judgment Day."

"But—"

"James 5:16 says: '*Therefore confess your sins to each other and pray for each other so that you may be healed.*' If you refuse to reach a point of godly sorrow, then all of your progress will be for nothing." Heather rearranges her curls, a habit she uses for dramatic effect, and something I actually caught myself doing yesterday. "Now, on to other things."

The process turns out to be far from over. By the time

Heather is done with me, my list expands from a mere five items to thirty-seven sins, including masturbation (#8), my specific thoughts during masturbation (#9), rebellious attitude (#15), not imitating my DP—*her*—to my best ability (#29), and being confirmed into a different church when I was younger (#34). When she's done, I'm clutching my Sin List like it's the only hard copy of the combination to a nuclear bomb.

Just as I stand up, Heather says, "Wait. I know this has been very uncomfortable for you. I have one last thing, though," she says. "And it's really important."

I sit back down, my heart racing. What else could we possibly have left to cover? I've just told her the most embarrassing things I've ever told anyone before now.

Heather looks at me and pauses before speaking. "Have you ever hated God?"

A twinge of guilt pinches my chest. I'm suddenly afraid.

"I'm very serious, Emily. Are you angry with God for anything that's ever happened to you?"

I'm searching her face for clues, but her expression doesn't change. Something inside of me is resisting the urge to even consider a response. "I don't think so," I say carefully. I grip my knees. It never occurred to me to be angry at someone else for the wave of darkness that sometimes falls over me, and how once I inexplicably wanted to walk straight into the ocean at night with no plan to swim back. How the only thing that stopped me was knowing it would kill my father. And how sometimes I wake up with specific childhood memories, but I don't even know if they're real or imagined. I know I can never let myself form these words, even in private.

"Okay. Let me ask it this way. Do you blame God for taking your mother away from you when you were a little girl?"

Yes.

Her question—and my mind's immediate response—knocks the wind out of me. It's not just God I blamed. The image of my father that day on the beach—reading, not paying attention, complacent—pops into my head. *Why was she out there alone? Why did he let her go out there? Why didn't he save her?* Guilt and resentment mixed with a raw anger rise up with such force and speed I can't stop them. I try to press them down, down, down, until I can almost ignore them again like I'd been doing my whole life. My heart aches more than I can stand as tears begin running down my cheeks.

Heather swoops to my side, her arm around me. She lets me cry into her shoulder. "It's okay," she whispers. "This is why we confess, Em. I can tell you're broken. We just have to remember we can't carry our sins on our own." She pulls away with abrupt optimism.

She places my Sin List in my hand and I immediately fold it, trying to hold back the nausea rising in my throat. When I stand up, Heather has to steady me. Wiping my eyes one last time, I take a deep breath and follow her out of the room. I would do anything to make this horrible feeling go away.

Meredith is waiting for us in the kitchen amid an elaborate display of finger foods and fresh-baked cookies, all artfully arranged on their counter in a still life of normalcy. She smiles at me and raises her eyebrows in an I'm-rooting-for-you expression. I smile back weakly. Her gesture is kind, but it seems incongruous to the weight of the situation. How could no one have ever warned me about the seriousness of this piece of paper earlier in my life? Maybe I would've made different choices had I known. Maybe everything would have been different.

"Emily," Meredith whispers excitedly, pulling me back to the present moment. "I want you to meet my husband." She turns and waves toward a hallway, summoning a tall attractive man with wire-rimmed glasses.

"Well, hello. You must be Emily. I'm Will." He leans forward and shakes my hand as I squeeze my folded-up Sin List in the sweaty palm of my other. "And no mister last name formalities with me." He winks. His relaxed attention is comforting, and also sort of exhilarating, like when a professor wants to chat about an A+ assignment after class. Will even looks a little like my lit professor: young and approachable, with a quiet magnetism, definitely the opposite of Meredith's overly charismatic brother on stage at church.

Will places his hand on my shoulder as he leads me to the French doors that open to the backyard. He leans

s skin seems pale beyond the nor-
ballor. "Now, Emily. This part can
ng to do is stay focused." He pats
remember this is one of the most
ever make," he says. I force a ner-
y Sin List, and follow him out to
ackyard where the other disciples
Heather is beaming at me, her

the group of us about to be bap-
e paved patio. We're all clutch-
s he arranges us in a semicircle
ming pool. A teepee of wood is
deep end; a large cross-shaped
ehind it. As Will slips off his
notice a large Band-Aid peeks
leeve when he lifts his arm to

ples! This is a very important—
p in your path to salvation, so
structions. First, I need you to
t hand out, palm up."
her hand clutching my Sin
y right hand. Its cool touch

notches. "Can anyone tell

No one answers. I swirl the sharp object in my h
anxious to speak.

"A thumbtack?" someone to my left guesses.

"Yes, but it's far more powerful than a mere ol
your ticket out of sin. Far away from Satan's grasp,

A few awkward "amens" break through the
silence.

"Now I want each of you to squeeze the tac
little bit—into your palm," Will says. "Can you fee

My tack is sideways. I readjust the sharp point

"Do you have an *inkling* of an idea as to what J
have felt when they hammered those nails into
You know why it was necessary, don't you? I
because of you. Do you know the *agony* he felt
committed—and when you continue to comn
those sins on your lists?" he bellows. "You *mu*
with your prideful behavior. You *murdered* him
rebellious attitude. You *murdered* him when you v
with your boyfriend. You *murdered* him when yo
drag off a cigarette, or that sip of beer.

"And it *kills* him—all over again—when yo
stand there and ignore his Word. It's the *only* t
of you. That piece of paper you're holding in yo
hurts him more than *ten thousand nails!*" Will is

I'm quiet and still as shame blooms inside c

"You *put* him on that cross, where he ble
agony, and it is *time* you all answered for that!"

A few nearby disciples sniff. The same guilt and resentment and anger I felt earlier bubble up again, but this time it's directed toward myself. The same question keeps repeating in my mind: *What have I done?* I try to focus on the soothing sound of water flowing into the swimming pool through an elaborate stone fountain.

"But I have good news." Will's tone shifts to comforting. "Tonight, we're giving you the opportunity to start fresh. To give yourself over completely to the cross of Jesus Christ. To open your eyes to his will. *Open your eyes.* Now take that tack and pierce it through your sins. This is your chance to lay it down at the foot of the cross."

I push the tack through my Sin List and follow the line forming along the pool. The other disciples before me fasten their lists to the pile of wood in front of the cross and walk away. When it's my turn, my pulse quickens as I tack mine to a piece of wood.

"Emily," Will says.

I wince, surprised to hear my name first.

He beams at the faces lining the pool and descends, fully clothed, into the shallow end. Then he turns to me and extends his hand. I take off my shoes and step in. The warm water is strangely comforting. My clothes swell and bloat, making it difficult to maneuver. Will rests his hands on my shoulders before speaking to all of us. I stare at the cross, which looms taller from this angle.

"Emily. Do you promise to commit to living a life as a

true disciple as outlined by Jesus Christ in order to receive forgiveness for your sins through the Holy Spirit?"

My heart is pounding. My negative emotions are more distant now, as if they're detaching from me, preparing to float away. "I promise," I say.

I hear a loud *whoosh* as someone lights the wood holding our Sin Lists. Will gathers my hands into his own, places them over my nose, and pulls me back in one overpowering splash. My eyes pop open underwater, a reflex I've never been able to correct. A distorted tower of flames quivers above the water. The chlorine burns my nostrils as I accidentally inhale some water. Just as I begin to gurgle and thrash, Will's arm pulls me upright releasing me from the silence. My ears clear to the sounds of cheering and clapping and "amens" as the raging flames crackle loudly through the bonfire.

I scan the faces of those lined along the edge of the pool, where every disciple appears serene and happy for me. Hot tears stream down my face. Relief rushes through me as the anxiety from Heather's interrogation washes away.

The warmth of Will's hands rests on my shoulders as everyone cheers. An intense flood of joy hits me. It consumes me the same way the pieces of wood burn through my handwritten past.

As I struggle up the steps, another disciple sloshes into the water. She gives me an enormous hug and takes my hands into her own.

"You're *saved*," she says, her face manic with exhilaration.

She releases my hands, leaving a smear of blood where her right palm was. Before I can say anything, she rushes toward Will, leaving a thin strain of red swirling behind her. It's suspended for several seconds, illuminated by the underwater lights, and then it dissipates into the big mass of water around it.

(REPEAT) STEP 1: Introduce yourself to someone new. Try a student sitting alone, or someone who seems upset or out of place. Invite them to an informal activity.

Sidelined

"Excuse me, do you have a second?"

A girl hauling an overstuffed backpack shoots me an aggravated look as she continues through the quad.

No? Okay, then.

This isn't going well, and it's my fault. It's barely been a week since my baptism, yet my responsibilities have multiplied—with inviting others to join our studies being highest on the list. I'm consumed with a restless fervor, as if someone lit an inner pilot light I didn't know I had, but I haven't figured out how to use it. I just can't get beyond the weirdness of approaching strangers, even though they're students like me. I can hear my Southern accent every time I speak. Then I become self-conscious and clam up, or just stand there panic-stricken, completely forgetting what to say. I'm worried if I can't generate more interest, I'll have to skip more classes and I'm getting close to maxing out my absences.

A clean-cut guy wearing a fraternity cap is heading my way.

I can do this. "Excuse me," I say.

He stops. His eyes shine a clear blue in the brightness of the sun as he smiles.

"I just wanted to invite you to a campus Bible study group," I stammer.

I wait for his resistance, but he tilts his head as if intrigued. "Bible study, huh?"

"Yes. We're a non-denominational group of students studying what the Bible teaches about life."

He smiles. My hopes soar. *Please, please, please say yes.*

"Do you know how many invitations to your study I've received this week? *Seven*," he spits. "Don't you have anything better to do than harass people into joining your weirdo cult?"

He stalks away, leaving me stunned and confused. *What is his problem?*

I look for Heather's guidance and spot her across the quad near a spire-topped building, chatting with three well-dressed girls. They look so happy and at ease, like the stock photos from all the university brochures. I can't help my jealous admiration of Heather's nonchalant way of bringing people in.

I edge over in their direction until I'm within earshot.

"So, we'll see you later today at the volleyball game?" Heather says to the girls.

Volleyball game? Heather hadn't mentioned that as a thing I could say.

I'm about to approach them just as two giant hands gently cover my eyes.

"Guess who?" My stomach flips as I recognize Josh's voice.

I put my hands over his. "Josh?"

He laughs as I turn around. "Are you recruiting?" he asks.

"Trying," I say.

"Ah. Not going so well?"

I wrinkle my nose in response.

"Hey. Don't worry about it. Listen. Here's a tip," Josh says quietly, leaning into me. "Look for people you'd want to talk to anyway. They'll be more likely to connect with you."

"Yeah. I guess you lucked out when you stumbled upon me, then," I joke.

"Sure did." His fingers sweep my hair behind my ear, and it's almost enough to erase my insecurity about this process.

"I don't know," I say. "Maybe this part just isn't for me. Heather is so good at it."

Josh puts his hand on my shoulder. "Heather has a way

with people," he says. "She brings more students into the Kingdom than any other DP on this campus. Just be yourself." His hand slides down my arm from my shoulder to my hand. He intertwines his fingers with mine.

"Um, hello?" Heather interrupts in her most annoying schoolmarm voice. "PDA while recruiting is a bit inappropriate, don't you think?"

Josh automatically drops his hand to his side. My cheeks redden—with shame or annoyance, I'm not sure. Now that I'm baptized, Josh and I are allowed to be together, but Heather hasn't let up on her vigilance or judgment.

"So." Heather turns to me. "How many people have you invited?"

Her confrontational tone makes me uneasy. "Ten total, so far?"

Heather's brows furrow. "Why does your answer sound like a question? Any seem interested?"

"Maybe," I say optimistically.

Heather has that look—the I'm-about-to-give-advice one. I cut her off before she has time to embarrass me in front of Josh.

"Why didn't you tell me about the volleyball game?" I ask.

She looks surprised for a moment, and then composes herself with an assured toss of her hair. "Oh, it's just an event we're sponsoring for the Kingdom on Campus group." She turns to Josh. "You're coming, right?"

"You bet," he says.

"I would have mentioned it, Emily, but I was worried you'd be uncomfortable. It's mostly *experienced* DPs and potential new members," she says with authority.

Josh puts his arm around me in a defiant gesture. "It might be good for Em to *watch* the recruiting side of things, rather than just throwing her out here in the quad without any preparation," he says to Heather in an authoritative tone.

Heather shoots Josh a fake smile. "Fine, then. Now some of us have to get back to work. So many souls, so little time," she says before walking off to approach a girl sitting alone on a bench.

With Heather's back turned, Josh takes me by surprise with a quick kiss on the cheek. "I'll see you at the game at four—I have to run to class," he says, smiling as he goes.

I watch him stride off, my cheek tingling.

At the volleyball event, Heather flits from person to person without taking a single break. She doesn't bother to acknowledge me beyond her smile-and-nod "sorry I'm busy" gesture, so I walk around until I run into Andrew. He pats my arm when he notices me worriedly tracking Heather. "Don't worry, Em," he says. "We can't all be as productive as your DP." I almost detect a hint of sarcasm in his voice, but it's so subtle that I tell myself it could be my imagination. "Anyway, I spy your boy." He points to Josh standing at the volleyball net. "You should go find a seat and enjoy the view," he says with a wink before walking toward a concession table.

I take his advice as the deep punching sound of a fist launching a volleyball prompts cheering from the sidelines. "Go, Jessie!" a girl sitting nearby yells with her hands cupped around her mouth. Jessie laughs as she shuffles back and forth, her arms outstretched with hands connected into a *V* in front of her.

This is exactly what I imagined college would be like amid the bustle of large activities. I clap for the players, happy to feel like I'm a part of something. And it's a relief to be able to sit on the sidelines instead of actively recruiting, stuttering and sweating. Josh is playing volleyball, while Andrew and Ben keep score. I spot Heather talking to the same group of girls from the quad.

A familiar voice breaks through the outdoor commotion. "Why, hello, Miss Emily. How are you doing?" Meredith sits down next to me, but I don't recognize her at first. Her tight blond ponytail—the perky kind fastened high at the crown—makes her seem very young. With her lean build in a white button-down shirt and khaki shorts, Meredith could easily pass for a senior. It's the jewelry that gives her away. Most college girls don't wear full-carat studs and drop necklaces to a volleyball game.

"I'm great," I say.

"No, I mean, how are you *doing*? You know . . . spiritually." She looks at me with a caring expression.

"Oh. Fine." I sound like I'm questioning my own answer. I'm worried she'll bring up the fact that I can't even convince one new person to come to our study groups.

"I've heard good things about your progress," she says. "You've been staying on track with your QTs and BTs, and I know it isn't easy with a full load of classes. Some students struggle in their spiritual walk because of school and other outside distractions, but you've really shown your priorities are in the right place."

"Thanks," I say, a surge of pride lifting my voice higher than usual. After my baptism, Heather ramped up our study schedule, plus added in time for recruitment. I had to miss a few classes and stop volunteering at Senior Meals just to keep up. It was a small price to pay.

"So, have you thought any more about our meeting?" Meredith asks.

"Which one?"

Meredith stares at me. She doesn't seem put out, just serious. "About our world missions and the many opportunities for students to participate."

"Oh. You mean the internship?"

Her eyes widen with enthusiasm. "Yes. The internship." She leans forward. "We feel you've been called to be a part of this, Emily. All of us," she says with a conspiratorial whisper. "Including my brother."

The Leader? I sit up straight. I've learned enough to know the Leader's attention is a very big deal. My heart pinches at the thought of not being home for the summer to hang out in the Gulf of Mexico with my friends—no deadlines or scheduled pressures—just the hum of a boat motor and music trailing in our wake.

"I'm not sure about my summer plans yet—" I say, squirming.

Meredith interrupts. "There was a recent mission to Africa to see where we'd have the most effective impact in such an enormous continent with so many lost souls. And I can tell you . . ." Her eyes gleam through a dramatic pause. "*Miracles* happened there."

More than a little intrigued, I wait for her to continue. Meredith silently fidgets with her wedding ring as her eyes follow the volleyball with each bump keeping it airborne. Unsure of what to do, I turn to watch the game. Josh is in front of the net, where he leaps up to slam the ball into the ground on the other side. Everyone cheers and screams. His eyes scan the sidelines until he finds me, a huge smile on his face. Nothing could stop my own smile in return, and it's clear Meredith notices.

"Did you know I met my husband when I was your age?" she says, her attention turned back to me. "We were both at Vanderbilt, back in Nashville where I grew up. I was a freshman and he was a senior pitching for the baseball team. I spent so much time sitting in the stands and just watching him play. . . ." Her voice trails off as she looks down, still twisting her ring. She looks up at me with a quick smile. She seems embarrassed to have revealed something so personal, yet happy to share the memory.

She quickly shakes off whatever she's feeling and continues. "Well. I know Josh is hoping you'll join the Italy mission."

"Why do you say that?" I ask, playing dumb.

"Oh, just a hunch. I'm not *that* old, you know. I still remember what boys his age act like when they're interested in someone." Heat rises in my cheeks. *Italy with Josh . . .*

"What about Heather? Is she going?" I ask, trying to deflect the conversation and my own thoughts.

Meredith wrinkles her nose and pauses carefully. "Heather has a gift for turning the numbers by helping students find their way to Jesus. We believe that her gifts are best utilized here on this campus where she can do the most good for the Kingdom."

"She really wants to go to Italy. She could recruit so many people there," I say, out of obligation or guilt I'm not sure. Italy is Heather's dream, but when I imagine being there with both her and Josh, I'm conflicted.

Meredith's face shifts to the aloof expression I'd first noticed at church. "Heather will do what God asks of her," she says. "I told her to study it out while fasting and praying. God will lead her to the right decision. He always does."

I glance at Heather, already chatting with a new group of girls. She may be difficult at times, but she was my first real friend here. My gaze shifts to Josh, and a picture of just the two of us relaxing together in Italy flashes through my mind. A smile creeps across my face.

"I'll ask my dad about Italy."

Meredith's face brightens. "Wonderful! And we can make it super easy for you. You can store your stuff at our house over the summer—free of charge. That way you wouldn't have to mess with a storage unit," she says off-handedly. She sits up straight and adjusts her ponytail. Her blond hair shines in the sun. "We want you to think of us as extended family—people who look out for you when you're so far away from your own."

An unexpected sadness temporarily blurs the volleyball game and everything else around me. "Thanks. I'll tell him," I mumble.

"You do that," Meredith says just before popping up and dusting off her shorts. She leans down and puts a hand on my shoulder. "So good to chat with you, Emily. I'll look forward to hearing from you soon."

On the other side of the game, Heather is staring in my direction. When I catch her eye, she turns her back and starts talking to the same girls, who are laughing as if they're all best friends.

incentive effect: when a rewarded member serves as an inspiration—or a corrective example—to other members competing for the same incentive in a high-pressure group

A Gift for Numbers

Heather is late for our morning BT. And Heather is never late. I call her room, but her phone just keeps ringing. When I knock on her door, she's startled to see me. "What are you doing here?" I hold up my notebook and Bible. "I'm here to study," I say, confused.

"Didn't she tell you?" Heather says, distraught. Her eyes are red and swollen. "I'm no longer your DP. They're assigning you a new DP to prepare for the world mission to Italy."

I reel back. "What? But I don't even know for sure if I'm going," I say, panic in my voice. "I haven't even talked to my dad yet."

As a bunch of girls bump past me in the hallway, Heather

"You should leave," she says, as if talking to an annoying stranger.

I clutch my Bible and notebook to my chest. "Heather, *please*. I feel so terrible about all this. Can we please just talk?"

"No." She decisively slams the door in my face.

Her door magnet crashes to the floor. I stare at it in a state of shock, and then bend down to pick it up and put it back in its place.

The rest of the day is a blur. My emotions overshadow everything else around me. I go to class and back to my dorm. I call Josh, but he doesn't answer. I study and take a nap. I go to the cafeteria to eat dinner alone. Loneliness creeps in with its cold intensity—a reminder of life before I met Heather. I pick at my food and gaze at the metal napkin holder until I lose track of time. People sit down, talk to each other, eat, and get up again, only to be replaced by other people. I sit there until my legs begin to fall asleep. I picture my dorm towering above the noise and traffic. I have to make myself go home. *Home*.

As I walk across campus, a woman with short hair and glasses stops right in front of me. "Emily?"

At first, I don't recognize her. Then I notice the blue shirt with the Senior Meals logo. "Hi, Jackie," I say to the coordinator I used to work with at the soup kitchen.

"I was just on campus giving an informational workshop. You know, we really miss seeing you," she says with a genuine smile.

keeps her arm on the doorframe, blocking my entrance. Her mouth is locked into a frown.

"Well, it's not like you can say no." Her tone is distant and bitter.

"Maybe they're still deciding who's going," I offer helplessly. "There's still time for them to change—" I stop talking when I see tears streaming from her eyes.

Not sure what to do, I step forward to give her a hug. Her back is as straight and tense as a metal pole. When I pull away, she doesn't move. She looks right through me. "They said I have a gift for numbers, but that *your* gifts would be more useful for the special world missions," she whispers through more tears.

What could they possibly consider a gift better than Heather's?

Heather wipes her eyes with her sleeve and levels a glare at me. "I saw you talking to Meredith at the volleyball game. What did you say to her? You must have said something to change her mind. She told me I have a defiant heart."

"No! That isn't true! I didn't say anything except that I hoped you'd get to go too. She was talking about Josh." I flinch, suddenly realizing I may have said too much.

She scoffs indignantly. "Well, that makes sense. I guess my mistake was focusing on my salvation and not *seducing.* . . ." Heather exhales through her mouth to compose herself. "Let me guess. Josh is going too."

I look down at the floor.

A smile covers my embarrassment. I've been so busy with Heather and the Kingdom that I haven't even thought about how long it has been since I was over there helping out. Now all of my time and donations are going to a cause that's "more effective and reliable," according to Meredith.

"You know, Helen has asked about you," she continues. She looks at me with concern. "How are you feeling? You look . . . not quite yourself."

I try to find the words to express my guilt and shame when I think about Helen waiting for me to come back, but I can barely speak. "I-I'm so sorry," I stammer, unable to hide my emotions. I say it again as I rush away.

I head back to Heather's dorm, determined to make it right with her. Despite her coldness, she's become my best friend in Boston. And I hope that a trip to Italy won't change that.

When I knock on Heather's door, no one answers. I try again. Still no response. "Heather?" I turn the knob. It's unlocked. I walk inside. The room is dark, the blinds completely closed. It's too quiet.

"Heather?" I say again, quietly, in case she's asleep.

An abrupt sound alarms me.

It takes me a few seconds to register what it is, exactly. I look around the room. No one is there. Plastic bags are strewn all over the floor, which is unusual for Heather, who always keeps everything in its exact place.

Then I hear the sound again, coming from the bathroom.

I rest my ear against the cool metal door, where a sliver of light glows underneath.

"Heather?"

I hear violent retching with loud moans and sobs in between. *"Heather?"* I try the knob, but it's locked.

I bolt out of her room and down the hall to get the RA, who is sprawled across her bed reading a magazine.

I try to catch my breath long enough to speak. "My friend on your wing is very sick. She's locked herself in her bathroom."

"Let me guess," the RA says as she flips the page of her magazine, unconcerned. "Heather the Jesus freak." She sits up to mute the television and turns to me. "You must be her—what is it called—disciple?"

"Yes," I say, bristling a bit. "And her friend."

"Well, don't worry. She'll be fine." The RA looks at me in that condescending upperclassman way and says, "All I'll say is, you reap what you sow."

Frustration courses through me. "She's *sick*. Someone should help her."

The RA looks me up and down, this time as if she feels sorry for me. "I don't understand why you all curl your hair to look like hers. It's just *weird*."

I touch my hair, confused. *It looks better this way.* I open my mouth to tell her off, but she's already flipping through her magazine again, so I slam the door without responding.

I run to the lounge area down the hall and rummage

through the kitchen in search of crackers and ginger ale. I find an unopened package of water crackers and grab it, promising myself I'll replace it later.

I burst back into Heather's room, and I'm surprised to see her at her desk with an open Bible under a lamp—the only light on. The room is completely picked up, all of the plastic bags gone. Her hair is pulled back and twisted into a giant clip, and the lamp gives the fuzzy curls around her face an ethereal glow. Her expression is distant and serene.

"Heather?" I say tentatively, walking toward her. "Are you okay?"

"Of course I'm okay. I thought I was clear earlier when I asked you to leave." She doesn't look at me, and I can tell by her posture that she's still hurt and upset. She doesn't appear to be sick, though.

"Is your roommate here?" I ask.

"She's been in the library all day." Heather pauses to glare at me. Then she looks back down at the Bible as if I'd just rudely interrupted her.

"Are you sure you're okay? I thought you were sick, and—" I awkwardly hold up the crackers. "I brought you this." As I step forward, right beside her bed, a loud crinkling sound under my foot causes me to jump back.

Heather's eyes widen when she sees the Oreo cookie package that I just crushed. All three sleeves inside are empty, except for a few crumbs nestled in the shiny white ridges. Her face turns so pale that it almost seems translucent. I stretch over to the trashcan beside her and politely throw it away. Heather looks down at her desk as if I'd never walked in to check on her, as if I'm not even in the room.

It's as if I'd never existed to her at all. I gently place the crackers on her desk, right beside her Bible and a large tin of Altoids. "I'm so sorry. I thought you needed this," I say.

When she doesn't respond, I tiptoe out of her room and pull the door shut.

milieu control: a tactic that isolates members of an insular group; enforces limitations on communications between the group and the outside world; creates a sense of general alienation; can deepen bonds between isolated members

The Bridge

Back at my dorm, I pull out my room key, and stop when I notice something taped to my door. My heart leaps when I see what it is: an origami airplane.

I drop my keys on the ground to undo the paper folds hiding the message:

> *There's only one place (but it's nearby)*
> *Where boats drift under as planes cross high*
> *And cars and trains pass in between.*
> *Meet me tonight at eight fifteen.*

Happiness briefly overcomes my sadness and confusion as I step onto the down escalator at 7:30 p.m. The sky has darkened to a vivid blue that makes everything against it more visible and radiant. The nagging memory of Heather ignoring me at her desk drifts further and further away as I take in the countless lit-up windows outside—Heather's one tiny room among city blocks packed with buildings glowing top to bottom with squares, all so small from this perspective. I grip the moving rubber handrail and watch the thousands of crisscrossed lights travel with haphazard purpose.

The walk isn't far from my dorm, but the winding staircase to the top of the BU Bridge is steep and noisy. I'm dizzy by the time I reach the top. A jogging professor huffs an acknowledgment as he passes and thumps down the metal steps. I walk to the middle of the bridge and stop to see the buildings' staggered glowing curve along the water. I remember at orientation someone saying the BU Bridge is the only place where you can see an airplane above a car above a train above a bike above a boat. It's been one of my favorite spots since then—the perfect place to achieve distance.

"You're early," Josh says into my ear.

I jump.

"Hey," he says, laughing. He puts his hand on my shoulder affectionately. "I'm always scaring you, right? I'm sorry."

"No. It's okay. I just didn't see you coming," I say.

His hand drops down to my arm and searches for my hand. "That's funny, because I saw *you* the moment I got to the top of the stairs," he says. "You know, I still remember the first time I saw you reading a book in that chair, completely oblivious to the rest of the world around you."

"That's me. Oblivious." I laugh bitterly, my interactions with Heather creeping forward again.

Josh puts his other hand around mine and leans into me. "No," he says. "You're the opposite of that, actually. You're observant and kind and adventurous." He kisses my hand. "I admire you for all those things," he says.

Cars *whoosh* by us in a steady rhythm as we step aside for a pack of students heading toward Cambridge with black guitar cases covered in stickers. I pull away from him to lean against the cold, metal rail where the wind is stronger.

"Come back here," he says. He drops his hands to my waist and pulls me closer.

"Josh . . ." I want to ask him so many questions about Heather and Meredith and Italy, but I don't want to break our connection, so I don't say anything else.

As I wrap my arms around him, my butterflies give way to something warm and exhilarating. As the cars pass, it's like time is suspended.

"Did you make a decision about this summer?" he asks.

I think about Heather. How cold and cutting she was this afternoon. I think about my family back home, unaffected by my absence. I think about how I've felt alone and lost for so long now. And, finally, I think about my mother and desperately wish she could help me decide. *Life is fleeting. How could I not accept this opportunity?*

"I'm coming with you," I say, my face pressed into his shoulder.

He kisses the top of my head, his other hand clutching my hair, and I let him hold me like that for a long time. The wind whips around us and people continue to pass by in both directions, yet it somehow feels like we are separate from the rest of the world.

In this moment, I'm certain of one thing: *Josh and I were chosen for this. I was chosen.*

(continued)

They will tell you the numbers don't lie.

The weekly Victory Bulletins confirm multiple successes in their mission to save the world. The bulletins are crammed with figures, along with words like, "Awesome!" "Glorious!" "Amazing!" The statistics are made into artistic graphics, which are then projected onto large screens for the members, who often stand and cheer for each success every Sunday.

Here are just a few "Kingdom facts" from past bulletins:

Average attendance in Boston this year: almost 8,000

Baptisms in Boston YTD: 727

Largest single special church contribution for missions: nearly $1.5 million

Give to Boston nonprofit volunteers: close to 5,000

Funds raised for the poor and needy: almost $700,000

Kingdom Publications sold: nearly 10,000!

Chosen interns for world missions: 79

Number of major cities with successfully planted Kingdom churches: 67 . . . and counting!

How is it that one of the world's fastest growing organized religions has recently been banned from 39 U.S. college campuses?

INTERVIEWS FOR EMILY X—

Article by Julia O. James

HEATHER: Emily *never* should have been chosen over me, so, yes, I was furious. I didn't even get credit for recruiting her. *Josh* did, even though I did all the work.

I know it's a sin to say this, but what happened in Italy serves all of them right.

RACHEL: I didn't want to go to Italy. My mother didn't even want to go to Italy. We were busy packing for the move to California so Dad could meet us there in August. Then my uncle came over one night, handed her a ticket, and told her she didn't have a choice. "It's up to you to fix this," he said to her. He slammed the door when he left.

UNIVERSITY CHAPLAIN: I was aware of the official campus club. We had no idea it was connected to something like this. We banned them from our campuses even before Emily's father threatened the lawsuit. We take the safety of our students very seriously. After twenty years as chaplain, I can honestly say the Kingdom is one of the most destructive groups I've ever seen.

ANDREW: Emily is one of those people you feel instantly connected to because she's such a genuine person. Looking back, I wish I had talked her out of going to Italy, but Josh and Ben would have—literally—killed me.

RESIDENT ASSISTANT AT EMILY'S DORM: That girl was a crazy bitch. Heather was. Not Emily. Emily seemed nice. I didn't know anyone named Kara.

MEREDITH: I had never even heard of an intern named Kara.

PART TWO

Italy, May 1994

"Those who can make you believe absurdities can make you commit atrocities."

–VOLTAIRE

Crossing Over

The phone call went like this.

"Daddy?"

"Hi, sweetie. How was Boston Garden?" The sharp pinch of homesickness threw me off for a few seconds, and I had to make myself focus on the purpose of my call.

"Oh, fine," I said in my breeziest voice. "I mean, it was really cool to see it."

"Did you go to a game?"

"Uh—" How could I explain everything that's happened? Where would I even start? "More like a tour." It was easier to lie.

"Patti loved the pictures you mailed of you and your friend. And she was thrilled you were wearing the outfit she sent, but I almost didn't recognize you! You must be ready to get back to some good old Southern food—get some meat back on your bones!" He laughed. "Oh. Hang on just a—" He said something to Jean in muffled demands. "Sorry. I've got a conference call with a judge in five minutes. So. When will we see you back here, sweetheart?"

My heart fluttered as I took a deep breath. "I wanted to talk to you about that, actually."

"Go ahead."

"Well, there's this internship—"

"Whoa," he interrupted. "An internship during your first summer in college? Impressive."

"It's in Europe. Italy, to be exact."

He whistled the cartoon falling sound. "I didn't realize you were interested in world travel."

"Well, I hadn't really thought about it until I was selected," I said.

"Selected," he repeated. "So, *for whom* will you be *working*?" His voice had shifted to a formal business tone. I always forget how intimidating he can be without warning.

I paused again, not sure how to answer. "It's through the university, so it would be with other students from my campus," I said tentatively. It wasn't really lying, since Kingdom on Campus is an official university-approved group. He wouldn't have understood even if I did explain.

"Sounds promising, especially if you pull another four-point-oh this semester," he said. His voice momentarily faded as I realized in a panic that I had no idea how I was doing in my classes. But it couldn't be good. After maxing out my absences, I meant to touch base with my professors, but I was too distracted by everything else going on. ". . . Tamara might be able to provide you with some good advice about traveling over there. Also, don't forget my friend Deborah teaches law in Zurich now. It's not too far away, and she hasn't seen her very own goddaughter since you were little. I'm going to miss having you home though. You're still my baby, you know."

My heart constricted with an overwhelming ache. "I know, Dad," I say.

A sound beeped on his end of the line. "Sweetie, I've got to take this. Listen, it sounds like a great opportunity. I can't wait to hear more about the details. I love you," he said.

"Love you too, Daddy."

I still haven't shaken my sadness since we hung up.

Trust Games

My first two days in Europe are pure motion.

Will and Meredith set up a competition to see which intern could get to the villa with the most money saved from frugal planning. I researched every route in *Let's Go Europe* and I ended up with a flight to Amsterdam (the cheapest one I could find), train to Florence with a student-rate Eurail Pass, and, now, the public bus, which is supposed to stop at the base of a hill leading to the villa where Will and the other interns will be waiting.

Meredith called me the morning after I met Josh at the BU Bridge to coordinate my travel plans, even taking me to lunch at a fancy restaurant, where we worked out the details and logistics of getting me to the Italy mission. We met almost every single day until I left—a welcome distraction since Josh had to fly out early with Andrew and Ben to help prepare for the mission.

There wasn't enough time for me to fly home before leaving for Italy. Dad wasn't happy about it, but he was in the midst of a trial, so he eventually agreed to deposit the money I needed for the trip so I could fly directly out of Boston. Meredith hired movers to transport my things from the dorm to their pool house. And I was so busy with the logistics of leaving that I didn't return messages from Summer or Tamara—both calling to wish me a good trip.

Meredith had even driven me to the airport and walked all the way to my gate. She must have sensed my anxiety about leaving the country alone when she pushed my hair back with softened eyes. "Oh, honey, don't be nervous. The experienced interns are already there waiting for you." She grasped both of my hands in hers. "Listen. Just between us, the Italy mission is the most important one of all."

"Really?" I'd heard there were missions everywhere from Hong Kong to Russia. Why was Italy so special?

Her eyes gleamed with a proud excitement. "Not many people know this, but Will and I are becoming coleaders in the church. In *California*. There's been talk about it since Africa, only with the top elders, so we've kept it hush-hush. The most important thing your group can do is to stay focused and never lose sight of our goals. The more success-ful we can make this mission, the faster we can spread the

Kingdom's message like a wildfire across America extending all the way to California."

Her expression was both adamant and expectant. This wasn't the first time Meredith had brought up Africa and how it had changed so much for her and Will. She was always so reverent and secretive when bringing it up—sometimes even using the word "miracles." I asked about it once, but she looked at me in the same way she used to chide Heather for doing the wrong thing. "Unwavering belief is what will get you into heaven someday. Questions of doubt only lead to a prideful heart." After that, I was scared I might ask the wrong thing, or in the wrong way, and it would be construed as doubting her. So I never asked again.

A vague uneasiness prompted me to take a deep breath as I watched a plane touch down on the nearby runway with the silent motion of a successful landing. I looked back at her and squeezed her hands. "We'll do our best," I said.

"Don't forget you were chosen, Emily," Meredith said. "And I think you know at least one girl who would have killed for your spot."

Now after two days of constant travel, I'm not sure even Heather would want to be in my spot anymore. I'm desperate to get to the villa. Besides having no access to a shower and very little money for food (everything was going toward the mission competition), I wasn't prepared for the sense of loneliness while traveling solo. I've been surrounded by people everywhere I've been, yet I can't remember the last time I actually spoke to someone. It reminds me of the period of time after Sadie left, before I found the Kingdom—before Josh found me. I replay my time in Boston with Josh like a secret movie. It will be a huge relief to see a familiar face—though deep down, I know Josh has become so much more than that.

I rest my head against the bus window as we enter a small town near Florence, weaving through curved strips of stores, apartment houses, and ancient buildings. It's like a dimension where the Middle Ages somehow collided with modern life. Even though I can't read or speak Italian, I recognize certain words: *"perfumeria," "pizzeria," "caffetteria."* It's strange to see camera shops, grocery stores, and restaurants labeled in another language. People file in and out of doorways performing ordinary tasks. They must pass right by all this beautiful stuff every day without even a second glance, carrying out tasks in their glamorous-yet-ordinary everydayness.

My bus pulls into an empty parking lot and whines to a stop. Everyone around me gets up to leave. I grab my bags and follow the crowd, not sure of what to do next. I look around and panic when I don't see anyone familiar. An Italian man wearing a soccer jersey helps me with my bags. His smile seems genuine.

"Grazie," I say timidly.

He asks me something in Italian, and I freeze up. I have no idea what he's saying. A female voice behind me answers him in Italian, and he smiles politely and walks away.

I turn around to see a tall, skinny girl with long, black hair. "You must be Emily," she says. If she hadn't said my name, I would have mistaken her for a local.

"Hi," I say. "I mean, yes, I'm Emily. And you're . . ." Talking is awkward. It's been days since I've held a conversation. I try to remember all the Kingdom students I'd seen around Boston, yet I can't place her.

"The person who'll show you where to go." She smiles. It isn't the reassuring kind, more like an amused "private joke" one. "I'm Kara," she says with a brief laugh, extending her hand. Her fingers are adorned with stacks of rings.

"Emily," I say. I shake her hand, and her eyes wander to my mother's charm necklace resting against my chest.

"Love the necklace," she says.

"Thanks . . ." My voice trails off. My hands fidget with it instinctively. Kara is looking around as if scanning the area, already on to the next task.

I sway, suddenly unsteady from exhaustion. *Why would they send a total stranger to meet me? Where is Josh? And Will? Or even Andrew?* I reach down and grip my suitcase handle, ready to follow her lead. Everyone we pass is speaking Italian. Across the street, the green-shuttered apartment buildings loom over us. My jet lag kicks in again, like a wavy brightness infecting my peripheral vision.

"Are you all right?" Kara touches my arm to steady me.

The stress from the journey catches up with me as my

hands begin to shake. I try to remember the last time I slept or ate.

"Hey. It's going to be okay," she says. "The first few days can be a little rough, but don't worry. I'm a pro." She laughs. Even my thoughts seem upside down. Just putting one foot in front of the other is a challenge. Questions spin through my mind like manic sound bites from somewhere else. *Who is this girl?* being at the top of the list. I do my best to suppress them as I follow Kara. I feel like I'm gliding just above the ground.

Kara takes my bag as if sensing my instability. "The villa isn't far from here. It's right up this hill, actually," she says, rolling my bag behind her with a grinding racket.

I grip my backpack straps, trying to hide how I feel about having to trek by foot up a steep hill after days of nonstop traveling. *Some welcome wagon.*

The narrow road is just wide enough for two small cars, and we have to step into the grass when we hear one coming. There's hardly any traffic as we make our way up the hill. I look around at the landscape dotted with ancient build-ings amid olive groves and vineyards. Majestic cypress trees stretch into jagged points against the sky. Bright red poppies sprout wildly across the fields and through cracks in the stone-lined wall. The wall curves all the way to a tall rusted gate anchored by two of the most enormous cypresses I've ever seen.

I'm embarrassed by how much I huff and puff as we make our way up the hill. "There isn't a car or something

JENNIFER MOFFETT

to take us up and down?" I ask, wiping sweat from my fore-head.

"I thought after your long bus ride you'd want to stretch your legs," Kara answers. I prickle at her almost mocking tone. "I swear we're almost there—it's just through that gate."

Our footsteps crunch through a wide path of pea gravel for a couple more long minutes before we pass the cypress trees and go through the gate. We step into an open court-yard, where a tangle of flowering vines spills over a rick-ety pergola in desperate need of repair. Andrew is the first person I see. He looks happy and rested, and I feel a smile spread across my face when he sees me.

"Em!" Andrew yells, running up to give me a hug. "It's so good to see you!" I'm overwhelmed with relief to see he's here. Other than assuring me Josh would be here, Meredith was very secretive about who else made the cut. I inhale his cologne—the familiar smell of Andrew: Calvin Klein's Obsession.

"You too," I say, suddenly overwhelmed, unexpected tears springing to my eyes.

Andrew steps back. His eyebrows furrow in confusion. "Are you okay?" he asks.

I don't know. I don't say it out loud, yet I hear the words so clearly in my mind.

Kara taps me on the arm. "Hey. You can leave your bags here, but let's go inside and check in at the office."

"We'll talk soon," Andrew says, giving me a small wave,

his expression still showing concern. *I must look like a wreck.* I almost hope I *don't* see Josh right away.

We walk through a concrete archway and a long hallway, at the end of which stands an ancient, imposing wooden door. Kara knocks forcefully. I hear the rustling of papers through the door. "Come in." I recognize the voice. *Will.*

Kara pushes it with one hand, her other on my shoulder. "Look who's here," Kara says with an optimistic tone.

His face lights up when he sees me. "Emily! Come in! How was your trip?" He seems more relaxed here. His hair has grown out, making it seem even more disheveled, and he appears to be growing a shadow of a beard. I can't imagine Meredith approving of his look. The intense amount of time I spent with her before flying out taught me that she loves order, neatness, and groomed appearances.

"Great," I lie. I'm doing my best to keep it together, but lightheadedness and hunger are threatening to overcome me.

Will straightens the various stacks of papers and passports on his desk. "I'm keeping our items in a safe here in my office so nothing gets stolen," he says.

"Oh. Okay." I pull the pouch hanging around my neck over my head and dig out my passport, Eurail pass, credit cards, and the traveler's checks Meredith had helped me get at the American Express office in Boston. She said I could sign them over when I get here, but until then they could be replaced if stolen. I touch my collarbone, checking for my mother's necklace, which slipped underneath my shirt.

Rather than ask him to put it in the safe, I quickly decide to keep it hidden.

He looks up at me. "Are you okay, Emily?"

"Uh, yeah. I think so. I mean, I haven't really slept since . . ." I hear my voice trail off as I search my brain for today's date to match it with the day I left Boston, but it's all jumbled.

"It's a long journey, I know. And you took the *really* long route to be more fruitful and generous to our mission. We appreciate that kind of dedication. So . . ." He backs away and slides behind his desk. "Let's see how you did."

My brain is like a stalled car trying to crank itself into motion. Kara nudges me. "The competition," she whispers. Kara hovers over Will as he counts the money and taps numbers into a calculator.

He looks up and smiles. "We have a winner," he says. "That means you and Kara may have the private building."

"Yes!" Kara says under her breath.

"We'll hold on to all of this in the safe for you," Will says. "Then you'll get everything back once I'm finished with the books and our budget." He sorts through the cards, cash, and traveler's checks, making neat stacks for each.

I notice the phone on his desk. "Can I call home? I promised my dad I'd call him when I got here."

Will shuffles through some papers on his desk. "We prefer to make the initial call. Parents like knowing you're in good hands. I plan to take care of that this afternoon. Here.

Fill this out," he says, handing me a form for emergency contacts.

"Oh. Okay," I say. I fill it out, hand it to him, and turn to leave with Kara, who is almost out the door.

"Wait," he says. He digs through a drawer and pulls out a blank airmail letter. "You'll need to write home today so we can go ahead and mail it." He glances at Kara.

"I can help her with that this afternoon," she says.

Will pushes his chair back and stands dramatically. "All right, then." His voice echoes through the room. "It's time to get started."

"Oh," I say, surprised. "I was actually hoping to clean myself up, maybe take a nap. . . ."

Will's eyes flash for just a moment. "There isn't a moment to waste, Emily. There are souls waiting to be saved." My head droops in shame. My first day—my first *minute*—here and I'm already disappointing Will. Meredith's words echo in my head: *Our future depends on Italy.*

Kara nudges me forward and leads me out of the office. We pass through an open space, and into a large room where the other interns are waiting.

Josh is the first person I see, and relief floods through me—any concerns about how I look are gone. He raises his eyebrows and smiles at me, like he wasn't sure until just now that I'd actually be here. My heart pounds as I smile back. I make to move toward him, but Kara gently grabs my arm. "You're over here," she says, guiding me toward a semicircle of chairs. I turn to look at Josh. He only offers an apologetic shrug. After weeks of imagining this scenario, it's disappointing to see him in passing and without the opportunity to talk.

Kara instructs me to sit down beside a girl I've never seen before. She's very small and seems younger than the rest of us. Kara leaves me to hover with the other DPs, including Josh, toward the back of the room.

"Hi," I say quietly. "I'm Emily."

"Lily—"

She barely gets her name out before another girl, standing closely behind her, snaps, "Hush! We're about to start." Lily runs her hand through her thick, brown hair and smiles nervously. Everyone else sitting in the circle of chairs is solemn and silent while the DPs chat quietly. I look around. After seeing so many amazing places out of my train and bus windows, this dingy room with cracked stucco walls and minimal décor is more than a little disappointing. *You're not here for a five-star vacation. You're here to save people*, I remind myself.

Will enters at the front of the large room.

"Disciples," he bellows. "Emily. Lily. Andrew. Todd. I need you to stay seated in the chairs."

Our semicircle is facing a wooden table pushed against the wall. The table is topped with large brown paper sacks, like oversized goodie bags waiting to be collected at the end of a birthday party.

"Kara. Shannon. Josh. Ben. Please come stand behind your disciple."

I watch Kara and the rest of the DPs make their way toward us. Kara whispers something to Josh in passing, making him smile. A pang of jealousy shoots through me. *Stop. It's nothing*, I tell myself. *We have the whole trip to spend together.* I compose myself as the DPs settle in behind us. Will continues: "Now, I want you to blindfold your new disciples."

What?

He hands each of them a red or blue bandanna to place around our eyes. Mine's red. I breathe in deeply through my nose as Kara ties a knot against the back of my head, securing total darkness. I strain my eyes to peek. I can't see anything.

"Now everyone listen carefully, because I want you to understand the importance of your Discipler-Disciple relationship. This is the basis for every single thing you will do on this mission." I sense Will pacing before us. "Yes, we are here to multiply our ministry and spread the Word of God to the lost souls here in this beautiful country, but each one of you here in this room is also here to advance your personal relationship with God. And we all know the way to accomplish that is by discipling each other.

"In order to be discipled, you must have a teachable heart and you must have a trusting heart," he continues. "Disciples, you have to be willing to do whatever your Discipling Partner—DP—advises you to do, without question. Proverbs 3:5 says: 'Lean not on your own understanding.'

You must not filter what you choose from your DP; it's all or nothing. A trusting heart will allow you to trust beyond your own understanding. How can you do what's right if you aren't willing to fully obey?" His voice moves in front of us, around us, behind us, back in front. Mixed with my exhaustion and hunger, the effect is almost dizzying.

"Now I want everyone to stand." He pauses. "Emily, Todd, Lily, Andrew. Your DP will lead you through this next step. Will you accept this test of faith? Will you trust them without question? Will your heart be open and obedient?" Each question ends with the lifted pitch of a revival preacher. He sounds more like the Leader than the Will I remember from my baptism.

Kara's hands warm my shoulders as she steers me forward with deliberate effort. I stumble a few times to keep up with her pace. Will continues a steady patter of words as we circle around his voice. It's like we're surrounded by him, and he's closing in. "Trust. Follow. Imitate. Only these actions will lead to being a disciple of Jesus. Your Discipling Partnership alone can guide you to a successful relationship with God."

He pauses as we continue moving around him. "Fear. Pride. Doubt. A rebellious heart. All of those things add up to that dreaded three-letter word: S-I-N." As he hisses the letters, my thighs bump into the table, and I almost cry out. His voice stops. The room goes quiet until Will begins speaking again, this time softly and very close to me.

"Now, Emily. I need you to put your hands
outside of the bag in front of you," Will says, his v
ing farther away again.

I touch the scratchy paper with the tip of my
Something shifts inside the bag—a living someth
immediately jump back.

Kara holds her ground behind me, gripping my sho
der. She nudges me back to the table. "You can do this," sh
whispers. "The DPs are watching. You'll be fine, I promise.'
I can barely hear her reassuring words even though she's
whispering them directly into my ear. My head is thrumming from jet lag and, now, from fear.

Will raises his voice, as if speaking to everyone. "Emily?
Do you trust Kara without question? Do you trust Jesus to
speak through her? Will you accept the challenge He has
given you?"

His provocation hits me with a sudden immediacy, like
the moment in a wedding ceremony when a public response
is required. I can sense everyone waiting in silence for me
to react.

My hand trembles as I trace the rigid edge along the top
of the paper bag. In a quick burst, the thing in the bag strikes
my finger. A scream that doesn't even sound like my voice
fills the room. I instinctively lift my throbbing finger to my
mouth and taste blood. It feels like everything around me
is upside down, and the only thing keeping me up is Kara's
steady hand on my back. I can hear everyone around me

ENNIFER MOFFETT

stirring nervously. One of the girls lets out a brief, anxious shriek. Will shushes them quiet.

I fight the urge to rip off the bandanna and yell at everyone, or push someone else to do it. Kara touches my hand and guides it back to the bag.

"Trust me," she whispers.

Her voice is sincere. And I realize I don't really know her, but something in this moment tells me to fully trust Kara. *It's a sign.* I feel the DPs watching me, and I sense the fear of the fellow disciples who were blindfolded. My fatigue gives way to a giddy sort of apathy. *What's the worst that could happen?*

I hold my breath and reach deep inside the bag, slowly this time, and my fear melts away the moment I feel a small mass of soft fur and hear the abrupt mewing sound of a kitten. It reaches for my hand, gripping it with its sharp claws to gnaw on my thumb. As it begins to purr, tears flood my eyes and seep into the cotton bandanna. My heart pounds in a jagged staccato from my chest to my fingertips. I want to fall on my knees and wail.

Kara gently removes my blindfold. The other blindfolded interns shuffle around silently. The girl, Lily, who sat beside me, is pushing nervously at the air with her hands, obviously unaware of what just happened. Their anxiety is palpable. Josh and Todd—the male interns who could see—are grinning broadly, trying not to laugh and break the carefully orchestrated tension.

Will barks more instructions as he gives me a quick wink.

150

"Kara, take Emily to her room. Emily, take your bag with you. And remember that trusting your DP is exactly like trusting in God. You will be rewarded with countless blessings. Amen?!"

"Amen!" everyone answers.

I follow Kara through a rustic kitchen with a farmhouse door that leads to another courtyard. I carefully pull the kitten out of the bag and cradle it to my chest. It wiggles in my arms as I take slow steps forward, still a bit shaky. The sharp scent of fresh herbs fills the air as Kara steps up our pace. My left foot drops with a crunch into the pea gravel. The warm Tuscan breeze hits my face. I stop to take a deep breath and look at the world around me where multitextured hills slope away from us in every direction. The view is so beautiful it almost looks like a fake backdrop.

Suddenly Kara stops and takes the kitten out of my hands. She carefully pulls it up to her neck. "I already named it," she says.

I hear feet crunching across the gravel behind us. Someone is laughing. "You were so freaked out. It was just made of rubber," a distant male voice says to someone else. Nervous laughter fills the distance, the kind of laughter that says, thank God the worst is over. I wonder what was in their bag as I notice Kara is halfway down the hill.

She disappears inside a tiny stone building with no visible windows other than an open-air rectangle of crisscrossing clay embedded into one side.

I rush to catch up with her.

Inside, the walls are stone like the exterior, and I'm relieved to see that there's one small window on the back wall. A metal bunk bed flanks the wall near the window. Both beds are covered with old, mismatched quilts, and there's a sink on the other side of the room.

"This is your bed. Mine's up here," Kara says from the top bunk.

I look around. "Where's the bathroom?" I ask.

"At the main house. Or out there." She points toward the window that frames a small view of the nearby vineyard. Kara stretches out on her bed to play with the kitten. She must have noticed my surprise. "Don't worry," she says. "We'll have a lot more freedom out here."

I notice my luggage is neatly stacked at the foot of the bed. "How'd that happen?" I ask.

"I know. It's like a miracle." She laughs. She sounds sarcastic, but it's hard to tell. "I'm sure one of the guys brought them here for you." She looks up to gauge my reaction. Did Josh already tell the others about us? Either way, I decide not to respond. I don't know how close Kara is to him, and I don't want to say anything out of turn.

I look at Kara with the intent to scrutinize. Her carefree goofiness makes it impossible. Her hair dangles above the tiny kitten as it leaps up to repeatedly attack it. She giggles. "Dolce says sorry about the scratch." She digs something out of her pocket. "Here," she says as she reaches down to hand me a Band-Aid. "This should fix it."

I smile. "I like the name." I wrap my finger, which still stings but isn't bleeding anymore. I want to like Kara. I know it will make life here a thousand times easier if I do. Already I can tell she's far more relaxed than Heather. We could maybe even have fun together.

I want to ask her so many questions. I have the odd sensation that I've walked in on a movie set and don't yet know my lines. I look around for a place to put my things.

"Where's the closet?" I ask.

"There isn't one," she says, "but we can share the drawers," she says.

I roll my suitcase over to the old wooden chest, unzip it, and begin unpacking.

"So how did you meet Josh?" she asks a little too casually.

"Josh?" I try to play it off.

"He's the reason you're here, right?"

Now I'm on guard. "I guess. He's the one who invited—I mean, I came here to be a part of the mission."

"Are you in looooooove with him?" she asks teasingly.

The sting of embarrassment triggers a sudden heat across my face. I guess living with Kara isn't going to be easy. Thankful my back is to her, I fold a cotton top and place it in the drawer. I fold another one before answering. "Does it matter?"

"Hmmm," she says, as if pondering with a vague sense of authority.

Heather and I had our share of awkward confrontational

exchanges back in Boston. It was exhausting because Heather was the master of deflection. At least I knew what to expect with her. Starting over with Kara is new territory, and frankly a little scary.

"So what brought *you* here?" I ask, hoping to change the subject. I try to hold myself together by refolding all of my clothes and putting them away neatly. This somehow keeps me calm.

"Me? I didn't have a choice." She's giggles at something Dolce does.

I'm not sure whether she wants me to ask questions about that, so I don't. I know better than to make a DP uncomfortable or defensive.

"If you really want to know the truth, my mother sent me," she volunteers.

"So she knows why you're here?"

"Yep," she says. A pang of jealousy hits me. There's no way my dad would have given me his blessing if he knew the truth about my mission here. *And that's exactly why I'm here instead of there.*

"Is your mother in the Kingdom?" I ask, brushing off my bitterness.

Kara pauses. "You could say that."

I zip up my empty suitcase and start on my backpack, but there isn't really anywhere else to store my things. Why this so-called house with no bathroom or closet and an open-air section of a wall counts as some sort of reward, I can't tell.

"Can I ask why you wanted us to live out here without a shower or toilet?"

"I prefer to keep my distance from the others." She looks at me. "Believe me. You'll understand soon enough."

Her statement seems odd, especially from someone who just asked me to blindly stick my hand into a bag. I don't want distance from the others. Especially when Josh, the only other person I really know, is one of them.

"Didn't you know Shannon from Boston?" she asks.

"Shannon?" I draw a blank.

"The girl unpacking the boxes in the courtyard? Lily's DP."

Oh. I suddenly remember Shannon. I saw her at Will and Meredith's house in Boston the night I was baptized. I try to remember what Heather said about her. I just remember it was critical—then again, anything Heather said about anyone usually was.

"I may have seen Shannon at a church event," I say. I close a drawer and look up at Kara. "I think my DP—I mean, former DP, Heather, knew her, but I don't really know her at all," I say.

"Hmm. I'm guessing Heather didn't like her. Shannon is a trip," Kara says. "And not necessarily the good kind."

"Did you know Heather?"

"Not really. I've heard about her though. From Shannon, actually. She said you took Heather's spot, which is kind of a big deal. I hear that makes you special." She smirks at me.

My defensiveness flares again. "I don't think that's true.

Heather is more valuable in Boston. She's the big deal."

"Yeah, I heard that one too."

Kara's voice is full of sarcasm. Suddenly I want nothing more than to get out of this villa and away from her—and find Josh. "Will we be meeting up with the others again today?"

Kara smiles at me, and it almost seems sympathetic, like she feels sorry for me. "I think you should get some rest," she suggests.

It's like her just saying the word—"rest"—has cast a spell on me. My exhaustion overcomes me once again, the small rush of adrenaline from my blindfolded brush with Dolce rushing right back out. I practically stumble over my suitcase as I go to collapse on the lower bunk.

When I come to, my brain begins to sift through recent events as I try in vain to remember falling asleep. I reach down and feel my blue jeans, stale from the train ride. I want to go back to sleep, but clips from yesterday (*or is it still today?*) begin to replay in my mind, as Kara's breathing on the bunk above me forms a soothing rhythm. *I'm not alone.* And that's comforting. My body is heavy, but my mind is alert. Nocturnal sounds fill the room: leaves rustling, the faint screech of an insect, the swell of the night air. I close my eyes again to let my body drift, hoping my mind will follow.

Then I hear a footstep.

I open my eyes and focus on the interconnected springs under Kara's mattress. I hear it again, this time in a brazen succession heading toward our building. I turn onto my side to lift myself on my elbows. My heart races. I hear someone shift right outside the clay openings in the wall. A shadow passes by. I watch it trail past silently. I look over at the window. It's closed shut by two wooden shutters connected with a rickety latch. I hear the shutters move. "Hello?" I whisper. I get up and tiptoe to the door. I glance at Kara's back before leaning outside.

"Hello?" I ask louder.

Everything is quiet. I walk all the way around our building, my fingers trailing the bumpy stone exterior and the grid of clay. No one is out here.

The night is bright and clear. I perch on the nearby ledge and look at the darkened vineyards, the tall cypresses marking the existence of other villas. I watch a colony of tiny bats swooping erratically around a nearby tree. I rub my arms just as Dolce leaps up right beside me, causing me to gasp. My breath turns shallow and quick. I wonder if someone is watching me, if they are trying not to laugh at the fact that a kitten nearly scared me to death—twice now. I look around again. It's completely quiet. The distant lights of other villas gleam silently against the night.

"Stop scaring me," I say to Dolce, exhaling with relief. She meows at the vineyard. I reach out to scratch her head, but she moves just out of range. I watch her scale the ledge with a languid, knowing stride, then leap down and disappear into a long row of grapes.

Just Like Family

Dear Dad,

Greetings from Italy!

My flight took forever, but I really enjoyed the train ride. I think Italy has the most beautiful scenery, and Germany is a close second.

So far, I'm learning a little Italian and seeing lots of churches. All the cathedrals are so amazing.

The other interns are super nice. Our place has a view of the Tuscan hills, and we even have a cat! I've made lots of new friends already. I

can't wait to get my photos developed
so you can see for yourself!
   Hugs to Patti and Tamara!
Arrivederci!
   Oh, and one more thing. I never
knew Italian food could be this good!

                              Love,
                                Emily

My stomach grumbles at the last line. Breakfast was a small roll and two slivers of an orange that I inhaled way too fast. "Do you think there's any more food?" I ask Kara, handing her the letter.

"Probably not," she says with a shrug. "We're under a strict operating budget."

"Oh. Well, maybe we could run into town? I can take us to breakfast. I just have to get my documents and money," I say.

Her eyes flash a hint of concern before glancing at my letter. "We'll have to wait until our activities are over, but they're safer locked in the office anyway. Trust me."

I open my mouth, and then hesitate. "Look," she says, her tone appeasing. "What's important right now is to show your family that this trip is a positive, life-changing experience." She folds my letter back and waves it for emphasis. "Happy people at home leave us free to prove our mission is a success. And the sooner that happens, the sooner we'll have things like better food."

Will's voice drifts from the courtyard through our open door calling everyone to a meeting. Kara and I rush to the main villa where some of the interns are already sitting on the floor. I spot Josh immediately. He's too deep in conversation with Andrew to notice me. I'd hoped to talk to Josh alone by now, but between trying to sleep off my jet lag and the scheduled activities, we haven't had a moment to ourselves.

Will raises his arms to signal the need for our attention. "Everyone on the floor in a circle," he says. I sit beside Kara, and Shannon plops down to my left. After the paper bag incident yesterday, everyone seems wary of organized activities.

Will sits in a chair, smiling vaguely at the window as if lost in thought. As soon as everyone is still and quiet, he scans our faces. "Before we dig into the mission of sharing our faith with new souls, we need to strengthen the spiritual bonds between each other. So I want everyone to offer something about themselves that will help us get to know you a little better. Be sure to include a fact that most people wouldn't know."

I try not to show my displeasure with this announcement. I've always hated these get-to-know-each-other scenarios at school. It's just so awkward when everyone is watching, expecting you to say something either profound or self-deprecating or witty about yourself. I've always felt like I fail under the pressure of trying to talk while thinking of what to say at the same time, especially when talking about myself.

Will leans back as if relaxing before a show. His chair puts him higher than the rest of us, who are sitting cross-legged on the ground. He leans down and puts his elbows on his knees, just enough to bend to our level. "Look. I can see you guys are a little uneasy. That's understandable," he says. "The trust game was an intense way to start. Right, Emily?"

Heat rises in my cheeks as his gaze falls on me, along with the stares from other interns. "But we all survived," he says with a chuckle. A gentle rumble of laughter from the others seems to calm the circle. "And here's the point. You trusted. You didn't filter or resist even though some of you just met your DP for the first time, for goodness' sake. You knew your DP wouldn't do anything to hurt you because they are appointed disciplers in God's Kingdom. It is your DP's sole job to lead you to be more like Jesus through trust and imitation. Don't forget that your faith in God is directly reflected through your faith in your DP."

The "amen" that follows is from several male voices, including Josh's. This time, the sound is stronger and more reverent. The voices converge to lift me up as someone to be proud of, someone who succeeded. Kara leans into me for a friendly *it's all okay* bump with her shoulder, but I still don't want to be first right now.

"So," says Will, straightening in his chair. "Emily, since you were the first to fully trust, we'll let you be last in the circle today."

I exhale with relief. It's almost like he read my mind.

"I guess that means we'll start with . . . Andrew." Will puts his hand on Andrew's shoulder affectionately.

Andrew sits very still, a sign of either total calm or hidden terror. "Well," he murmurs. "I'm Andrew. I go to MIT, where I study engineering—"

"Andrew," Will interrupts. "Don't be humble. Tell them why you chose your school. And speak up."

Andrew hesitates, and then continues. "I'm on a full scholarship there." He glances down as if embarrassed. "Hmmm. What else? I'm from the Midwest." Long pause.

"Tell them about your father," Will says cheerfully.

Andrew looks taken aback. "What about him?"

"Tell them who he is." Will glances at us. "He's a big deal."

"He's an elected official," Andrew says quickly. He looks down as if embarrassed by this. Just as Will is about to say something else, Andrew lights up and interjects. "Oh, my most interesting fact is that I won a statewide spelling bee contest in the sixth grade."

"Dude," Todd interjects. "You might not want people to know that." Todd laughs at his joke, prompting us to laugh with him. I'm relieved to see Andrew smiling.

I look at Josh, who was appointed as Andrew's new DP

back in Boston a few weeks before we left, just after I committed to join the mission. Josh stares ahead into the middle of the circle. Maybe he's thinking about what he'll say when it's his turn. It occurs to me that I don't know what his interesting fact will be—should I?

"Todd?" Will says. "Your turn."

"Hi. I'm Todd. I'm from Georgia, and I go to Boston College on a different type of scholarship. I pitch for the baseball team, which leads me to my secret fact. Well, I guess it's not really a big secret—I can throw a baseball ninety miles per hour." Todd looks around with a smug expression on his face, as if this announcement usually earns praise.

Something sparks in Will's expression when Todd speaks, and I don't think it's just because Meredith had told me about Will being a baseball star back in the day. Todd is the perfect example of what Heather always called a "sharp" member, one of the things she said to watch for when inviting people to our activities—tall, muscular, and outgoing. Athletes and social butterflies are coveted recruits in the Kingdom, and the more attractive the better. DPs like this tend to get assigned high-priority new members, which is why Ben is Todd's DP.

Ben is next. "I'm Ben and I'm a senior biology major originally from Florida." I turn to Kara to catch her reaction, to see if maybe they know each other, but she isn't even looking at him. "Oh, and I almost forgot," Ben says nonchalantly. "I was recently nominated to be an apostle."

This elicits a few gasps. I look around for clarity. I haven't heard of the term "apostle" yet, so I'm not sure what he means.

Will sits up straight in his chair. "Congratulations, Ben. I didn't realize that." His smile is tight.

"Well," Ben says, his eyes level at Will. "The Leader said it all depends on the success of this mission."

Will doesn't respond as he pointedly shifts his attention. "Josh?"

Josh glances at Ben before he speaks. "Hey. I'm Josh. I'm from Louisiana, in case y'all didn't know from my accent." Everyone laughs. "I can't really think of a secret or an interesting fact. I can't throw anything ninety miles per hour, that's for sure."

Todd laughs out loud. "Not many can, dude."

Will steps in to coax him on. "Now, Josh, remember we're just like family here in Italy. As brothers and sisters in Christ, we must trust each other by being open. Plus, as Ben reminded all of us, our success in God is interconnected." The remark sounds unexpectedly sharp. I look to Ben for a reaction. He's as stoic as ever.

After a pause, Josh continues quietly. "Back home, my dad was in law enforcement. Kept me in line, I guess. Not many people know about that." He doesn't emphasize the word "was" but doesn't explain it either, and it hangs around us like a palpable question mark. "And my mom . . ." Josh's voice trails off, like he stopped to think of something to say and then zoned out from lack of sleep.

"Looks like Josh needs to sleep off that jet lag," Will jokes, quick to end the awkwardness with a glance at Josh before scanning the group. "And now for our lovely ladies."

Shannon speaks first, as if she's just been addressed directly, even though Lily is sitting next to Josh. Shannon's bleach-streaked hair is pulled up in a scrunchie and teased into a perky shape, her makeup thick with eyeshadow and mascara. "I'm Shannon, and I'm pretty sure I'm the oldest intern here. If I'm not the oldest, then I've been in the Kingdom the longest. I grew up in Boston, and my parents have been in the church since I was little. I'm not even sure if I'm a senior yet, since I've changed my major so many times. It's just so hard to decide which path would best benefit the Kingdom." Something about Shannon's overeagerness reminds me of Heather, although Heather would probably balk at the comparison. "Oh," Shannon continues, "Lily is my disciple in Christ." She touches Lily on the knee, as if to signal her permission to speak.

"Hi, I'm Lily. I grew up in Mexico City, where my father owns an international trading company. I've traveled my entire life and I speak four languages." She smiles and sweeps her long bangs to the side. Lily is naturally beautiful and would never require much makeup, especially not Shannon's heavy-handed technique. "Shannon is my DP *and* my best friend. And many of you may not know I am a twin to my brother, Marc. He's my other best friend." I smile at Lily's genuineness. She's someone I could see myself becoming close with, which is nice to think about considering my relationship with Kara is off to a rocky start. On cue, Kara elbows me to attention.

"Oh. Hi, I'm Emily. I'm from the Gulf Coast. I don't know my major yet, but I love art and literature. Hmm. Interesting fact. I think I was born with gills. I mean, I love to swim. The 'gills' thing is something my dad always told me because I teach kids to swim during the summer. Well, not this summer, since I'm here. Every other summer." *Crap.* I hate that I ramble when I'm nervous, but I've never been able to stop myself.

In an attempt to end my turn, I look at Kara, who appears amused. She leans back, her demeanor totally calm and cool—almost like she's above this activity, above the rest of us. "I'm Kara. Interesting fact: I am *not* in college. And my one purpose in life is to advance our efforts in this worldwide mission. We should all feel lucky we were chosen to be a part of this opportunity to change the world." The words seem almost sarcastic coming from her. When she glances at Will, he smiles at her in a way that's almost grateful.

"Well," says Will. "I guess it's my turn."

"Many of you know I was chosen to lead our worldwide mission exploration a while back, when we visited different countries to look for possible church plantings." He speaks carefully, as if cautious about his choice of words. "What many of you *don't* know is that when we were in Africa, I died."

Murmurs go up around the room. It's pretty obvious no one saw that statement coming, but Kara seems unfazed. Meredith's words about Africa pop into my head: *Miracles happened there.*

"It's okay. I promise I'm not a ghost," Will says in a soothing voice. "You all are probably wondering, 'If he died, then how is he sitting right here telling us about it?' Well, that's easy. I lingered on the other side, for quite a while, actually, but the Lord ultimately decided it wasn't my time. And when I came back, it was in a tiny hut in the middle of a far-away village. I had no earthly idea I'd been in a coma for days."

Will leans forward and whispers forcefully, "God was not ready for me to leave this world, brothers and sisters, because *this* was His will for me."

Shannon is crying (and making sure we all hear it). She wipes her eyes dramatically with the sleeve of her shirt, leaving a dark smudge. "How did it happen?" she asks.

Will shifts in his chair. "That's irrelevant now because that was *nothing* compared to what we've been chosen to do here. Now we're facing the real challenge. One even greater than the fight for my life on earth." He leans down again and raises his voice. "Disciples, first thing tomorrow, I want you to go with your DPs and bring in souls to save. Do not lose sight of our *great mission*. I want to see this villa *full* of new believers this week. This is why we were put on this earth. *This* is why we were sent here."

Will ends the meeting with a prayer as we hold hands in a circle. "Now follow your DP for your BTs," he says with a shooing-away gesture. Back when I first heard the unexplained acronyms out loud in Boston, it sounded so odd. But here it's reaffirming that a combination of simple letters could mean so much to us yet sound indecipherable to others, and it's only because we haven't had a chance to share our positive message with them.

"Let's go," Kara says, as I watch Josh and Andrew slip into another room deeper inside the villa. Kara leads me to a veranda near the courtyard overlooking the hills. "If we're gonna pray in Italy, we might as well enjoy the scenery God created for us, right?" she quips.

The landscape sprawled in front of us *is* stunning, yet instead of inspired, I can't help but feel unsettled, especially after Will's story at the end. Back in Boston, prayer was always the answer. I close my eyes tightly and pray for our mission, for our souls, for guidance—still, I have to make myself ignore the sharp pains stabbing through my empty stomach. I can't stop thinking about decadent breakfast food—ham and cheese omelets, pancakes with bacon, buttery croissants. My eyes burn like I'm about to cry. I'm not sure if it's because of hunger or faith. I open my eyes to see Kara staring at me as if waiting for someone to finish something that has nothing to do with her.

"Ready?" she says cheerfully.

Back in our room, Kara climbs on her bunk to listen to

music. She's been quiet and distant since the meeting, so I hold back on all the questions I want to ask her. Will's revelation is chewing at my brain. I can't stop picturing him laid out in a distant hut fighting death with all his might. I stand there awkwardly, wanting to talk, but not knowing what to say. She turns her head and smiles as she pulls one side of her headphones away from her head. "Hey. Let's just rest. Okay?" she says before repositioning it over her ear, putting an end to a potential conversation. My jet lag takes away any will to argue. I lie on top of my sheets and close my eyes, drifting off to the muffled static from songs I can't decipher.

It's dark outside when I come to. As my ears search for recognizable sounds, I hear two people talking outside our open wall. One I know is Kara, and the other sounds like a male.

The phrase "I don't know" is all I can make out of Kara's side of the conversation.

I hear the word "chosen" from the guy, but it sounds like part of a question.

Then silence.

I carefully roll off my bed without making a sound and tiptoe toward the door. I freeze at the sound of the guy's voice. *Ben.*

Kara is louder this time. "I said I have no idea what you're talking about."

Ben: "The book of Acts, chapter 28, says that Paul—"

"I know what it says," Kara snaps.

"Well, I guess you *do* know what I'm talking about, then." Pause. "Sister."

"Careful there, *Brother*. No one knows each other's biggest struggles like family."

Someone stomps off. I rush back to my bed and shut my eyes. I hear Kara step back inside and rummage through our drawers. By the time I gather the nerve to open my eyes, all I see is her walking out the door. I close my eyes again, pushing back my frustration at not understanding what's going on.

My eyes are heavy. Another wave of exhaustion pulls me down, smothering my questions with the promise of unconscious bliss. Since arriving at the villa, these waves have overtaken my body like an inescapable force. Jet lag and hunger are a powerful combination. Every time I wake up, I can't remember how or when I fell asleep. Sometimes, I completely forget where I am until the interlocking metal springs under Kara's mattress come into focus above me. I quietly study them as if they hold the answers.

Sticky Smiles

The next morning, a hand nudges me awake. The smell of Kara's clean, wet hair stirs my senses. I open my eyes and rub them awake. Sunlight projects a bright rectangle onto the floor of our room.

"Time to save souls," Kara says cheerfully, head tilted to the side while combing through shiny dark strands of hair.

Too sleepy to talk, I trudge across the room to find something to wear.

"I'll be outside drying my hair the good old-fashioned way," Kara says. It takes me a minute to realize she means under the sun. My brain tries to catch up and process the here and now, but I'm too exhausted. The conversation I overheard last night lingers in the back of my mind until it finally fades into something like the fragment of a half-forgotten dream.

Will is waiting in the courtyard for us. "Okay, I need everyone to confirm you have your bus passes by raising your hands." Everyone confirms. "DPs," he barks. "You are in charge. And disciples?" He smiles as if to assure us. "Your only instruction is to follow your DP. Got it?" We say "yes" in unison before breaking off into different directions. I try to walk slowly, hoping to catch Josh, but Kara is nearly running toward the bus stop. I glance back one last time to see Josh and Andrew talking to Will and Ben before I have to sprint to catch up to Kara.

The bus pulls up right after Kara and I get to the stop. By the time the others arrive the engines are revving and there are hardly any more seats. Josh offers me a small smile as he walks past, toward the back of the bus. My hopes sink as another chance to talk passes.

The bus wheezes down the narrow street. Kara stares out the window while I sit patiently awaiting our destination. The bus route parallels a river flanked by a redbrick wall where people lean over as if watching something on the low-lying banks below. Old, narrow buildings line the opposite bank of the river. We turn onto a side street just before a lemon-yellow building with dark brown shutters, all tightly closed.

I have no idea where we're going. I glance at Kara sitting beside me, her backpack in her lap, her lean arms casually wrapped around it. She shifts in her seat then glances at me, smiles, and looks out the window again, a sequence of gestures that makes her seem friendly and unknowable at the same time.

Everything I know about Kara says she doesn't care about what may happen around her. It's all "blend in and just be." It's hard to blend in here, though, especially when everyone around me speaks Italian. I feel like I'm in the way—on trains, on the bus, on the streets—because I don't yet *know* the way, and Kara acts like she's lived here for years. She takes charge in a way that seems effortless, not like Heather's "take charge or take over" personality.

Kara taps the side of my arm. She points to the Duomo in the distance.

I smile in appreciation, realizing I'm seeing the thing from photographs in our textbooks right now, in real life. The bus passes by unceremoniously, and I try to ignore my disappointment. It's weird to be so close without any plans to go there. I'd ask if we could stop, but Will has to approve any funds we spend, and I already know what the answer will be. Whatever we have is for the mission, not sightseeing.

"Do you know where we're going first?" I ask.

"You know, the cool thing about being a disciple is that you don't have to worry about any of that, right?" She seems cheerful. I notice she cuts her eyes at me as if checking my reaction.

It's like Kara is constantly testing me, but I'm too

exhausted to decide whether it's just because I don't know her yet or because I'm starving or— *Stay focused*. My memory of Ben's voice talking to Kara last night flickers back into my thoughts. If I'm going to be spending most of my time with her, I probably should try to get to know her better.

"So did you know Ben in Florida?" I ask.

Kara seems momentarily caught off guard by my question. Her expression is pleasant when she turns back to stare out the window, though. She's quiet for a few seconds. "We have mutual friends." Her tone is honest, but I can tell she's choosing her words carefully.

"Josh?" I immediately regret asking this.

"Nooooo," she says dragging out her answer with a slightly mocking tone. She gives me a funny look, or a look that says she thinks *I'm* funny.

I pick at my finger that Dolce scratched. You can't really see the wound anymore, but it still throbs.

I decide to change the subject. "Do they speak English where we're going?" We hadn't strayed far from the villa yet, and no one had even mentioned learning any Italian.

"It won't matter," Kara says, this time never turning from the window.

Question time is clearly over. I turn away from Kara and spot Shannon and Lily a few rows back, giggling about something together. A pang of familiar loneliness hits me. Italy is starting to feel like Boston did before I met Josh and Heather.

Our bus rounds a bend and glides to a stop in a parking lot, and Kara nudges me to stand. We step off the moment the doors *whoosh* open. Cigarette smoke thickens around us as the locals pause to light up before veering off in different directions. When we reach a vacant part of the sidewalk, Kara stops to open her backpack.

"Are you ready for this?" she asks, pulling out a roll of stickers. She holds them up. Each circle is a bright yellow smiley face.

"What are we supposed to do with these?" I ask.

"Our goal is to make as many Italians as possible . . . *smile.*"

"Seriously?"

"I'm always serious about the Kingdom." It's impossible to tell if she's actually serious, but I accept the fat roll of stickers and smile anyway.

"What am I supposed to say? How will people understand me?" I ask.

"It doesn't matter. Just smile, be friendly, and give *every single one* of these away." She reaches into her backpack again and hands me a stack of cards with words printed in Italian, the symbol of the cross filling the top right corner. Dread creeps over me as I remember the day by the birds sculpture at BU. It was hard enough recruiting when I did speak the same language as everyone else. This is beginning to seem impossible. It feels like that was a year ago, but it's barely been a month. I think about Josh and his hand covering my eyes. I wonder which direction he and Andrew went in after they got off the bus. I hold on to the hope that maybe we'll run into them while we're recruiting.

Kara nudges me away before approaching someone walking into a storefront that looks like a supermarket. I peel off a sticker, place it on the edge of my index finger, and walk up to a short stocky woman in a black dress carrying a canvas bag. I smile and hold my sticker out for her to take, forgetting about the cards in my other hand. She snatches it and sticks it to her bag, then shoots a string of words at me in Italian as she rushes off. I'm strangely elated watching the bright yellow face smile at me as she walks inside.

After handing out more cards, Kara pulls me aside. "This is taking way too long. We need a better spot." She turns around as if thinking, and grabs my arm. "Follow me," she says.

We run through the shadowy cobblestone streets where shops buzz with activity. I start to giggle despite myself—I'm running in *Italy!* Skinny women hover in front of doorways, smoking and chattering in Italian. Restaurants are clinking with lunch preparations where savory aromas leak into the street. I'd give all the money I brought to eat whatever it is they're cooking. With a sudden twinge of worry, I remember I don't have access to *any* of my money right now. I focus on following Kara.

We continue moving toward an opening at the end of the street where the cobblestones are drenched with sunshine. As we approach a large piazza, bells ring from a distant church. Pigeons scatter in gusts across the square. My heart leaps when I see Ben and Todd standing near a fountain. They're talking to a blond girl who is taller than both of them. I turn to Kara just in time to see her eyes narrow with concern.

"Let's go say hi," I suggest, grateful for familiar faces, but Kara grabs my arm.

"Wait," she says.

The tall girl has a card in her hand just like the ones we handed out. Her legs are so long and frail that they make her seem awkward, like a baby giraffe trying to balance itself. Her effect on Todd is evident. She laughs at something Todd says. Ben is off staring at a statue as if trying to figure it out.

Kara pulls me in the other direction. "We need to get busy. Trust me when I say we do *not* want to be the only team without any guests at our first meeting."

We wander backward, deep into a different winding street. My mind starts spinning again. I'm completely disoriented. I try to figure out where we are, but I only see plaques I can't understand. *VIA DEL* this and *VIA POR* that. If Kara left me here, I'd never find my way back. She's the one with the map and, I assume, the money. I try to clear my racing thoughts and simply follow without questioning. Kara slows down in front of a bustling café packed with locals sipping cappuccinos and espressos while standing against a bar. The crowd overflows onto the sidewalk where a few young Italian guys are talking and teasing one another. I wish I could understand what they're saying, and I wonder again why no one encouraged us to study Italian before the mission.

Kara walks right into the cluster of guys. I linger outside the group, self-conscious, as if I just violated someone else's territory. This is just as absurd as addressing a group of bikers outside the seedy bar under the bridge in my hometown. I imagine Kara could stroll into that very bar and no one would bat an eye. She has a commanding presence that transcends any barriers, including language, apparently.

The guys pause as Kara approaches. One of them makes a noise, almost like a friendly hissing sound. Kara peels off a sticker and puts it on one guy's nose. The group erupts in laughter. There's another one who's noticeably different from the others: taller, a little more confident, a lot more attractive, clearly the alpha of the group. I watch Kara figure this out. She pulls off a sticker and walks up to him, stands right in his face, and waits for him to take it. He extracts the sticker from her finger and puts it on his coat, looking to Kara for approval. The others around him begin to circle them with singsong-y banter. *Bella, BEL-la. Bel-LIS-sima.* Then Kara stretches on her tiptoes and slowly kisses him on the mouth. She pulls away, hands him the entire roll of stickers, and slips the rest of her postcards into the back pocket of his jeans. She gives it a suggestive pat, and walks back to me.

The other guys are laughing and passing the cards around. One of them breaks out in some sort of song. The one Kara kissed seems very pleased with himself.

What in the world is she doing? "I've never seen *that* recruiting method," I say to Kara.

"Emily. If you want to succeed in the Kingdom, you'd better prepare yourself to do anything necessary," she says. She takes my roll of stickers and shoves them into her backpack, zipping it with a calm finality.

I try to imagine Heather's reaction to this scenario had I done the same thing back in Boston. "What does kissing a complete stranger have to do with our salvation?"

"Everything," she says, giving me a serious look. Then she laughs.

She must see the concern and confusion on my face. "Emily." She pulls on my arm. "How many of them do you think will show up?"

"I'm guessing all and then some."

"Okay, then," she says with finality. "Let's go celebrate. You can't tell anyone else, but I got us some money. And I know a place with the *best* paninis."

"What do we do with mine?" I ask, holding up my postcards.

She grabs them from my hands, never breaking her stride. She throws them into the first trash bin we pass, decisively and without a second glance.

\\\\\//

When we return to the villa, full and elated from a day of unplanned sightseeing, I hear Will yelling in anger. As we get closer, every ounce of satisfaction from eating the best sandwich I've ever tasted is replaced with a rising nausea.

Will paces near Josh and Andrew in the courtyard; all the others are gathered nearby.

Oh no, I worry. What if we're in trouble for being the last ones back?

Will holds a stack of cards like an exhibit in a courtroom. "Did you smile? Did you make eye contact? Did you attempt to greet them in their own language?"

Josh is looking at the ground, and Andrew faces Will, who is red-faced and livid. Ben stands to the side as if assisting in this very public lesson. My stomach drops as we inch closer to the courtyard.

"This is not a joke, people. These are *souls* we are talking about. *Lost*. Souls." Will glares at Andrew as if speaking directly to him. "We. Are. At. War. With. Sin."

I'm scared Will is going to yell at me and Kara, but instead he backs away from Josh and Andrew as if to include us in his lecture.

"Do we not understand this yet? You are the chosen ones—*chosen*—sent here to bring these lost souls home to Jesus. This is what you signed up for, and if you don't feel like taking this seriously, then you all can just hop right back on a plane and head home."

Will makes a disgusted sound and tosses a thick flurry

of cards at Andrew, then motions for Josh to stand beside him. I try to catch Josh's eye, but he keeps his gaze to the ground. Will turns to the rest of us. "You know, this is a good opportunity for a lesson. I want all of you to listen and understand this." He puts his arm around Josh's shoulder. "Josh and Andrew split up, and Andrew did not hand out one single card, but Josh didn't know until they returned here. So somebody please tell me. Who is at fault here?"

Everyone is silent. Andrew stoops to the ground and begins picking up his cards.

"The DP," Ben finally says. His tone is authoritative, as if he's assisting Will, rather than simply answering his question.

"That's correct, Ben. A failure to control your disciple is a failure to the Kingdom. But Josh is new at this, and so I'm going to give him a chance to do something pleasing to God in order to make up for this failure. Amen?"

"Amen." We all say it.

"Now I want you all to go into your BTs to talk this through. We. Must. Do. Better. Go!"

Kara gives me a "told you so" look, and we rush to our room.

"What was that about?" I ask. I can't shake the look of shame on Josh's face.

"Simple. They didn't give all their cards away." Kara is feeding Dolce from a cat food bag that somehow appeared in our room while we were out. I can hear Dolce purring and crunching her food in ecstasy.

"But it's not their fault," I argue. "It's harder than it seems for some of us. And we don't even know the language! No one gave us any instructions before leaving other than to spend as little money as possible actually getting here." My voice fills our room and I suddenly realize how upset I sound—how upset I feel.

"Why do you think I didn't make you pass out cards?" Kara is staring at me, her eyebrows raised. "My advice? Stay out of it."

I'm confused and grateful all at once. My eyes well with tears. I dry them with my T-shirt.

Kara tilts her head as if she isn't sure what to do with me. "Look. As far as I'm concerned, this mission is every man for himself. And, right now, you and I are fine."

I breathe in through my nose and tilt my head all the way back. The ceiling cracks spread in every direction like fossilized electrical currents. The room smells stagnant and dank. I want to crawl into my bed and sleep until I wake up at home.

Kara grabs her backpack again. "Come on, Em. Let's get out of here. I know the perfect place."

Out of the Bag

At the top of the road, Kara pauses under a brick arch that opens up into an enormous field of cypress trees. The view is startling. The hills below roll out in patchworked squares of diverging green and brown, and villas line the roads that curve downward into distant towns. I pause to pull my damp hair back with the ponytail holder on my wrist. I had no idea Italy would be this hot.

"Ach. Who knew Italy would feel so much like Florida?" Kara says, as if reading my mind. "We're almost there, though."

She's deep into the field, weaving through the trees. They stretch upward in massive dark columns like natural remnants of an ancient time. I finally catch up and settle across from her, just under a block of shade. It's a small but welcome relief. She opens her backpack and pulls out a sheet of paper from a thick folder. She looks up at me, silent, as if thinking about what to say next. "I know this is supposed to be our BT, but I just want to talk first," she says, still holding the sheet of paper.

Okay. With Kara, there's no way to predict what she will say or do, so I blink patiently and hope for the best.

"Let's start with how you met Josh."

My mind flashes to the Sin List I burned, to the invasive questions Heather asked about my previous relationship. I'm worried this conversation is headed in the same direction. "We met in Boston. At school," I say, hoping it's enough.

"Yeah, I know that. But I'm just curious about the exact path that brought you over here. You came here because of Josh, right?"

"No, not exactly," I say. Kara raises her eyebrows expectantly. With a resigned sigh, I give in and start from the beginning. I tell her about the coffee shop, and a sense of relief surprises me. So I tell her about the Pictionary game. The origami shapes Josh made for me. The day by the river when Josh asked me to come with him. It all spills out as I tell Kara everything that happened in Boston—everything I couldn't tell Heather. She listens, patient and quiet, without emotion, chiming in only when I start talking about Heather.

"And how did you meet Heather?"

"She was friends with Josh and Andrew."

"Was she your only DP?"

"Yes. Well, until right before I left for Italy. I was reassigned to the Leader's sister—Will's wife—but we really met only a few times before I left. She's great, though. She let me leave my stuff at their house so I wouldn't have to figure out a storage unit."

Kara arches an eyebrow. "And she was Heather's DP too?"

"Yes."

Kara looks away. She seems distracted by the tree beside us. She reaches to pluck a large purple berry from a branch, glances at me, and looks back down at it while turning it with her fingers, as if checking for flaws. For the first time since I've met Kara, she seems vulnerable when she asks me what Meredith was like.

"She's pretty, like model-pretty. And she can be really nice. It's hard to explain, but people are just drawn to her," I say, knowing I was one of those people. "She does seem to have favorite disciples, though, and she's tough on the others."

"Were you one of the favorites?"

"I guess, but she never said that or anything." I'm suddenly self-conscious. "She was always on Heather about dieting and losing weight. She never bothered me about that kind of stuff."

I search Kara's face for a reaction. Her expression doesn't

change. She throws the berry away from where we're sitting. Kara gets quiet before asking in a tone that says it's the main thing she really wanted to know all along, "What's she like with *him*?"

"The Leader?"

"No, Emily. Her *husband*."

I shrug. "I never really saw them together that much outside of church events. I mean, they were always together, like in the same room, but they were always talking to different people or doing different things." Sweat begins trickling down my forehead and back, the shade no longer helping fight the afternoon heat. Heather always controlled the BT by talking and "guiding" (as she called it), and then she would leave me alone to finish my QT and total up an Accountability Sheet. It was always very orderly and businesslike. Not off topic like this. "I'm confused. Is this not supposed to be our BT time?" I ask.

"It can wait. Do you know why she didn't come to Italy?"

"She said they're getting ready to move to California."

"You mean Florida," she says.

I wipe my forehead. "No. She told me they're going to Los Angeles. She and Rachel stayed in Boston to pack and coordinate the move."

"Rachel . . ."

"Their daughter." I can hear the frustration in my voice, and I almost start to apologize because Kara looks really upset.

Her eyes dart around as if processing something. She

inhales deeply through her nose and gets up while shoving the notebook into her backpack. "Listen, I've got to go help with something at the villa," she says.

"Oh. Okay. Should I come?"

She seems distracted. "No. It's just for DPs. You should stay here and finish your charts and QT. It's the perfect place to be alone."

"Wait. Did this count as—?"

"Yes," she interrupts, handing me a sheet of paper. She slips her arm through her backpack strap and disappears behind a cypress tree.

As I begin to total my Time Evaluation Chart, I notice a new verse printed in small, tight handwriting at the bottom of the page: *Ephesians 5:15-16: Be very careful, then, how you live—not as unwise but as wise, making the most of your time, because the days are evil.*

I drop my forehead into my hands. How am I supposed to make the most of my time when my DP runs off and abandons me in the middle of a field? Why does Kara always make me confused and frustrated? Yes, Heather was overbearing. And definitely judgmental. Even annoying, at times, but I always knew what she was thinking. I'm not sure why I was assigned to Kara in the first place, only to live outside the villa away from the other interns. It doesn't help that I haven't been able to speak to Josh even in passing yet. A strong breeze stirs through the field. I look around. It's just me and the trees. I stand up. If I hurry, maybe I can catch up with Kara.

\\|///

I'm on the wrong road. I know it. I've never had a good sense of direction, and I wasn't paying attention to where Kara led me because I had no idea she was going to bolt. I must be turned around. All of the cypress trees look the same, and I can't remember where we entered. Dread hangs over me, seeps into my gut, but I keep walking, hoping the next turn will reveal a familiar path.

I walk by a patch of poppies—have I passed by those before? I stop and turn all the way around. The vineyards and groves of gnarled olive trees all look the same. The twisting narrow roads look the same. Even the villas look the same. My doubt sharpens into fear, as I try to ignore my lingering sense of panic.

Keep walking. You'll end up somewhere. But what good would that do? I don't have my passport or any money.

As I'm wiping my eyes, a cat darts across the road and onto a narrow path, too quickly for me to get a good look. "Dolce," I call out, but she keeps walking as if on a mission. I follow her bouncing tail through a row of vineyards. Twigs snap under my feet as I rush to keep up. The cat stops and rubs her side across the grapevines. Her tail curls high in the air like a question mark, just before slipping through another row. I stand still, waiting for a sound. The rustle of the trees tickles my ears. I walk to the end of the row, where I see large slate steps leading up a hill.

I climb the steps. The slope is steep, and at the top, a

blue rectangle of water shimmers in front of a small villa. The grass is neatly trimmed and the pool is clean, but the villa appears unoccupied. The cat is scratching her back against the concrete surrounding the glistening pool. Her feet point to the sky, and I see that one is orange. *Definitely not Dolce.*

For the first time in days, I laugh uncontrollably. I feel elated and unhinged and disconnected from everything I once knew. I sit beside the cat and take off my shoes. Scooting to the edge, I ease my feet into the cool water. All of a sudden, being alone seems fine. I lean all the way back, my feet still in the water, and absorb the heat of the sun.

I squint my eyes against the bright sky. Plump clouds drift slowly overhead. I imagine what it would be like if I wasn't here for our mission, if I was just a student abroad, free to roam and travel. No invitations or stickers to hand out, no strangers to approach. No pressure. *I could leave these people. I could get Josh to come with me.*

A metal door suddenly rattles open. I slosh my feet out of the water just as a gray-haired man emerges from a small shed beside the pool. His eyes dart in my direction just as he begins mumbling in rapid Italian.

"I'm so sorry," I say as I scramble to put my shoes on.

He continues talking in Italian as if expecting me to understand. He doesn't seem angry, just confused.

I look at the cat rolling around on the concrete. "The cat? I thought it was—"

He cocks his head to the side. "California, yes?" he asks me slowly.

Not sure what to say, I smile and shake my head no. I instinctively rush to the steps. When I reach the bottom, I pause, surprised not to hear any protests from the man. He's whistling as he resumes his work.

I make my way back to the road with no idea where to go, yet this time I'm calm and at peace, as if the absurdity of the situation will somehow spontaneously fix itself. In that exact moment I look down the hill and see a giant cross wavering against the sky. As I get closer, I see Andrew holding the cross upright while Josh digs a deep hole. Just beyond the cross, I see our villa. The relief is overwhelming. I keep walking until I reach them. I smile.

"Hi," I say.

Josh appears surprised to see me. He's sweaty and out of breath. "What do you think?" he asks.

"I think you saved me," I say.

Andrew's eyes widen, but Josh is smiling just like he used to back in Boston.

"No. I mean, I was lost. Literally. Kara took me to a park for our BT, and then she had to leave and I couldn't find my way back."

"I saw her going into the office earlier," Andrew says. He freezes as if checking himself, unsure of whether he should have blurted that out before thinking it through. He keeps glancing at Josh while trying to balance the cross, which must be heavy.

I desperately want to talk to Josh privately. "Hey," I say to Josh. "Do you think we could . . . talk?"

He glances at me, and quickly turns back to help Andrew. "I'm a little busy right now."

I exhale my frustration. Even though he's probably still upset about Andrew, why wouldn't he jump at the first opportunity we've had in three days to talk one-on-one? My cheeks flush as I turn to leave. The sharp sounds of digging continue as I walk toward the villa to find Kara. If Andrew just saw her, then she's probably still there.

The office door is closed shut, but I can hear Kara's muffled voice inside talking to Will. I start to knock, then pause. The voices sound tense. I hear Kara say, "You promised." Her voice is soft but angry.

"God has a plan for me," he answers. His voice is calm and distant as if he's patiently waiting for her to finish throwing a fit so he can finally be alone in peace.

"In California?"

"Stop asking her questions about my wife, Kara. I knew better than to trust you to be a DP."

Kara speaks in a lower tone. "Really? What were your other options? To have Shannon be mine and ask me about all of my sins so she could tell her family back in Boston?"

There is a long silence. I hold my breath.

Kara speaks so quietly that I almost can't hear what she says next: "My entire existence is a sin and you know it."

I hear movement in the room and hurry away, my mind

racing faster than my feet as I rush back to the safety of our building.

I slow down my pace when I round the corner to our private entrance. As I get closer, I see our door is cracked. Kara locked it when we left; I remember her struggling to get the key in right the first time. Or maybe that was yesterday? Time has already begun to blur here.

"Hello?" I push the door into the dark room.

Quiet.

The shutters are fastened tightly. My eyes take a moment to adjust to the darkness. A wave of exhaustion leaves me dizzy. I start to crawl into the bottom bunk to rest, not even bothering to shut the door. I pause. There's something at the foot of my bed—a bulky cloth pillowcase secured with brown twine, strung through a small piece of folded paper. I pull the twine, open the note, and hold it up to the light from the doorway.

TRUST ME is written in all caps.

The pillowcase moves. I freeze as I realize something is inside it.

My first thought is Dolce. Then I hear her loud hiss from the top bunk followed by a guttural growl. I look back down at the pillowcase to see it gliding to the edge of the bed, moving of its own volition. *This is ridiculous.* I reach out to grab the bag to stop this nonsense just as it tips and falls beside my foot with a significant thump, the twine securing it loosening.

Before I can react, an enormous black snake slides out of the bag, slowly curving itself to the side. It's one of those moments where one would imagine you'd scream, but real terror is a funny thing, and sometimes it leaves you unable to move, as if weighted down with ten thousand pounds that won't even allow for breathing. I stand there and watch the snake slip to the corner of the room in a horrifying fluid motion as if it's trying to find a way out. It lifts its head to test the air, then races through the sunlight toward the door.

I have no idea how long I've been sitting on top of Kara's bunk, my knees up under my chin, all of her sheets and pillows strewn across the room, when she finally walks in.

After one glance, she rushes up to me. "What's wrong?"

I'm still clutching the tag that says *Trust me.* I thrust it at her, my hand shaking violently. Kara's eyes furrow over the message. She hands it back to me, but I let it fall on her bed. My breathing turns shallow, and I start to suck in deep breaths. The room appears wavy as my vision narrows into a dark tunnel.

"Oh my God. Seriously, Emily. What happened?" Kara tries to make me get down, but I slap her hand away, too scared to stand on the floor.

"There's a snake," I say.

Kara exhales. "What? Emily. You have got to calm down."

"There. Was. A. Snake. On. My. *Bed*. And you want me to *calm down*?" My trembling voice is beyond my control. I swat her arm away again when she tries to guide me down.

"I don't see anything." I notice Kara is looking around the room. She picks up the sheets and shakes them out. "Are you sure?" she asks me.

"It went out the door," I say. I curl up onto my side trying to take in air. *Just breathe.*

She glances at me with concern as she folds the sheets. She places them in a neat stack on top of our dresser. She kneels down onto the floor and looks under the bed. I hold my breath until she pops up again. "It's okay. Honestly, Emily. You can relax. There's no snake, I swear. Nothing is in here but us."

"Kara. There was a snake. In a bag. With a message."

Kara gets quiet, pensive. "It wasn't meant for you," she finally says.

"What do you mean?"

Kara crawls up onto her bed and sits cross-legged by my feet. She puts her head in her hands for a few seconds. Then she looks up at me, her eyes straightforward and honest. "It was meant for me."

"I don't understand," I say. The words are far away, like they aren't my own. I can't tell which way is up or down. Everything that's happened settles on top of my chest and I suddenly can't breathe.

"Whoa," I hear Kara say. I lurch forward with the overwhelming desire to run, but Kara stops me and guides me to lie down. The words "I need to leave" repeat on a constant loop in my mind. I feel my chest heaving. It actually hurts and the sensation scares me. My mind whirls as if someone spun it too hard. I cannot form a coherent thought. As soon as the spinning begins to slow, a terrifying realization blooms inside of me: *I'm going to die.*

I roll over to rock back and forth.

Kara shakes my shoulders. "You're going to hyperventilate if you don't listen to me," she says. Even her long black hair seems threatening as she unfolds her legs and leans over me.

I'm going to die. You don't understand. I am going to die.

Tears stream down my face, pooling into my ears, yet I feel completely detached from my body.

I hear Kara jump down and hurry across the room. She rustles a paper bag from her drawer, steps up onto my bed to reach me, and puts it over my mouth. "Here, breathe in this. Slowly."

I concentrate on breathing. *One, two, in. One, two, out.* A nagging sense of panic slithers back into my thoughts, threatening to capture my breath and never give it back. *One, two—oh my God, I'm going to die because I cannot breathe.*

My eyes fill with tears again as the terror refuses to let up. I try to move my arm. It feels like it's already floating upward but when I look down, it's actually planted deep into my blanket. My airways feel constricted. I gasp for air.

Kara fumbles through one of her bags and extracts two blue pills. She shows them to me in the palm of her hand.

"Emily, you have to listen to me. You have to open your mouth and swallow these. They will help make it easier to breathe."

I'm too scared to even speak. Her fingers push them between my lips. She unscrews the cap from a water bottle. The pills are already expanding in my mouth, filling it with a putrid acidic taste.

"Drink," she says, tilting the bottle to my mouth. I take a swig, surprised that my body is allowing me to swallow anything. "You're having a panic attack, but you're going to be fine. Those were Xanax."

The world slows down as I try to relax. *How could I lose control of myself so suddenly?*

"Why would someone leave you a *snake*?"

She pauses. "I'm sure it was just a joke."

"A joke? Who would think that's funny?" I'm scared all over again. I try to focus on the cracks in the ceiling. I follow them outward to each endpoint.

"I promise it isn't a big deal, Emily. Like an inside joke. Please don't worry."

My body begins relaxing into slow motion.

"I'm *so* sorry it scared you. I really am," she says.

I smile to show her I'm going to be okay, even though my thoughts are telling me the opposite.

She smiles back, but there's a distant worry in her eyes. She goes to the dresser, gets new sheets, and moves them to the lower bunk. "Don't worry. You can sleep up there if e bed underneath. "Think about

ool today," I say. I have no idea

houghts. I remember how the

clouds moved slowly through

ne something important. And

ng nice. I'm calmer now, my

ipping the blanket onto the

can take me there. Okay?"

ber her saying.

lete failure.

smile. They

e of meat, but

e chance to be

of the time—

r conversation

Some join in.

, and then they

back, but we all

Tuscan hills and

us with a sense

returning will be

A Saved Soul

Our first big Bible study proves to be a com
Strangers with stickers show up. W
smile back. Kara's guest eyes her like a pie
leaves as soon as he realizes he won't have t
alone with her. She sulks in a corner mos
she's been quiet and distant ever since o
during my panic attack yesterday. We sin
We pray. They listen. We study with then
leave one by one. They *say* they'll come
know, even as the sun submerges into the
bathes us in a golden light that should fi
of hope, that the chance of any of them
unlikely.

Will stomps off to his office with Ben, as the rest of us disperse in silence. I sense the doubt and disappointment— it's already infecting the group. *What if the mission fails?* I'm too scared to ask this out loud as Kara and I walk toward our building. I see two figures shifting in the vineyard.

"Look," I say, nudging Kara.

Todd and the girl he invited are huddled in a private conversation.

"Well, look at that. Todd saves the day," Kara says. "Or night." She yawns.

"Why didn't you talk to that guy you invited?" I ask Kara.

"What's the point?"

"Maybe he would have committed to coming back."

"I doubt it," Kara says. "Anyway, the key is to stay just one step ahead. We'll just invite some new people next time to keep our numbers up."

Keep our numbers up? "I thought the key is to save people," I say.

Kara shoots me a look. This time I can tell she's studying my expression, looking to see if I mean it.

"Do you think anyone who showed up tonight will come back?" I ask.

"No," Kara says. She sounds like she doesn't even care.

I pause inside our doorway, scanning the corners of our room.

"Em, stop it," she says. "How many times do I have to tell you? It. Was. A. Joke."

"Yes, one that you never explained to me, and I'm still not laughing."

"Trust me," she says, climbing into the bottom bunk again. "See? You can have the top bunk permanently. That's how worried I am."

"I'm way too wired for sleep," I say. "I think I'm going to take a walk." I glance around the room again for any signs of movement.

"Whatever," Kara says. She pulls her headphones from under her pillow and puts them on.

I step out into the night and look around. Todd and his friend are gone, so I decide to walk through the vineyard. I'm thinking about Josh, wondering where he is and if he isn't too "busy" now to talk, when I see a figure between rows. My heart races as I try to focus. It's a male, but too short to be Josh. I see a tiny light near his hand lift up to his mouth just as I smell the cigarette smoke. I try to sneak around him, but he hears me and turns around.

"Emily."

I pause, not sure what to do.

"Oh, don't worry. It's just me." I recognize Andrew's voice.

I walk toward him. "I thought we aren't supposed to smoke. Is it not against Kingdom rules?"

"Eh." He shrugs. "Do you want one?" He gestures to his pocket.

"No thanks. But how did you get those? Did they give

you money?" I ask. As far as I know, Will still has all our passports and travelers' checks stored away in his office.

"Shhhh," he says. "I stole them from Todd's new girl-friend."

This catches me off guard, and I laugh without thinking. It feels so good to laugh.

"*Shhhhhh,*" he says again, laughing through an involuntary cough.

"Hey, I'm sorry about yesterday," I say.

"Oh, the lecture on what a disappointment I am?" He rolls his eyes in a forced gesture to seem unperturbed. He takes another drag and exhales. "Let's just say I'm very used to it after all these years. It kind of reminds me of being at home when my dad was actually around."

A wave of sympathy takes over my thoughts. "I'm sure your dad doesn't really feel that way," I offer. "Dads who are busy like ours have trouble communicating. Or that's what my stepmother always says, anyway."

"Well, at least you're lucky enough that yours are divorced," he says. "Mine are too caught up in appearances to ever have a shot at happiness with other people."

He obviously doesn't know about my mother, and I don't bother telling him.

"I'm sure they're both really proud of you. MIT is a big deal," I say.

"Nope," he says nonchalantly. "Try again."

We stand through an awkward silence.

"*This* was supposed to fix me."

I stare at him in confusion. "This?"

"The Kingdom. It can fix anyone. For anything. Even if you've tried everything else. Any soul can be saved if you follow the right path. Didn't they tell you?" His authoritatively sarcastic tone is making me uncomfortable.

"So. Do *you* know what we're doing?" he asks.

"What do you mean?"

"What we're all *doing*. Here. There. All of us interns. Scattered across the world."

I stare at the ground. I'd be lying if I said I hadn't been wondering the same thing since we'd arrived.

He takes a drag, tilts his head back, and exhales into the air. "Have you ever been to the Leader's house?"

I think about it and realize I've only seen the Leader up on stage, preaching. "No. Have you?"

"Well, I know where he lives. And no home is less than a million in his neighborhood."

I furrow my brow. "What are you saying, Andrew?"

"I'm saying all of the mandatory tithing, those extra world mission fund-raisers—they are obviously not paying for our mission in this crumbling villa with barely enough food to survive. The reason I couldn't hand out all my cards was because I was too nauseated from hunger. Josh and I thought Will would understand, but . . ."

Stop. Stop. Stop. Stop. I close my eyes and think of Heather praying with me. Of my mother in heaven. Of how the Kingdom found me when I was lost. Yet my heart aches at the thought of my family and friends enjoying their summer without me at home. I'd imagined this trip as an adventure, Josh and I together at last. Confusion consumes me as new fears creep into the periphery.

"My parents actually tried to convince me not to come here, you know," Andrew continues. "They showed me articles in the *Boston Globe* about our church, but Ben said those articles are 'spiritual pornography.'" He laughs. "Can you believe that's the term for articles about our church? How ironic."

"I have no idea what you're talking about," I snap, suddenly uncomfortable. As I start to leave, I catch a glimpse of his expression and stop. He looks like he's about to cry.

He takes another drag and blows out smoke in a long exhale. "Ultimately my parents left it up to me. They said it's time I made my own decisions, including my own mistakes. They wouldn't give me any money at all, so I had to work three different jobs up until the day I left just to meet the minimum tithing required."

"Why did you come, then?" I ask.

Andrew quietly stares at the ground as an uncomfortable silence lingers between us. "The funny thing is, I joined this mission for *them*. Will promised this would make me a stronger person—the kind of son my parents could . . ." His voice cracks before trailing off. He stares into the distance.

"Hey," I say gently. I desperately want to make him feel better, to help him see we're doing something important.

"I'm sure if your parents understood what a big deal this is, they would be *so* impressed. We were chosen. We're here for a reason—we have to be." I can't tell if I'm trying to convince him or myself, especially since I didn't even have the guts to tell my own dad certain details about this mission. It's like if I can convince Andrew it will assuage my own needling fear that this could all fall apart—that maybe it already is.

Andrew gently squeezes my arm with his hand. His eyes are puffy and red. "Keep believing it, Em. You do what you have to do." He pulls away and looks into my eyes with sincere affection. "Just don't lose yourself in the process."

"Everyone come inside *now*! We are having an emergency meeting!" Ben's voice echoes through the property.

"Sounds like we're being summoned," Andrew says flatly. He takes one last drag of his cigarette, crushes it under his foot. He extends his arm to me with a sad smile. "Shall we?"

I link my arm into his, and we walk back to the villa in silence. When we arrive, everyone is already gathered in a semicircle in the dining room. Will paces at the front of the room. Ben stands off to the side, his arms crossed and stance wide. He cuts his eyes at us. "Sit," he hisses.

I jump slightly at the sharpness in his voice. I hurry to take my place next to Kara, and Andrew finds his next to Josh.

After a moment, Will stops pacing to face us. He's paler than usual and is sweating profusely, but the anger in his eyes makes up for his ragged appearance. "Africa? *Thousands*. India? *Thousands*." He starts to move again with an almost feral quality. "They've reached one thousand in London alone! I just got off the phone with the Boston elders, and do you know what they said to me?" He leans down directly in Andrew's face. "Our numbers *don't . . . look . . . good*."

I tilt my head down so as not to draw attention to myself. I notice Andrew gazing at the wall in silence. His hands are shaking.

My heart is pounding as Will backs away to address everyone. His tone shifts to pleading, and for a moment, he seems on the verge of tears. "Where is our focus? Are we lukewarm? Have we forgotten our mission? Have we allowed sin into our lives? Do we need to pray and fast it out?"

No one moves or speaks.

"Look. I could stand up here all day and chew you out, but that would be a waste of time." Will lifts his arms and we all stand up. Shannon begins swaying with her arms in the air just like some of the students in Boston would do at church. Lily follows along timidly. Kara and I stand still and quiet like the others.

Will continues pacing, much like the Leader in those Boston Garden services. "We need to be out recruiting, amen?"

We shout, *"Amen!"*

"Showing the path—the only way—to salvation in God's Kingdom."

"Amen."

"Baptizing brothers and sisters."

"Amen."

"We cannot lose sight of our focus. Not even for one single minute."

"Amen."

"We are here to multiply members."

"Amen."

"To crank the numbers."

"Amen."

"Tell me why we are here," Will shouts.

"To save souls," we say.

"What was that?"

This time we practically shout: "TO SAVE SOULS!" I barely recognize my voice when I say it.

Such a Person

We baptize Eva Jane Johnston in our bathtub.

We crowd around holding hands when she sloshes into a reclining position, her jean shorts and DKNY T-shirt darkening in the water. Being crammed together in that tiny bathroom reminds us that we're a close family, and converting someone like Eva makes us feel important. Will is beatific, his enthusiasm contagious, and we're all smiling more now than we have in the whole week we've been here.

Josh squeezes in between me and Kara for the ceremony. His warm hand closes around mine. We have not had a single moment alone, yet as I stand here holding his hand, I can tell we're still connected like we were in Boston. Our hymns echo against the tile of the small bathroom, our voices intense and ethereal, like sounds in a tightly contained cathedral.

Will submerges his arm under Eva's shoulders. Her long blond hair fans out as she eases down into the water. The tub is too short for Eva's legs, so her bony knees stick out of the water awkwardly. Will closes off her nose and dips her head under, then pushes her knees to the side to be sure she's completely submerged, and, in that moment, Eva becomes the most important member of our family in Italy.

She breaks the surface with a dramatic gasp and a squeal. We clap. We hug one another. We sing praises. Eva stands up and the water pours off her body. She hugs each one of us, leaving a wet imprint down the front of our clothes and puddles of water on the floor. She throws her arms around Will and kisses him on the cheek. "I'm so proud to be a part of this," she says, beaming, looking around the bathroom at each one of us. We have to steady ourselves and hold on to each other so we don't slip and fall on our way out.

Eva is assigned to Shannon for intense discipling. She follows Shannon around like a hyper puppy, constantly asking her what to do, what she thinks, what she wants. "How do I handle this?" is her signature question. Something about their dynamic makes me feel sorry for Eva.

Will decided Eva may continue working as a model, so long as she stays on track with her BTs and QTs and contributes her part to the mission. From what I can see, Eva doesn't seem to have any interest in money, or even a concept of its power; she's so eager for approval, she probably would've consumed that entire tub of bath water just to stay in the good graces of the Kingdom.

Shannon is delighted to have two disciples, but it's clear that Lily is being slighted. Shannon and Eva begin fasting together. "To improve the odds of our mission," they say, their arms around each other's shoulders. It's hardly been a week since Eva's baptism when I'm on my way to take a shower one morning and see Shannon rummaging through Eva's clothes. I look around the room, but Eva isn't there.

"What are you doing?" I ask.

"Eva's working," she says distractedly, still checking herself in the mirror. "She said I could borrow something to wear."

Shannon looks so different standing there in black stirrup pants and a loose sweater. Her crowded facial features and permed hair seem out of place in Eva's clothes. The only thing they have in common physically is clothing size. Shannon has been fasting off and on since the day I met her. For once I'm grateful to be paired with Kara as my DP.

Kara's approach is so different, or maybe "hands-off" is the better way to describe it. I still don't understand what Kara expects of me. She hasn't offered me much spiritual direction beyond making it clear by her general evasiveness and long bouts of silence that she prefers being left alone. Even at night, Kara is rarely around when I fall asleep. I usually take advantage of the alone time to catch up on my

QTs, but this one particular night I decide to go for another walk in the vineyard. Something about Tuscany has started reminding me of home: the winding roads lined with wildflowers, the quiet landscape, the night sky cracked open with stars.

When I stop to catch my breath, the faint sound of voices drifts from beyond a row of vineyards. Lily is talking. As I edge closer, I hear Andrew. In a small clearing beyond a patch of gnarled olive branches, I can see both of them sitting on a blanket. They sound cheerful and at ease, so I follow the voices.

"Hi," I say awkwardly, afraid I'm intruding on their time together.

Lily gasps. "Oh! Emily, you scared me!" She laughs nervously.

Andrew stands up. At first, he seems afraid. "What are you doing here? Are you following us?"

"What? No. Just taking a walk." I gesture to my gym shorts. "What are y'all doing? Where's Shannon?" I ask Lily. It's an innocent question, but I can see why they don't take it that way at first. We're supposed to stick close to our disciples, and I've never seen them apart. Also, technically, we're not supposed to be alone with the opposite sex, a strict Kingdom rule. I belatedly realize why Andrew is defensive, but I was with him for a while the other night, and he didn't seem fazed.

"Probably with Ev-ah," she says, adding emphasis to the

"ah" sound, as if giving it a snooty accent from somewhere other than a small town in Texas, where Eva grew up. Lily gives me a defiant look. "Where's Kara?"

"Asleep," I lie. I don't think Lily's trying to be confrontational, but sometimes it's hard to tell under our strict circumstances. The truth is I never know exactly where Kara is. I do know she's rarely in our room or with me when we're supposed to be recruiting together.

"Lily and I were just talking about family," Andrew says. He glances at Lily as if to say he knows I'm cool with all this.

"Oh. You mean our new addition? Well, I don't think Eva is having a difficult time adjusting," I say.

"No, Em. Back *home*." Andrew sounds annoyed that I don't get it. I'm even a little embarrassed that my actual family wasn't my first thought.

"I've been missing my brother," Lily explains. "I've been having these weird dreams lately, and I really want to speak with him. We've never gone more than a week without talking."

"Then call him," I say nonchalantly, but I suddenly realize it's been almost two weeks and I haven't called home yet either, partly because I haven't had the opportunity, partly because I'm scared Dad will ask too many questions and I'll say the wrong thing. I'm hoping the letter was enough.

Then Lily begins crying. She looks so small and vulnerable sitting on the ground, her long dark hair falling over her face. "I *can't* call him."

"Shannon won't let her," Andrew says.

"Why?" I ask.

"Are we allowed to ask questions like that?" Andrew asks sarcastically. He stands up and levels a glare at me. "What does Kara allow you to do, Emily?" he challenges.

"Pretty much anything."

"Well. Lucky you," he snaps.

"Hey. I didn't ask for Kara. I honestly don't even really know what I'm supposed to be doing half the time."

"If you've been blessed with that luxury, then why don't you just shut up and appreciate it. I would kill for that opportunity," he says. And, without even a polite good-bye gesture, he walks back toward the villa. I can't tell if he's mad at me, or maybe just at the entire situation.

"Please, *please* don't tell Shannon about this," Lily says to me, her arms are wrapped around herself awkwardly as if she's afraid. I sit down beside her. She gets very still and quiet.

"Emily," she says. She lifts her head to look at me, her eyes full of pain. "I just miss my family. I want to make sure they're okay." She pauses. "I want to go home," she whispers.

"Oh, Lily. I'm sure you'll feel better if you can just call them. I'll help you. We'll figure this out."

Lily throws her arms around me in a violent hug and pulls away. Her eyes are wild. "You're such a nice person. Would you really do that for me?"

"Of course," I say.

The next morning, I ask Kara if I can recruit with Lily.

"Sure," she says without hesitation.

I study her mood.

Kara widens her eyes with impatience. "Really, Em. It's fine. I need to take care of a few things around here anyway," she says.

"Okay. But can you convince *Shannon* to let me recruit with Lily by ourselves?" We both know this is the real obstacle, yet saying it out loud makes it sound like an odd request.

For a second, Kara seems intrigued, like she's going to ask questions, but her expression quickly shifts. "On one condition."

"Yes," I say. "Anything."

"*If* you'll take me to that pool you found," she says.

"Deal," I say. "Wait. Do you really think you can convince Shannon without her suspecting anything?"

Kara gives me a look that says I'm an idiot for even asking.

As soon as we get to town, Lily finds a pay phone and inserts an orange card.

"Where'd you get that?" I ask.

"Andrew." She smiles a wide smile as she dials a succession of numbers.

"What was his problem the other night?" I ask.

"Oh. I don't know. He just gets so cranky about everything. Will really has it out for him." Lily turns to the pay

phone and breaks into rushed Spanish. I try reading her tone and expressions. Her eyes widen and glass with tears as she says her brother's name. And then a word I understand: *No, no, no, no, no.*

She hangs up the phone and staggers, her chest heaving with each breath.

"Lily? Are you okay?"

She looks at me almost as if she doesn't know who I am, and then she starts to run. I take off after her. "Lily!" I yell, but she keeps running down the winding narrow street. I can barely keep up. She's screaming as if she's in physical pain. I run faster until I nearly fall over her body slumped against a building. She's sobbing violently.

"Lily. Hey. It's okay. It's Em. Tell me what's wrong." I stroke her back gently, then sit down beside her and put my arm around her. "It's okay. It's okay," I say. She looks up at me, the tears still rolling down her face. "*Alguien ayúdeme,*" she whispers. She begins rocking, chanting it like a prayer.

"It's okay, Lily. Let's just get back to the villa and get some help. We need to figure out what to do."

She grips my arm and begins to moan. She's mumbling in Spanish again.

"Lily. Can you tell me what happened? I want to help you."

Then she screams again, this time so loudly that I don't know what to do. A few Italians poke their heads out of nearby shops. An elderly Italian man wearing a white apron

moves closer to us. Lily grasps his arm. She seems to be pleading with him.

"*Alguien ayúdeme!*"

Several onlookers turn to stare at me standing there. The old man looks at me with caution, and I wonder if he thinks I hurt her.

I carefully put my hand on her shoulder. "Lily. It's okay. It's okay. Let me help you."

Lily turns to me, her eyes glazed with a faraway sadness. She puts her head against my shoulder. The man in the apron nods and walks away, back-glancing with concern while mumbling something in Italian. Lily speaks quietly, as if telling herself something. "Marc was in an accident. He's in the hospital. I don't know . . ." Her voice trails off. She holds my arm, as if for support.

"It's going to be okay," I say. "We'll get you a flight home. We can all pray for him. It's going to be fine." I try to make my voice soothing and confident like Kara's.

We go straight to the villa to look for Shannon, who is studying with Eva in the room they all share. Lily starts crying uncontrollably when she sees Shannon. Eva pops up to comfort her, but Shannon motions for her to back away.

Shannon turns to me, livid. "What did you do to her?"

"Her brother was in an accident. That's all I could figure out. She's been hysterical."

Shannon seems concerned for a second, and then narrows her eyes at me. "Wait. Where did she hear that?"

Suddenly, I remember we weren't supposed to make any phone calls and Shannon had specifically told her not to call home. I don't say anything about Andrew giving her the card—he's been in enough hot water. Lily is hysterical again. Shannon rubs her back, glaring at me the entire time. Eva, seemingly bored by the lack of attention, leaves the room.

"Remember what we talked about?" Shannon says to Lily as if convincing a child of something through a series of easy questions. "Remember what we studied about family? Luke 14:26?"

"Yes," Lily whispers.

"Remember your soul, Lily. You don't want to lose everything, do you?" Shannon prods. Lily looks down at the floor, nodding her head as tears stream down her face. "No," Lily whispers. Shannon guides her to lie down on the bed and gently covers her with a blanket.

Shannon turns and motions for me to leave. "Go," she snaps.

I look at Lily, who is calm now. She stares vacantly at the wall, her expression serene, but silent tears continue to fall down her face.

I can't get this vision out of my head as I walk back to my room.

The Deep End

Kara is digging through a Tampon box full of her mix tapes when I walk in. Still dumbfounded by what I just witnessed, I try to convince myself I misinterpreted their interaction. Kara looks up at me. "Whoa," she says, her eyes widening as she stands. "What happened to you?"

I try to ignore the weight on my chest—the pressure that makes it so difficult to breathe. If only I could get Lily's dazed expression out of my mind. She looked dead-eyed, saying yes or no like an automated response. My anger surges like a rising heat as I think about the way Shannon treated Lily. But within seconds, my mind begins to rationalize Shannon's behavior—maybe she was simply trying to calm Lily down by reminding her to focus on our mission.

My thoughts are like an uncontrollable tug-of-war.

"Hey," Kara says, her head tilted with concern. "Do you want to talk about it?"

"I . . ." Ugh. I don't even know where to start. What if Kara goes over and agitates Shannon, making it even worse for Lily? "I'm okay." I swallow awkwardly.

"I think I know something that will cheer us both up," Kara says.

"And what is that?" I ask, wary of her possible suggestions.

Kara in her *duh* voice: "The pool you found?"

I let out a laugh because I can honestly admit I wasn't expecting *that*. "Do you even have a swimsuit? Besides, there was a man there cleaning it. Don't you think the owners might care?" I'm not up for a spontaneous adventure with Kara, especially after what happened with Lily. Kara's mood seems mischievous, and so far breaking the rules hasn't been working out. Still, I would love nothing more than to get far away from the events of this day.

Kara looks at me like I'm an idiot as she closes the box of tapes and carefully puts it back in its hiding place. "Emily. First of all, we're in Europe. You don't even need a swimsuit to go to the public beach, and you said the old guy was Italian. He's probably the caretaker. Most of these villas are rentals." She opens a plastic case and inserts a tape into her Walkman. "We can sneak over there tonight as soon as it gets dark. He'll be long gone by then."

"But what about Lily?" I say instinctively.

Kara puts her headphones around her neck impatiently. "Look. It sounds like you need to tell me what happened today."

"There was an accident. Something happened to Lily's brother and she got really upset in town—"

Kara's eyes grow big. "Emily. How did she know this?"

I freeze. I really thought I was helping Lily—I didn't realize it would be such a big deal to everyone else if Lily called home. "I may have . . . helped her call home."

"*Shit*," Kara mumbles. Her expression grows serious. "Tell me exactly what Shannon said. Word for word if you can."

"Shannon got really mad at me, and then she told Lily to remember Luke 14 something. Do you know what that means?"

"What verse?" Kara asks agitated.

"I can't remember. She said something about family and that she didn't want her to lose everything."

Kara inhales with anger. "It figures. . . ." Her voice trails off as she shakes her head.

"What?" I ask Kara.

She pauses as if considering what to tell me and then climbs onto her bunk without saying anything. After a few seconds of silence, Kara starts reciting the verse. "'If anyone comes to me and does not hate father and mother, wife and children, brothers and sisters—yes, even their own life—such a person cannot be my disciple.'"

"Why in the world would she say that to Lily right now?"

"You really don't understand how this works, do you? Shannon is a lifer. Her parents are Boston lifers. They are hard-core when it comes to discipling. Gray areas do not exist with them."

"That's . . . awful. My DP in Boston was pretty hard-core, but I can't imagine her ever quoting a verse like *that*."

"Only because you were never in Lily's situation. If she felt like you had to choose sides, you'd be surprised by what she'd say."

I remember how I wasn't allowed to call my dad that first day. A pit deep down in my stomach forms; it tells me that what Kara is saying is true.

"Are your parents lifers?" I ask.

An awkward pause follows. "Dusk. That's when we'll sneak off to the pool," Kara says, ignoring my question. "And don't worry about Shannon," she reassures me. "I'll talk to Will. You won't get in trouble." She clicks play to end the conversation, sending muffled tones through her headphones.

When the pink and orange sky starts to color the hills, we slip out of our villa and I lead the way to the pool.

"If anyone sees us, we say we're going to our spot for BT. Got it?"

"Got it," I say. My stomach is turning somersaults. *What if we get caught?* After seeing how Will yelled at Andrew, I don't want to find out how he would react. And yet I left with Kara without a fight because she seems so reassuring, as if she has control over the others. Seeing how Shannon treated Lily made me grateful for Kara as my DP, thorns and all. I'm taking Andrew's words from our last conversation to heart: *Why don't you just shut up and appreciate it?*

The air is crisp and earthy. Our footsteps are barely audible as we make our way up the hill. Distant lights from the city twinkle from miles away, as if mirroring the stars. Anticipation and excitement surge through me. Who knew it would feel so good to get away for a while?

The pool seems menacing in the dark, much different than I remember it. The quiet trees seem to watch us. I start to walk over to where I can see the nearby villa. The sound of Kara's huge splash stops me mid-step. Her clothes are in a jumbled heap near the shallow end, but she's in the middle of the pool. I hear her swoosh to the surface. "What are you waiting for? Hurry up!" She dives back underwater and swims to the other end.

I pull my clothes off into a neat pile and ease into the cool water of the deep end. I push off the ladder backward and stare up at the stars. My skin tingles all over, and I let out a tiny squeal as I swim to the other side of the pool. The water is cold, but also comforting at the same time. It feels like home.

My feet scrape the shallow end where Kara is sitting on the lower steps, the water all the way up to her neck. I shift onto my knees in the shallow end, keeping a respectful distance. She seems deep in thought.

"Hey," she says. "Why are you here?"

"Because you made me bring you?" I can hear the playful sarcasm back in my voice. Here in the water, so far away from Will and the others, I embrace the sense of freedom. I'm feeling more like myself than I have since I got here.

"Stop!" She splashes water in my direction. "I'm serious. Why are you *here*? In Italy."

"I'm here for the mission. To make us better than we were before. To save others."

"Really. You buy that?"

"There's nothing to buy," I say, now letting frustration creep out. It's almost like Kara wants to prove I was wrong for joining. "I was saved, and now I'm better. Much better."

"So, the whole 'Sin List' thing. You made one, right?"

I pause. I don't even like *thinking* about the Sin Lists, much less discussing them out loud—*naked*. I can't stop the small laugh that escapes from my lips. It's funny: Compared to the "trust games" and having someone leave a random snake on my bed, sitting in this pool naked with Kara seems downright normal.

"Doesn't everyone have to make a Sin List?" I ask. Now I'm curious.

"That depends on how you define 'everyone.' "

The words I overheard Kara say to Will replay in my mind: *My entire existence is a sin.* I try to gather the nerve to ask her about it, but she interrupts my thoughts.

"So you believe your sins went away—just like that?" Kara asks.

"I watched them burn. And all I know is that it made me feel completely free from them. Like I could start over."

"It's amazing how much some people will believe total bullshit." Kara sounds bitter, not unlike Andrew the other night.

"Kara, stop . . ."

"What? I can't say the word 'bullshit' to describe bullshit? You're naked in someone else's pool right now. It's a little late to be uptight about the rules, don't you think?" She laughs.

I swish around in the water. "Hey. I was baptized in a swimming pool," I say, trying to shift the conversation to a lighter mood.

"Naked?" Kara jokes. "I'll bet everyone loved that!"

"No." I laugh. "But you're my DP and you *told* me to do this. One hundred percent imitation, right? You're completely responsible for me."

"Good defense. Maybe you'll be an attorney someday after all."

"What do you mean?" I ask her.

"Like your dad. Right?"

The way she says it makes me uneasy. And there's something else. "I never told you what my dad does," I say.

She pauses, running her hands over her wet hair. "Em.

If you haven't figured out that we are all open books here, then God help you."

I swim away from her to hold the edge of the pool at the deep end. I try to remember what I told anyone about my dad. Heather and Josh are the only people I can think of, but I don't think I ever said what he does for a living. An unsettling feeling sends a wave of chills through me. I clench my jaw to keep my teeth from chattering.

"Don't worry. Your secrets are safe with me." She swims to the middle, closer to me.

"I don't have any secrets," I challenge, slipping back down farther into the water.

Kara's smug smile is a victory in itself. "We all have secrets."

I hang on to the ladder and try not to shiver. Kara seems to enjoy throwing out random disconcerting facts on a daily basis.

"We could leave, you know," Kara says brazenly over the sound of her arms treading water.

My stomach flips at her suggestion. "What?"

"It's really never crossed your mind?" She swooshes back playfully, moving toward the shallow end.

"No," I lie. I think about Josh, and the guilt hits. *I didn't come here just for him.* "We're all here for a reason, Kara," I say, hearing my own doubt.

"Oh, come on. You and I both know this mission will never work. Boston already knows it. You think even a handful of Italians are going to chuck the Catholic Church and sign on to a mission that requires complete and total control of their lives? What would the Pope say? What would their *mothers* say? Besides, that's not what this is all about anyway. This is all about Will making himself look good to the Leader so he can keep moving up—and clearly that plan isn't going very well."

"That's not true. I mean, I don't feel that way." I try to think about my time with Heather, about what first pulled me in, about my own mother.

"Why *did* you join?" Kara asks, as if she can read my thoughts.

"What—you don't already know? I thought you said we're all open books," I spit back. Kara isn't budging, though. She stares at me, waiting for my answer. "I wanted to be saved." Then more quietly, "I want to see my mother someday."

"Oh. I'm so sorry." Kara's expression softens. "What happened to her? I mean, I know she . . ."

"She drowned when I was little." I say it matter-of-factly, reaching for the necklace around my neck. My eyes brim with tears, so I turn away.

"Hey. I'm really sorry. I wasn't thinking, and I'm really sorry I brought up your family," she says.

"It was a long time ago." I plunge myself underwater and swim back to the shallow end. I push my hands into the bottom of the pool and bolt into a back flip, like I used to do as a kid. I do it again and again. I'm dizzy, yet the thrill of being disoriented feels good as I exhale a violent spiral of bubbles into the dark abyss.

Suddenly, the water brightens like spotlights on a football field, only lit from underneath. I squeal through the water and surface for air. Expecting the old Italian man, I'm surprised to see a group of strangers towering over the edge of the shallow end. A tall guy in the middle casually holding an enormous basket-covered bottle has a half-smile on his face, while the others are frozen in surprise with their glasses of red wine and mismatched towels draped over their arms and shoulders.

"Looks like we have visitors," the guy with the bottle says.

Everyone is quiet as I sink down and turn to swim into the deep end, trying to hide the fact that I'm naked. Kara swims past me in the other direction where the strangers are still standing. By the time I get to the deep-end ladder where my clothes are strewn, I hear Kara say, "Thanks." I turn to see her wrapping the bottle guy's towel around herself. *"Kara,"* I say under my breath. The others settle into lounge chairs as if nothing odd is going on.

"Nice ink," he says to Kara.

A girl with black-and-blond streaked hair picks up my T-shirt beside her chair and tosses it to the ladder. "Thanks," I say.

"Are you guys backpacking or something?" the guy sitting beside her asks me.

"Um—" I start to say.

"Yes," Kara answers.

"Hey, Kevin," someone says. "Check out this tattoo." A stocky guy with a goatee wearing a plaid button-down shirt strolls over.

Kara grips her towel and tugs it around her chest then walks around to the deep end. I'd already slipped my T-shirt and shorts back on in the water, and now I'm somehow afraid to get out. Kara clearly does not share my apprehension.

"Tattoo? Oooo. I wanna see," the streaked-hair girl says.

Expecting Kara to walk over to show the girl, I freeze when I notice her toes curl over the edge of the pool. She drops her towel, arcs her arms overhead, and plunges deep into the glowing water in lightning-quick succession, but not before revealing the largest, most elaborate tattoo of a snake I've ever seen—the tail resting on the topmost region of her inner thigh, its body curving up all the way around her hip and disappearing around her back.

"Jesus. Christ. Where'd you get that done?" the girl who handed me my clothes asks Kara just after she surfaces from the dive.

Kara treads water in the middle of the pool and answers, "Africa."

Eva's Apple

Kara's bunk is empty when I wake up. It's so early that it's still dark outside. A sense of dread creeps through me. I try not to panic. *Yet*.

Maybe she's at the main villa taking a shower. I figure it's fifty-fifty at best. I sensed a spark between Kara and that guy, as did the quiet girl in the group who claimed to be too jet lagged to swim and chose to sulk at the edge of the pool, refusing all invitations to get in.

I remember walking back alone last night, dripping the entire way. When Kara refused to get out of the pool with her new friends, I came back for fear we'd get in trouble. Everyone was drinking wine and playing Marco Polo when I left, and I doubt they even noticed when I said good-bye. What if she didn't come home?

I climb out of bed and get dressed, reminding myself I'll have to be careful not to run into anyone, in case Kara isn't there and someone asks where she is.

The main villa is quiet and still, just one window alight with a shifting glow. I try to remember whose room it is as I tiptoe up to the side of the building. I hold my breath when I hear Ben's voice.

Will sounds perturbed. "We're running very low."

I strain to hear the muffled words. I take a few more steps and crouch down as close as I can to the window.

"Kara only brought one box," Ben says. "I can go into town and see if I can find a pharmacy, but I don't speak Italian, or know the local protocol for buying them, for that matter." Ben's voice is level and calm, like someone who doesn't care how this apparent dilemma turns out.

I lean forward, listening through a blooming silence.

Will's voice is low like a growl. "Figure it out."

I hear a door slam, then the creaking chair of an angry person sitting down. I carefully back up and peek around the corner to see Ben walking toward the road. His stride is not one of anger; it's one of surety, almost cockiness.

I sneak back to our room to find Kara putting on makeup, something I've never seen her do. Her headphones are on, and she's swaying her head in between touches to her face, which lights up in a smile when she sees me. I try not to seem surprised by her happy mood.

"Did you have fun last night?"

"Did you?" she smirks at me.

"Not really. I had to walk back by myself thanks to you. Did you even realize I left?"

"Of course. You're a big girl."

"Someone has to be." It sounds sharper than I meant it to come out.

"We're supposed to recruit this morning," she reminds me, changing the subject.

I sigh. "Okay. Where to?"

"To a nearby villa?" I watch her brush out her hair, only to twist and clip it into a messy bun. With her hair out of the way, and now that I know it's there, I can just see part of her snake tattoo.

"So, were you on the Africa mission with Will when he said he died?" I ask. Maybe she could explain the miracles Meredith spoke of with such cryptic reverence.

Kara turns to me, suddenly serious. "No. I made the Africa thing up. Besides, I really don't want to talk about our missions. I just want to pretend we're normal young people traveling through Europe. On an adventure, not a stupid mission no one wants to join. I've been done with the Kingdom for a long time now, in case you can't tell."

My heart jumps with frustration. And *fear*. "Why did you come here, then?" *And why in the world were you assigned as my DP?* I want to ask.

"Because my mother thought it would be a good idea

for too many reasons." She exhales an incredulous snort. "I tried to tell her nothing good could come of this, but she refused to listen, and now I'm just done."

I cannot seem to articulate anything.

"Emily, I'm going to be very honest with you. Do you mind?"

I wait for the explanation I've needed since day one.

"You need to stop asking so many questions and just come with me," she says.

I take a deep, frustrated breath. "Why?" I ask.

"Because, as your DP, I think it's the best thing for you." She puts her hands on my shoulders and tilts her forehead down as if communicating with a child. "I'm worried about your soul, Emily."

I squint at her in confusion.

Kara's tone fluctuates from one moment to the next, and sometimes it's very hard to tell whether or not she's joking.

She narrows her eyes in a serious expression. "I think you need to feed it a giant breakfast and take it for another cold dip in the pool."

"Naked?" I say. I can hear the judgmental tone in my voice, and I'm not sure whether to be proud of this, or embarrassed by it. I want to ask her about the tattoo again. About Africa. And Will. About the conversation I just over-heard. But it's clear I'll never get answers from her.

Kara laughs. "No, silly. We'll buy bathing suits."

"With what money? I still don't have my credit cards or traveler's checks. Or my passport and Eurail Pass, for that matter."

Kara grins knowingly. She has a plan. Of course.

"What will the others say when we aren't back here for lunch?" I ask, resigned. I've come to accept that once Kara has it in her mind to do something, there's no stopping her.

"I'm guessing they'll say, 'Yay! More food for us.'" She tilts her head back, laughing at her own joke. "Besides, they're supposed to be recruiting, which is what we'll be doing too."

"So are you recruiting Kevin and—"

"David?" She smiles a dreamy, faraway expression. "Absolutely *not*. No way. And they can *never* know why we're really here."

I'm filled with dread and confusion and an annoying sense of anger. "No thanks, Kara. Have fun," I say as I burrow back into bed and pull the covers over my head to tune out the sound of her tearing through drawers and shoving things into a suitcase. I'm relieved when she finally leaves, knowing she failed to convince me to follow her.

Soon after Kara leaves, I hear giggling, people talking in English, all in cheerful voices.

I hear Eva's Texas drawl outside, and then another round of laughter. A sense of dread builds in my chest as I get dressed and stumble into the bright sunlight. Dolce runs to me and rubs on my leg. I scratch under her chin and head down into the vineyard, where I hear more voices. As I approach, someone calls my name. *Josh*.

I stop at the edge of Josh's picnic blanket where he pats the ground for me to sit beside him. "Come eat," he says, holding out a plate. I take in the spread of fresh food on multiple blankets. *Where did all this come from?* Josh smiles as I sit beside him. *Finally we can talk.*

I'm pondering what to say to Josh when Eva jumps up with a bunch of grapes and yells, "Hey! Guess who I am?!" She's standing like a statue holding the grapes just above Todd's mouth. Everyone is busy eating, so she makes a dramatic whining sound and says, "The goddess of grapes! Duh."

I force a smile while nibbling on a lemon cookie. Everyone seems giddy, but in an off-kilter sort of way. It's like they're drunk off their full stomachs. *How am I going to pull Josh away without anyone noticing?* Just as I start to whisper to Josh, Andrew snaps at Eva, "There's no such thing as a goddess of grapes." He rolls his eyes. "There's Dionysus, the god of wine, but Dionysus is a *he*, so that doesn't quite work for you." His tone infects the picnic with a sudden tension, but Eva seems oblivious to anything except acting out this bizarre scene with Todd.

"Okay, fine." Eva pouts. "I was just trying to be a goddess, you know, like those Halloween costumes." Todd nips a low grape off the bunch in Eva's hand and dramatically moans with satisfaction as she smiles down at him and lifts the grapes higher, teasing him. I glance at Josh, hoping his reaction will give me a clue as to what's going on with everyone, but he's gingerly stacking salami and cheese onto a cracker.

"Eva!" Shannon barks, her hands on her hips. "You are not the goddess of anything. And we don't even joke around about pagan gods," she says in a shushing voice. "It's blasphemy to the Kingdom."

Todd stands to face off with Shannon. "Hey. Maybe you could tell us why we have all this food today," he taunts. I look to Josh again for guidance. He lifts his eyebrows in a this-is-entertaining-but-it-isn't-our-business gesture. Shannon's face flames red. I can't help but feel a tinge of satisfaction; Shannon's authoritative attitude as of late has gone from annoying to unsettling and she needed to be put in her place. But the air is charged with a sense of mutiny today, and the shifted dynamic is making me uneasy.

"Oh, I know the answer," Andrew chimes in, eager to stir the pot. "Eva bought us all food with her paycheck." He turns to point at Shannon. "And where'd you get that outfit, Shan? I've never seen it before until today. Is it *designer*?"

Eva smiles triumphantly. I catch Andrew sneaking an anxious glance back at the villa. I suddenly notice Lily isn't here. *What's going on? And where are Will and Ben?*

As Shannon stomps off to sulk, Eva immediately rushes to her side and puts an arm around her. "Oh, come on, Shannon. We're just kidding. You know that, right? I'm really sorry."

Shannon pulls away. "We'll discuss it later. We can add it to your *list* of things to discuss," she hisses.

Eva's expression changes to worry. She grabs an apple from our spread of food and walks to the edge of the vineyard toward my building as if getting away from Shannon.

"Josh," I finally say as he pops a cookie into his mouth.

"Sorry. I'm starving," he says, laughing with a mouth full of cookie. I laugh with him, relieved that things between us seem closer to normal again. Just as I reach for a cookie, a piercing scream echoes through the vineyard.

It's Eva.

She screams again.

Josh is already running toward her by the time I jump to my feet. He yells for us not to come back there, but it's too late. I'm already right behind him.

"*Holy*—" someone behind me says. Dolce is making a constant yowling sound that I know I will never be able to erase from my memory. Her front leg is swollen and bleeding, her tiny body writhing with every yowl. Her back legs convulse uncontrollably.

I choke in air, trying to process what's happening. Eva starts pacing around Dolce, her hands covering her high-pitched heaving sounds. She doubles over and stares at the ground like she's going to throw up.

Bile rises in my throat. *"What happened?"*

Todd leans over Dolce. "It looks like something bit her," he says. Dolce's legs slow and then stop twitching, as if suddenly paralyzed. Her eyes are vacant and afraid, and she never stops making the horrible sound. Todd shoots me a worried glance and looks away. Goose bumps spread like a rash on my arms as I remember the snake in my room.

My face turns numb. I want to scream, but my throat is so dry I can't talk. I scan the area in a panic. I don't see anything except Dolce crying in agony.

Josh shoves Todd aside and heads straight for the nearby shed. He emerges with a shovel, his face determined and red with anger.

"Turn around," Josh says.

We stand there frozen, staring back at him in shock.

"TURN. AROUND. *NOW*."

And as I do, the sound of the shovel slicing through the air and a dull thud puts an immediate end to the yowling, and our poor kitten's misery.

Eva sobs with short, erratic gasps in between, her hands over her eyes. Shannon shows no emotion. I notice her hands shaking as she steps up to comfort Eva. Filled with a mixture of horror and gratitude for Josh's willingness to take on the unthinkable, a roaring shockwave expands in my head.

Everyone else is silent until Shannon's matter-of-fact voice breaks through the chaos: "It was God's will."

I open my eyes to see Josh gently scooping Dolce with his shovel, before walking away to bury Kara's kitten. *Kara. I'll have to tell Kara.* I close my eyes and sit down on the ground, hugging my arms around myself. I press my forehead against my knees. I want to cry, but I can't. I want to scream, but I can't. Something has hijacked my ability to process any of this.

"It's okay. It was God's will." Shannon repeats it over and over again to no one in particular.

Rage begins to cloud my vision. I stomp off toward Josh.

"How am I going to tell her?" I sound angry. I *am* angry.

Josh looks up from the fresh mound of dirt. "That depends. Where is she?" he asks me.

This is the first real one-on-one conversation I've had with Josh since we got to Italy, and it's while he's burying a kitten. The whole situation is so absurd that it almost makes me laugh, but then I notice the blood splattered on Josh's legs as he tamps dirt over Dolce's grave. Nothing about this is funny.

"I can't say," I answer. This is not how I wanted this conversation to go, but I've lost control of everything, and it's clear I won't be getting it back.

He turns to me and leans into his shovel. "You can't say because you don't know, or because you refuse to tell me?"

I stare at the ground, trying to figure out how to fix all this. Where would I even start?

"You keeping secrets from me now? After this?" He glances down at the mound under his shovel. He looks up, his eyes pleading with me. "After everything?"

I want to scream, *After what?* I came on this mission for me, yes, but also for him, as pathetic as that may sound. And he's made no effort to even speak to me until now, as if changing time zones completely changed his feelings for me.

"I would never betray the confidence of my DP," I say defiantly. And with that, I stomp away.

\\|//

As I walk up the hill in the dark, I hear music coming from the villa where the Americans are staying. The windows flicker with lit candles. The sound of carefree togetherness feels out of place after what I've just seen. A sense of homesickness expands in my chest.

"Emm-y!" It's the girl with the streaked hair. "Oh, look! You're actually wearing clothes!" She laughs and pulls the knot on her silky wrap skirt. I'm surprised she remembers me at all, so I don't correct her for getting my name wrong. And, for a moment, I realize how easy it would be to simply become someone else, especially around this group. She leans in for a cheek-to-cheek kiss, leaving the syrupy scent of wine between us. "Let's get you some vino."

"Oh, I can't . . ." I start to protest, but she guides me through the living area down a hallway where I smell the lingering aroma of garlic and onions. I'm starving.

"Kiki is cooking. Doesn't it smell amazing?" She stops at a side table full of wine bottles with differing levels of emptiness to pour me a glass.

"Oh. No, thanks," I say, my hand up. "I'm okay."

She gives me a condescending look and waves the glass under my nose. "Oh, no-no-no. You have to try it. We went all the way to Montalcino yesterday and bought two cases. You'll never taste a better Chianti in your fucking *life*."

I smile politely and take a quick swig, even though I know it's against the Kingdom rules. "No alcohol whatsoever," Heather told me in Boston, which was fine with me since I'd never been a big drinker, but this Chianti tastes so good that even the one sip helps to calm my nerves. I make an approving sound and take another, hoping it will erase the memories of such a horrendous day.

"Jenna!" a male yells from the kitchen.

"Coming . . . ," she answers in a singsong-y voice as she rolls her eyes and slips away.

I sip the wine and walk down a hallway toward voices. *I am someone else. I am someone else.* Kara's voice startles me.

"Well, well, well. Look at you drinking the Kool-Aid. As they say, when in Tuscany . . ." I turn around to see Kara in a bikini with a man's button-down shirt as a cover-up. Her voice is sharp and sarcastic, and I honestly can't tell if she's happy to see me. She leans forward. "You're alone, right?" she whispers.

"Yes," I say. I take another drink of wine and my eyes well up. "There's something I have to talk to you about."

"I disagree," Kara says. "There will be no talking about anything tonight. And I make the rules, all right?" She takes my arm and leads me back toward the table of wine.

The guy wearing the same plaid shirt from the night at the pool appears from a nearby hallway. "Another rule? Oh, come on," he jokes to Kara as if they've known each other for years. I'm in awe of her ability to assert control over complete strangers so quickly.

"Where'd you get the swimsuit?" I ask, trying to hide my

extended stare at her tattoo. Even the scales on the snake are visible up close. I notice its open mouth is black instead of the red tongue normally depicted in snake images.

"Turns out I'm Jenna's same exact size," she says, pouring her own glass of wine.

The tall guy with round glasses walks up. His button-down shirt—suspiciously similar to Kara's—is as disheveled as his brown hair. Something about him is attractive, though not in a conventional way, and I'm worried for Kara. "Calm down, man," he says to his friend, pushing Kevin away from us. He puts his arm around Kara, his hand lingering suggestively around her waist, falling almost to her hip.

"Nice to see you back. You're just in time to eat with us." He takes my glass and refills it to the top with wine. "Emily, right? Kara's told me all about you," he says as he hands the glass back to me.

Kara lifts her eyebrows and nudges him.

"Okay. I guess I need to check on dinner," he says before sauntering off.

"What did you tell them?" I whisper forcefully.

"Oh, just that we're backpacking after graduating college and completing a stressful mission with the Peace Corps."

"What?"

She laughs abruptly. She's probably been drinking wine all day. *How am I going to get us back to our room without anyone else seeing us?*

"Kara. Seriously. What did you say about us?"

She takes another drink and smiles. "Peace Corps. Africa. Now backpacking." She points to the rounded curves of her breasts, barely contained by the patterned triangles of her top. "In a bikini." She snickers, clearly drunk.

I'm warm and light-headed myself. From a vague far-away place in my brain, I know I need to think of a plan, to focus. I need to get us out of here. "Kara. It's about Dolce," I say.

"Oh! I'm so glad you reminded me. Would you feed her for me?"

"Um . . . I don't— Wait. Where are you going?"

Kara narrows her eyes at me. "I'm not going anywhere." She adjusts the elastic on her bathing suit bottom with a decisive pop.

"Kara. I know you're having fun with these people, but you can't just stay here." My panic rises. It hadn't occurred to me that Kara wouldn't want to come back at all. Explaining why she's drunk is one thing; explaining why she disappeared is another.

"David invited me to go wine tasting with them tomorrow, so I am staying, actually."

"For the night?" My anxiety begins to rise.

"Seriously, Em. Don't be a buzzkill!" She pushes me, spilling my wine on her arm. Kara exhales in belligerent frustration as she wipes the wine with her—or I assume David's—shirt, leaving a dark stain. "Just go, okay?" she says.

I inhale sharply to contain my anger. "Okay. Fine. What

am I supposed to say when someone asks about you?"

"Easy," she says. "Just find Ben and tell him that his joke was *not* funny." She lowers her voice to whisper, "Also, tell him you recognize my tattoo, and I promise you no one will ask one single fucking thing about anything else we do."

My mind is spinning when I get back to the villa. I head straight to my room. I gasp when I open my door.

Josh is standing by my bed, just as surprised as I am. The room is a mess from Kara's noisy packing rampage before she left.

"What are you doing here?" I ask, my heart still racing from his unexpected presence.

"I wanted to see you."

"Then why do you seem so surprised that I'm here?" Josh's face falls and I immediately feel silly for being so defensive. "I'm sorry. I didn't mean . . . I'm just upset. I didn't get a chance to tell Kara about what happened today. I mean, I tried, but she wouldn't let me. She said not to—"

"Hey." Josh pulls me into his chest and wraps his arms around me. He begins smoothing my hair. "Hey. It's okay," he says.

I melt into his embrace, but I'm still upset. "It isn't okay. None of this is okay."

"Maybe I can talk to her. If you'll tell me where she is, I'll explain what happened and fix this. I can get her to come back. I can go right now and she'll be here within the hour."

He's right. I know we should go get Kara, but I'm afraid of how that would play out. Bringing her back drunk after essentially abandoning the mission? No. I'll fix this myself in the morning when Kara is sober. "I'm sure she's fine," I say.

Josh's jaw twitches. "We should really go get her, Em." An abrupt sadness overpowers me. I know he's right—we should go get Kara—but the thought that he would rather do that than be alone with me abruptly overpowers me with sadness. I heave a sigh and wipe the tears off my face with his T-shirt. He gives me an odd look.

"Have you been drinking?" he asks.

"No," I lie.

He lifts my chin up. "You sure about that?" His finger brushes my lower lip. I inhale deeply just as his mouth closes in on mine, and my thoughts spin into a dark and starry nothingness until he pulls away

"Wine?"

"Maybe," I whisper.

"Where is it?"

"Not here." He's kissing my neck now, lightly working his way up to my ear. I exhale. "Not there, either."

"With Kara?" he asks.

"Yes."

He kisses me again until he asks the next question. "Why can't you tell me where? What if I wanted some too?" he whispers as he slowly backs me into the wall. I can feel every horrible thing that's happened in Italy falling away as we kiss, and I imagine we're far away from this building, far from the Kingdom. The possibility of freedom needles its way through the bliss of the moment until the fear creeps in.

I break the kiss, but Josh holds the back of my neck, almost too tightly. I wrap my arms around his shoulders and kiss him until I can't tell which way is up. My back presses into the wall as our struggle to breathe amplifies, triggering a thousand fleeting thoughts, none of which I can pinpoint. His heart races against my chest, his hand gently slipping under the hemline of my top. His knuckles brush against my bare skin underneath as his fingers unlatch the front clasp of my bra and then the button of my shorts. He moves to the zipper.

Oh God.

"Oh God." I say it out loud, suddenly remembering he will have to tell Ben every detail of this. Or worse, *Will.*

I push him away, trying to catch my breath. He gently takes my face in his hands.

I exhale into the silence—half frustrated, half euphoric. "Josh . . ." My shorts feel dangerously close to falling. I fumble to refasten the button, but he stops me by taking my hands and lacing his fingers into mine. He presses our hands against the wall on either side of my face and kisses me again. Then his hands are everywhere as my thoughts reel way too fast to hit the brakes.

I mumble his name again between breaths. *We have to*

desperately want to stop him from leaving. Instead I stand there like an idiot.

"I'm really sorry, Emily." He sounds truly apologetic. "It's more complicated than that. I just . . . can't." He slips out the door and gently closes it behind him.

I stare at it as my heart fills with regret. *Why did I have to push him too far?*

Straightening my clothes in an attempt to pull myself together, I wipe the tears from my face, open the door, and run toward the vineyard. I don't even realize I've run head-on into Andrew until I hear his gasp. A searing pain rips through my head.

"Jeez, Emily." He's bent forward with both hands on his knees. "What are you doing?"

"Colliding with you, apparently," I say. Andrew stands straight, still rubbing just above his eye. "What were you ᵍ with Josh?" he asks boldly.

Are you spying on me?" I sound unhinged. *What if Josh ᵗ and Will what we did? What I suggested?*

ᵗ, relax. I'm the best secret keeper at this villa. Just " he says ominously. "No. I meant what are we still ᵉ?" His tone is serious.

ᵗ say something but realize I don't have an answer. ᵉ, Andrew."

ᵘis eyes at me, leans in, and whispers, "Haven't ᵗbout leaving?"

ᵉear me and Josh?

stop. Kara's reaction to my cautiousness about David (*Seriously, Em*) flashes through my mind. She was actually *mocking* me for following the rules. Maybe she's right. I'm too uptight about the Kingdom. And Kara *is* technically still my DP . . . *But what if someone catches us right now?*

I push Josh away, harder this time, even though everything in me wants the exact opposite. "What if we . . . left?" I say. The empty villa and pool flash through my thoughts Kara and her new friends will be gone for most of the ⟨?⟩ tomorrow. My mind is clearly functioning throug⟨?⟩ heightened senses because all I can think about is bei⟨?⟩ him like this anywhere but here, somewhere far ⟨?⟩ from the others.

He squints down at me, confused. "Wh⟨?⟩ drop as he steps back.

"Seriously. I know a place where we ⟨?⟩ at least, until we figure out . . . um . . ⟨?⟩ rassed, refastening my shorts. How ⟨?⟩ thinking out loud?

"You mean with Kara?" he ⟨?⟩

"No. Just *us*."

He pulls me close aga⟨?⟩ my arms around his b⟨?⟩ heart is still racing, b⟨?⟩ can't," he says. He ⟨?⟩ arms, his expres⟨?⟩

A wave of panic ⟨?⟩

246

"Well, I have," Andrew says. "And I know where the passports are."

My heart makes a hopeful leap.

Andrew leans in close. "I've already checked them. But you should know yours is missing and so is Kara's. Your Eurail passes are gone too. Among other things."

I'm dizzy with panic. Does Kara know about this? How will we get home? "What are you talking about?"

Andrew gives a harsh laugh. "Come on, Emily. You're smart enough to know things are going to get way worse. Where *is* Kara anyway? We're all going to have bigger problems than your missing documents if we don't figure out where she ran off to."

I rub my forehead. It still hurts from our collision, and this conversation is only making it worse.

"Look, Em." His tone shifts to sympathetic. "I wouldn't blame you if you're the one who took it. You know that, right? Backpacking through Europe sounds way better than begging Italians to join our meetings just so we can watch them eat all our food then take off the moment they figure out what we are." He glances at me, waiting for a reaction.

I pause, reluctant to confide in anyone right now, even Andrew. Kara may have lost her senses, but I understand her desperation to run away from impossible expectations—the crushing weight of guilt that follows inevitable failure. But Josh . . . Why would he refuse to leave with me, especially after what just happened in my room? What I was willing to risk just to physically be with him? Then it hits me. Maybe his faith is just stronger than mine. If we're here for the right reasons, everything will work out. I just have to have faith.

"You know what we are, don't you?" Andrew's voice is sharp. "Let me give you a hint. It starts with a C. And it's not church."

A sudden fury rises in my throat. "Stop it, Andrew. What is your problem anyway?" I snap. "I'll bet you were the one who left the snake for Kara."

"Snake?" His face is shocked, drained of color, as if I'd conjured a ghost from the vineyard.

"The one in the bag. On *my bed*. There was a note that said TRUST ME. Sound familiar? That's what killed Dolce, you know. Was that you?"

"No," he whispers, his tone completely changed. "I have to—"

I rub my eyes in frustration and exhale a deep breath. "Andrew, I'm so sorr—"

I look up, and Andrew is already walking away.

If only I could be more like Kara—more impulsive, irresponsible—maybe Josh would have left with me. Or maybe Josh is the one saving me from my own self-destructive doubts, even after I tried to tempt him to leave. A sudden anxiety lodges in my throat, making me want to scream. Instead I swallow it down and stagger to my room.

Devil's Music

By the time I wake up the next morning, Andrew and Lily are both gone.

My formal interrogation starts with Kara's mix tape.

The headphones sit on Will's oversized desk. I try to ignore them as I sit in the chair across from him.

"Emily. Did you lose something today?" he asks me as he looks down at the Sony tape player, careful not to touch something so consumed with sin.

A knot tightens in my throat.

"No, sir," I say. Being alone with Will is intimidating. He has a way of extracting guilt even from those who had no idea they'd done anything wrong.

His blue eyes reveal a mix of amusement and disg

their color a stark contrast against his pallid complexion. Will somehow grew paler since we got here, almost like the Italian sun drained his skin of color instead of tanning it.

"That's very interesting, since Shannon said she saw you wearing them earlier this week."

He must have seen Kara wearing them every day for weeks. So why is he trying to corner me? "Well, I guess I've borrowed them before," I answer.

His eyebrows shoot up. "Then, is this your . . . *music*? If it can even be called that." He mutters the last part as he picks up the tape player and ejects the tape. He handles it carefully using the tips of his fingers as if it were a razor blade fresh out of the box. The clear cassette exposes a long white sticker labeled *MY MIX* in Kara's unmistakable angular scrawl.

"It's not mine," I say, grateful to be telling the truth.

"You don't recognize these lyrics, then?" He pushes a notepad with words scribbled on it.

"Go ahead. Read it," he says.

I sit frozen, terrified of where this is leading. He seems unhinged. "Can you not read my handwriting?" he asks.

"I can. It's just—"

He looks down at the object in question, carefully inserts a pencil under the exposed brown tape, and begins pulling it out. As he extracts the cassette's entrails, the tangled heap of shiny brown loops glimmer like a pile of worms writhing on is desk. "Go ahead, then," he says.

I look at the lyrics and whisper the first line of Liz Phair's

"Flower." "Every time I see your face I get—" I stop and look away. There's no way I'm reading the rest of the explicit lyrics out loud.

"Is there something you'd like to confess?"

"No," I say quickly.

"Are you *sure*?"

A Vespa buzzes in the distance through the open window. The noise escalates like an angry insect as it passes the villa and fades up the hill, triggering me to question the absurdity of a mix tape interrogation in the middle of Italy. I have to stay focused. I have to get back to Kara without anyone knowing. *Just play along.*

"Listen. I promise this tape is not mine. The headphones are Kara's, but I don't know where the tape came from." *Shit.* Why did I bring her name into this situation, or even say it out loud?

"They came from your room," he says gingerly. "So I guess we'll have to ask Kara, then. Only she's not here to ask, is she?"

I struggle for a response.

In a sudden burst of anger, Will stands up and grabs the earphones, still connected to the tape player. "Since she's left you here to answer for this, tell me. Where are the rest of these tapes? There must be more." He sways to one side, as if off balance, and catches himself by pressing his hand into the desk. I can see beads of sweat on his forehead, even though the room is cool and breezy.

"I have no idea," I plead. "They honestly aren't mine."

He leans over his desk to hand the jumbled mass to me. I reach for it just as he grabs my hand. His hand is clammy and cold, but his grip is tight. I notice a large Band-Aid on his arm.

"Where is she?" His eyes seem wild.

"I don't know," I lie. I know he can sense it, and I brace for his anger. Something changes in his expression. He seems desperate, afraid even.

"We're talking about the success of our mission here," he says. "We *need* her."

His clammy hand is still gripping mine, but now he seems to be grasping it for balance. He lets go and falls into his chair. After a pause, he takes a deep breath. "Emily, look. If you know where she is, just *please* bring her back." He wipes his forehead with a tissue. "I know you're a good girl and want to help without betraying your DP. I know you'll do the right thing. Just think it over. I will have to address the music situation, since several DPs know about it," he says. "Don't worry. You won't be marked."

With a wave of relief, I stand up to leave before he changes his mind. He lifts his hand in a stop gesture. "We have a meeting."

My heart jumps into my throat. "But—I—" My mind is spinning too fast to think of an excuse.

"Right now," he says.

We all gather together in the main room where Will

wheels in a television on a large cart. A shocked silence blankets the room when an MTV logo flashes on the bottom right corner of the screen.

A collective gasp erupts when the video reveals an emaciated old man wearing a Santa Claus hat climbing up onto an enormous cross in the middle of a field of red poppies. Kurt Cobain's gravelly voice murmurs the lyrics of "Heart-Shaped Box" as Will lingers beside the television with an exaggerated expression of concern, as if someone is torturing him by forcing him to watch the ensuing blasphemy. I look around and see that Shannon is watching with the same horrified expression. "Oh my word," she says, looking away dramatically.

I'm not sharing the level of shock exhibited by everyone around me. The bizarre video seems to be reenacting someone's disjointed dream. A raven perched on a cross. A fat lady jumping in a Mr. Goodbody suit. Kurt Cobain in a coma. Hundreds of bloodred poppies just like the ones that cover the Tuscan hills around us. It seems absurd, though I imagine Shannon is having a different reaction.

The moment it ends, the spell is broken and we look at one another with anxious glances. Will shuts off the monitor and makes eye contact around the room as he waits for a response.

"Can you believe *this* sick excuse for music is what young people are listening to today? You could make an entire Sin List from this one video," he says. "Does anyone want to give it a shot?"

I'm lost in my own thoughts. Part of me wants to respond, to believe he's right. I hear words from various voices around me float to the surface: Blasphemy. Dark Arts. Drugs. Sex. The Pope. Abortion. Satan. Homosexuality. Gluttony. I have to keep myself from laughing out loud, and I'm scared of what that could mean. Summer and I used to listen to this album on repeat, and never once did we worry about the idea of . . . Satan. I try to picture Summer here with me now, but all I can see is her standing up to scream: *Why are y'all freaking out about ANY of these things?*

For some reason, the only word I can think to say from the video is "poppies."

Will is staring at me with his head cocked in curiosity. *Did I say that out loud?*

Perhaps not. He continues on with his rant and I can't process a word of it. I'm thinking about how something so natural and beautiful could be torn apart and distilled into something addictive.

Will paces in front of us. "Lily and Andrew are gone. Andrew left a note saying he cannot be a part of our mission. You need to consider what that means. We know Satan moves among us. He seeks to divide us from our work, from our Lord, and our salvation."

Everyone is silent. I stare at Josh, but he refuses to look at me.

"Do you really think Andrew and Lily were Satan's only ~ents here?" he continues.

A sharp fear jolts through me. I can't remember when I last saw Lily. The image of her staring at the wall is the last thing I remember about her. Her sadness was so horrible, and I'm rocked with an intense surge of guilt for not having gone back to check on her, to at least see what happened with her brother. What if Will is right? What if things happen in life to sow doubt in our hearts?

"As of this moment, both Lily and Andrew are marked," he yells. "You must never, under any circumstances, *ever* speak to either of them again. They have chosen to be selfish, to listen to the devil rather than God's calling, and they have chosen to turn their backs on the Kingdom. Both of them are like dogs returning to their vomit. Therefore, we must turn our backs on them for their own good and the good of our mission."

A sudden anger rises in my throat and spreads heat across my face. "Her brother was in a really bad accident. I'm sure she was trying to get to her family, and that this is a misunderstanding. Andrew just wanted to help her."

"Oh please," Shannon says. "Andrew has had a thing for Lily since day one, so they're choosing to live in sin. And her brother wasn't even saved. He was probably drunk or on drugs when it happened."

"But he's her family," I say.

"*We* are her family," Shannon says. "There was sin in his life, and that's what caused him to crash his car. His wreck was God's will."

I want to scream in Shannon's face. I remember how she said the kitten's death was God's will. Why would something so random and horrible need to be explained away as *God's will*?

Will puts his hand on my shoulder to calm me down— or keep me down. "Shannon is right. When you have sin in your life, bad things will happen and God cannot protect you."

Shannon glares at me smugly, and then looks around the room. "Where's Kara?" she asks me. "I haven't seen her in days."

Will cuts in quickly. "Kara is working on our mission elsewhere." To my surprise, he glances at me and quickly raises his voice. "Everyone needs to listen up, because we are being tested. Just listen to us fighting amongst ourselves. How is God supposed to protect *us* when we turn our backs on Him? The mission of the Kingdom must take *full* priority, even over our families back home. We have bigger issues than the fact that we've managed to lose two interns. The issue is sitting right here in this group."

We all shift uncomfortably.

"There can be only one reason for our failures," he says matter-of-factly.

No one says a word. Will drops his head and stares at the floor, and then raises it again with a look of sorrow.

"There is sin in this group."

With that, Will storms out of the room and slams his

office door. Ben scurries after him while everyone else sits in silence, glancing around with shocked faces. Before anyone can stop me, I bolt straight out of there to go find Kara, pausing only once to be sure no one followed me outside. I find her floating around the pool by herself. Her new friends are abuzz with activity inside the villa, so I charge to the edge of the water.

"So it's just you now?" I ask her.

"Em!" she says, rowing with her hands to the edge. "No. They're packing to leave."

I'm not in the mood for fake talk. "Andrew and Lily are missing."

"What? No shit."

"They ran off together. 'To live in sin,' as Shannon put it."

Kara laughs. "I highly doubt *that*."

"I really think he was helping her get back to see her brother, but I saw them in the vineyard the other night. And as I'm *sure* you're aware," I add sarcastically, "we're not supposed to be alone with the opposite sex." I press my fingers into my forehead to block out the way-too-detailed memories of Josh in my room.

Kara swishes her hands in the water. "I'm pretty sure Lily is safe from living in sin with Andrew. Also, they really should rethink that rule."

I fold my arms and tilt my head back, inhaling with frustration. "What's that supposed to mean?" She has no idea how weird Will's speech was just minutes ago, while she was floating around in this pool like she isn't even part of our mission anymore.

"Nothiiiing." Kara scrunches her toes on the side of the concrete and pushes away from the edge to the middle. "Why don't you swim with me? You can borrow a swimsuit. Or not. They'll be gone soon, so you don't have to be so embarrassed."

I try my best to keep my cool. "Kara. I don't want to swim with you. I need your *help*. Please come back to the villa with me. I can't do this anymore. Everyone keeps asking where you are." I pause, searching for the right words, but I just say exactly what I'm thinking. "They're starting to scare me."

Kara rolls her eyes and laughs. "Just stay here with me, Em. We'll float and do water flips and eat pasta. It'll be fun." I look past her at the distant green hills, trying to come up with the right words. I feel conflicted and so helpless. Trapped here so far away from people who could help us—who could help *me*. My eyes well as Kara blurs into the water. She paddles back to me and reaches for the side of the pool.

"Seriously, Em. Come here."

I sit on the hot concrete at the edge where we can talk quietly. "Stay here," she says. "I can get us out. I have a plan. You didn't tell anyone where I am, right?"

"No," I say, skimming the water with my fingers.

"Good. Has anyone ever followed you here?"

"Not that I know of."

Kara is whispering now. She's so close I can smell the wine on her breath, yet she seems completely sober—more focused than I've ever seen her, actually. "They may be watching you. I already got our stuff," she says.

I remember Andrew telling me mine and Kara's things were gone. "How did you get in? When were you there? *Everyone* has been looking for you."

"It's a long story. Listen. I just need you to get one more thing."

"What. Your Tampax box? Can't live without your mix tapes?"

"I have those here," Kara says.

"Apparently not," I say. "And I took a lot of heat for that, you know."

Kara's face turns serious. She almost seems afraid. She grabs my arm, almost pulling me into the water. "What are you talking about?"

"Someone had headphones with your mix tape in it. I had to answer a bunch of questions, and Will tried to get me to read some dirty lyrics out loud while he pulled the tape apart like a psycho."

This gets her attention. "Emily. Do you know which tape it was?"

"I think it said *MY MIX*."

Kara sighs in relief and lets go of my arm. But her eyes seem frantic. "Who's been in our room?"

I stare at the sunlight dancing on the water, hoping the question will disappear on its own.

"Emily?"

"No one," I say. The lie falls out of my mouth so easily. I stand up and pace along the edge of the pool.

An awkward silence fills the gap between us as Kara studies my reaction.

"I can't imagine why anyone in our group would want to take your stuff. I mean, what if it was just an accident?"

Kara twists her mouth as if deciding what to say next. "Emily, I know it's hard for you to understand, but you cannot trust *anyone*."

I want to scream. To demand straightforward answers from her, but seeing Kara's friends inside the villa windows makes me swallow my frustration instead. "Look," I say in a calm voice. "All I know is everyone has been acting crazy, and I can't do this anymore. But I don't know how to just . . . leave. I mean, I don't even know where my passport is."

"Your passport is here," she says matter-of-factly, swishing her hands in the water.

My body tenses with concern. "Here where?"

"Here at the villa. In David's room."

The realization rushes to my head: *She's really serious.* "Kara, what the hell?! Were you just going to kidnap me in my sleep?"

"No, silly. I knew you'd come back to look for me. And

here you are. It's so easy now. We can just leave." She flashes a triumphant smile.

"Kara. *What is going on?* They told me I had to bring you back, and then Will lied about the fact that you're missing. They marked Lily and Andrew—we can never speak to them again, which doesn't matter since I doubt they'll be back. And Dolce is dead." I immediately regret saying too much.

"What?" Kara's voice is quiet. Her eyes glaze with tears.

"I'm so sorry. I tried to tell you before. I think it was that snake. . . . *Please,* just tell me what's going on."

She dunks herself underwater then swooshes back up and grounds her arms elbows-out on the edge of the concrete. Her gaze is focused and determined without a hint of emotion.

"If you really want out, I can help you. I have everything we need, except one thing: You need to find some money, or better yet, your credit cards."

"Kara—" My head is in a fog. Leaving is the only way I can think of to remove the weight crushing my chest and the pressure constricting my throat, but something—a strong sense of dread—is holding me back. I'm scared, but I don't even know *what* it is I'm afraid of.

"Listen. David already invited us to meet them in Rome, beyond that would be iffy. And once we leave the villa, that's it. We can never go back to see anyone in the Kingdom. They won't even be allowed to speak to us." She gives me a serious look. "Not even Josh."

"I don't care," I say. Even as I say it, I tell myself Josh will eventually come around. Sometimes when you need to keep a clear head, you have to hide your decisions from your heart.

Kara smiles. "Okay, I got our passports and travel passes from the office, but the money must be in a different place. It's got to be somewhere in the office, probably locked up. You'll have to figure that part out when everyone is asleep."

"How did Lily and Andrew leave without any money?"

"She probably got her parents to wire it to her since she was calling home."

"I'm still confused. Why didn't they mark *you* and forbid me to speak to you if they don't even know where you are?"

"Because you're the only person who knows where I am, and I'm the only person who knows everything."

Light as a Feather, Stiff as a Board

I wait in the vineyard until everyone seems asleep, just like Kara said. I go back to the window where I overheard Ben and Will. The wooden shutters are closed. A slender bar of light glows underneath.

The villa is quiet as I rush toward Will's office. I reach for the knob and stop when I hear a voice on the other side of the door. *Ben.* And then someone else—a woman—says, "We have to pull this together before he gets here tomorrow. And you're going to have to take over this fiasco, because I've got my hands full."

A jolt of fear steals my breath. *Meredith.* I hear drawers opening and closing, papers being shuffled on a desk. "I see all the Accountability Sheets and BT checklists, but where are the SLs?" she says.

A pause, and then Ben: "We don't know."

Meredith laughs. "I don't know how y'all ran things down in Florida, but Boston is a whole different story." More drawers open and slam shut. "'We don't know' will not fly in Boston, I can tell you that."

"Maybe your husband knows." Ben's tone is sharp. "I've looked in every corner of this villa and still haven't found them."

No response. Just the sounds of more rummaging. My instinct tells me to tiptoe away, but my desire to hear what's going on overrides the risk.

"Can he talk yet?" Ben asks, his tone now more sympathetic.

"He's still resting. They said he needs some time to recover."

Recover. From what?

"Is it his blood sugar?" His voice sounds tentative. "He seemed really unsteady the last few days."

"Blood sugar? No. Probably dehydration or exhaustion." She says the words like someone else's improbable guesses. "But those are just sympt— What in the world are these for?" Her tone shifts to confusion.

"Oh. I just got those from town for his insulin shots. He was almost out."

"He isn't diabetic," Meredith says as if Ben must be an idiot.

"He said—"

"Well, he must be delirious from that fever because he's never taken insulin in his life."

"Then why would he—"

A car driving up the hill flashes a bright light into the hallway where I'm standing. I hold in my breath, trying not to panic. I exhale through their long pause as quietly as possible.

"Ben. This mission is doomed, and we both know why. The issue is clear-cut. This group came here with sin in their hearts. I can't believe you threw together such a divisive and rebellious bunch. Has anyone else fallen away other than Lily and Andrew?"

"Well, technically, no. Kara is working from another location. Or so they say. . . ."

"Who in the world is Kara?" Her voice is tight and irritated.

My minds reels in confusion. *How could Meredith not know Kara?*

"Kara from the Florida church. She was with her mom, the nurse, on the mission in Africa?"

"In *Africa*? How have I never heard of them?"

Silence.

"Well, I don't have the first clue as to what's going on here and clearly you don't either," Meredith continues. "I shouldn't even have to be here at all. We're moving to California in a matter of weeks. Do you have any idea how stressed out I am?"

"Look. I know how to handle this," Ben says, his voice now authoritative and closer to the door. "I'm already working to get this mission back on track if you'll just let me lead."

"Fine. Whatever. Go ahead and take over. But what we really need is a miracle."

"I completely agree," says Ben.

Meredith's laugh fills me with a nauseating dread.

"I know what to do," Ben says. "We just have to eradicate the sin. It's the only way." His definitive tone prompts me to slip away and down the dark hill to my building.

I'm surprised to find the bunk beds occupied. Kara never said anything about meeting me back here. The plan was to meet at the pool. I take a few steps forward and see Eva is in mine. A sleeping body is under Kara's blanket. Shannon's curls spill across the pillow. *Shit*. I tiptoe to the drawers and open one. It's empty. I squat to look under the bed where our suitcases were, but nothing is there. I open all the drawers, only to find them empty.

"What are you doing?" says Eva, half-asleep.

"What are *you* doing? Where's my stuff?" I say, playing dumb.

"Ben told us to sleep here tonight with you and Kara. I have no idea where your stuff is. He just brought us out here about an hour ago. Can you keep it down? I'm exhausted." She turns and pulls the covers up over her head.

Ben? I'm frozen with panic, not sure whether to run back to Kara or try to get back into the villa. I think better of the latter, as Meredith is probably still in there.

I hear voices coming toward the door. Suddenly it opens and Ben walks in with Josh and Todd trailing half-asleep behind him. If Josh is surprised to see me standing there, he doesn't show it.

"Here are your instructions," Ben says. He hands a folded piece of paper to Todd. "There's sin in this room, living in some or all of you. It's killing our mission, so you guys are going to stay in here until it's gone," he says calmly.

Before anyone has a chance to object, Ben walks out and shuts the door. Just as my eyes adjust to the darkness, a locking sound clicks from outside. I turn to see the wooden shutters are closed. I rush to open one, but it's secured from the outside.

Todd unfolds the piece of paper. "How am I supposed to read this?" he asks.

Josh clicks on a small flashlight. He shines the light on the paper:

> Put to death the sinful, earthly things lurking within you . . . God's terrible anger will come upon those who do such things.
>
> Colossians 3:5-6

I recognize the handwriting from the writing on the tag with the snake. I'm lightheaded, like I'm about to fall off a high ledge. "Is this Ben's handwriting?" I ask Josh.

"Yeah, why?" he mutters.

Shit. I hurry back to the shutters and try them again. When they don't budge, I start pounding them with my fists. Josh puts his arms around me and backs me away from the window. "Shhh," he whispers into my ear. "The last thing we need to do is wake up Shannon before we figure out a plan."

I know Kara said not to trust Josh, but after the bizarre conversation I just overheard, I don't even know if I can trust Kara. Why had Meredith never heard of Kara even though Kara was part of the notorious Africa mission? Kara herself has become an even bigger mystery than before. "There's something I have to ask you," I whisper back. "What are 'SLs'? I overheard Ben say he can't find them."

Josh stares at me, worried. *Oh God.*

"What's going on?" Todd is right beside us. "Why are you guys whispering? Do you know something? Why in the world would Ben lock us in here?"

Josh lightly nudges my back, a signal to be careful. I stay composed. "I have no idea," I say. Josh's hand stays on my back. It's a protective gesture, but I can't help thinking about what happened when we were alone in this room.

Todd paces and rambles out questions. "How are we supposed to know who is sinning? Don't we all sin every day? I mean, isn't that why we need DPs, so we can confess?"

"Well," Josh says, cutting his eyes at me. "Emily's DP is

God knows where, so I'm not sure what good that would do here."

"Maybe Eva and Shannon could have a BT session," Todd pleads. "Maybe that would make Ben happy. I can't do this for long. I get claustrophobic."

"Please don't wake them up," Josh says.

"It's too late." Shannon, who obviously heard everything, sits up in bed. "I don't understand why *we're* the ones being forced to fix things in here, while our biggest sinner is out there, probably shacked up with some guy. *Kara* is the issue, and we all know it. Ben knows it too."

"What are you talking about?" I ask Shannon.

She climbs out of bed and gets in my face. "I don't know. Maybe *you* know what I'm talking about."

"I know! I know," Eva says. She's manic and animated. "We can pretend *I'm* her. I'll confess for her! Will that work?"

Shannon narrows her eyes. "No, Eva. That won't work." Her condescending tone sends Eva into silent despondency. Shannon turns to me. "But *you* could do it. You and Kara are close. And she knows all about you, so your sins are a part of her, which makes you permanently connected." Her rambling logic is frightening. While Kara knows a lot about me, she's more of a mystery to me now than the first day I met her.

"Come on, Emily. Take one for the team," Todd says. Eva is beaming at Todd, nodding.

Everyone looks to me expectantly, but it feels like a

threat. It's as if I'm the prey, and they're all about to pounce. I look to Josh for any kind of support. He's silent as if deep in thought, as if . . . he might be willing to go along with whatever the others decide.

Suddenly the door opens and slams shut and locks again. Everyone breaks away in confusion.

"Hey," Todd says from the other side of the room. He's staring at the base of the door. I open my eyes. He bends down to pick up a small black box with a silver rectangle inscription.

"What does it say?" Josh asks.

I'm heavy with exhaustion.

"'For purification,' and there's a cross on it."

"Open it," Shannon says.

The red-velvet lined interior holds a row of small clear drinking vessels, almost like tiny shot glasses. The bigger screw-top vial in the middle is filled with a tawny liquid. I notice Josh tense up.

"I think Ben wants us to take communion," Todd says. He holds up the liquid-filled vial. "But this isn't grape juice."

"What is it, then?" Eva asks.

"I guess we'll have to find out," Shannon says.

"No," Josh says.

"Are you going against Ben?" Todd asks.

Josh nudges me behind him. "I'm not doing it. And neither is Em," he says.

Shannon steps toward Josh and gets in his face. "Are

you kidding me? You would go against the Kingdom's plan because of *her*?"

Josh stands still, his entire body rigid as if ready to strike if necessary.

Shannon looks at me condescendingly. "Well, I think we've identified the sinners in the room." The others turn to me.

"How long have you two been hiding as a secret couple?"

"We aren't a secret couple," I say.

"Well, maybe Josh thinks so." Shannon walks up to him. "I'll bet you think impure thoughts about her. And Kara, too. Maybe even about both of them at the same time."

"That's enough, Shannon." I've never seen Josh angry like this.

"You two obviously need the communion more than *any* of us." Shannon cocks her head to the side and turns to me, so close that she's spitting words into my face. "God cannot help you until you repent and cleanse your soul."

"Leave her alone," Josh says.

"Oh, really," Shannon says. "Don't you want to explain to your girlfriend how you got that tape out of this room? What else have you been doing in here, Josh?"

I turn to Josh, who looks horrified. My head is churning. "What is she talking about?" I ask him.

Josh stares down at Shannon.

"Go ahead. Tell her the truth," Shannon says.

He looks at me with a pinched expression.

No. When he was in this room the other day, he *was* looking for something—it just wasn't me. *Kara's mix tapes.* But why would he want Kara's stuff? Nothing makes sense. My eyes sting with tears as Josh turns away.

"Ha!" Shannon says. "I knew it."

I have to get out of this room and back to Kara. I turn to the window again. There has to be another way to unlatch it. Kara is probably wondering where I am by now. *What if she leaves me here?* Then I see a dark line slip by my feet and off to the other side of the room. Eva screams. My head begins to spin so fast that I can't tell which way is up. I'm pushing the window, but it's bolted shut from the outside. I pound my fists against it. I'm so dizzy I can barely stand. *Please help me!* I can't even tell if I'm saying it out loud or in my own head. Then a sudden uplifting—almost ecstatic—sensation releases through my body just before I hit the floor.

EMILY X—

(continued)

Cory Daniel gets up every morning in his Florida garden home at 5:45 a.m. to make coffee for his wife and feed his German Shepard named Ace.

At 8:00 a.m., our designated time, I tap lightly on a metal door flanked by the freshly painted beige stucco exterior of his garage. I'm here to meet Cory and see his collection. He's still holding his coffee when he opens the door, revealing a dim room with a concrete floor.

A fluorescent light casts a manufactured glow over a wall of Tupperware containers lined with newspaper. If not for the light, one would imagine this as an ordinary storage room in the back of a garage, the plastic containers full of Christmas ornaments and itchy, out-of-season clothing.

Upon first glance, the containers appear mostly empty, but if you stare in their general direction, you will see that they contain living shapes, some curled up in a corner as still as a rubber toy, but others in perpetual motion, their heads exploring, searching for a way out of their clear prisons.

"Most of my clients are other collectors," Cory says. "They have to have permits, though. I can't just sell them to anyone."

He cheerfully offers to demonstrate his expertise in

what he says "pays for the hobby and the Harley in my garage." I instinctively back away toward the door.

He walks to the sink to find a suitable shot glass and rips a small square of plastic wrap from a yellow Saran Wrap box. He carefully stretches a clear film tightly across the top and secures a rubber band around the glass as an extra precaution.

He turns to the wall of crates, as if thinking through a crucial decision.

"Now comes the hard part," he says.

INTERVIEWS FOR EMILY X—

Article by Julia O. James

WORLD SECTOR LEADER (BOSTON): Yes, the Italy
mission was the biggest failure in the history of all active
missions to date, but we like to focus on our countless
successes, as outlined in the Victory Reports I sent for
your article. Would you like to hear the most current
statistics?

BEN (GAINESVILLE, FLORIDA): The Remnant was
inevitable. Without the Remnant, the Kingdom would be
nothing.

JOSH (LOCATION UNKNOWN): I feel terrible. It was
a nightmare for all of us. Especially for me. [long pause] I
loved her.

JULIA: Which her?

JOSH: [silence before hanging up]

PART THREE

Europe, July 1994

"There is n

In Remembrance of Me

I wake up outside under scattered stars.

I try to move but nothing happens. I'm too heavy, too numb. A breeze brushes across my face, stirring the smell of dirt under my hair.

My hand is clenched around gravel. I remember the sound of rapid crunching underfoot. The pain when I fell. A voice in my head. *Get up. Run.*

A hand strokes my hair. I hear my mother's voice. *Sweet girl,* she says.

I'm frozen with panic. "Did I die?"

Shhhhhhhh. She's stroking my hair and humming.

A breeze rustles against my ear. I try to scream, but my mouth tastes like it's full of metal. My tongue is heavy and thick. Something is crawling on my arm. No, under my skin. Spiders. Ants. Millions of microscopic bugs. Every pore on my body is taut, covered with goose bumps. My palms burn with scratches. I clench the gravel in my hand as the stars begin to gyrate into a pattern, like headlights moving along invisible interstates in the sky.

A raw terror overrides my discomfort. The humming stops.

Mama? I squeeze my eyes shut. They open again to the same sky, the stars now a jangled blur. I'm alone.

My memories are out of reach, careening ahead of my questions in scrambled clips. *Running. Running away—where is—oh my God.*

My first coherent thought is like a shot of adrenaline: No one can save us.

The clipped memories continually reorder themselves.

I can't remember everything. There are blank gaps of time—blacked out with an expanding whine, and punctuated with horrifying fissures in between.

Eva begging, *no, no, no, no.* And Shannon's voice. "As your DP, I'm telling you that you must repent in order to receive salvation.

"Just drink it," Shannon snapped.

Todd grabbed her arm. *No.* Someone pushed Shannon. Was it *Josh?*

Then I'm running.

Eva's scared voice still chanting *no*.

The memories scramble and run over each other again: Eva moaning and coughing, almost choking. I'm running. Slipping through the gravel. Grasping for traction, but getting nowhere. *Ben. No.*

Ben was on top of me, straddling my torso, holding me down.

"It's the only way, Emily," he said. His warm finger brushed gently across my lips and pushed its way inside of my mouth, methodically rubbing something bitter and metallic into my gums. A slow-blooming shock followed.

His eyes looked down at me with tender affection, like he was trying to save a wounded animal intent on running away. "Do this in remembrance of me."

A blank terror. The quiet sky. Then nothing.

I feel tears on my face. *Mama?*

I can hear myself screaming, but everything is black.

Shhhhh. Sweet girl. It's okay.

It's okay.

I wake up again to a brightening dawn. I squeeze the gravel. This time when I let go, my hand opens all the way. I hear the rocks gently click against one another as they fall out. I grab another handful and drop them. I immediately reach for my face and look down at the rapid rise and fall of my chest. I reach my arm above my head where I feel a tangle of grapevines. A vague determination begins to formulate and direct itself to my arms as I grasp the vines and pull myself up. I hear a car on a nearby road. The villa where the Americans were staying sharpens into view. I must have lost consciousness in the vineyard trying to get to Kara.

Kara.

I stumble a few times before I manage to run.

Kara comes into focus, stretched out in the grass beside the pool. Relief washes over me. I start to run toward her, attempting to call her name with my strangled voice. Then I notice her long wet hair swept in front of her face. Her leg twisted at an unnatural angle. Her arm swollen and bent against her gray T-shirt. Her other arm seemingly reaching out to me, palm up, fingers gently curled, as if she just gestured for me to "come here." A needle lies in the grass beside her swollen arm.

No. No. No. No.

A strange knowing sensation billows inside me, covering everything that was once normal.

I step toward her, my feet heavy and numb.

"Kara?" I can barely choke out her name. I need her to answer, to see her stirring. A deafening static fills my ears. Her face is a pearlescent light blue.

"Kara!" This time I'm loud. Stillness.

A high-pitched tone vibrates in my throat, but my mouth won't open. My teeth clench so tightly that it hurts. *No. No. No.* I turn away and look at the villa, my fist jammed against my mouth. Without looking at her again, I bolt inside.

"Help! *Please help!*" No one answers. I run into David's

room, nearly ripping the door off its hinges. It's empty. Kara's backpack is zipped up and sitting on top of the bed. Our documents are beside it. I look down to see my rolling suitcase on the floor. My heart fills with hope and remorseful gratitude. Kara was going to get me out of here. I look out the window where her body lies twisted and unmoved in the distance. *This can't be real.*

"*Hello?!*" I scream. My hysterical voice echoes through the empty villa. Sunlight streams through the open window in a cheerful glimpse of normalcy. I tear through the house until I find the phone in a hallway by the side door. Grabbing the receiver, I dial 0 with no idea if that's the correct number for an emergency.

Someone says something in Italian, and I whisper, "Help. Please help." My hand begins shaking so violently that I drop the receiver. It cracks against the tile as an avalanche of fear immobilizes me. *It's pointless. You can't save her.* My mind flashes to Ben on top of me, to the sheer helpless terror of not being able to move or get away. *You have to save yourself.* The vision of Kara alone by the pool nearly stops me. I don't want to leave her like this—like that—but there's no choice.

In a blind panic, I rush to grab the documents, put on Kara's backpack, and grab my own bag. I tear through the vine-tangled arch, past the stone wall, and onto the narrow road snaking down the steep Tuscan hill. I have to run. I move as fast as I can to get away.

Rows and rows of vineyards smear into the periphery as I sprint, never slowing down until I get to the concrete highway at the base of the hill. I stop on the pedestrian bridge that hovers over the traffic. The incessant roar of cars below echoes my confusion.

My emotions catch up with my thoughts. I try to scream, but I can't seem to catch my breath. Something like a primal groan comes out of my throat. I cover my mouth with my hand and force myself to keep walking. The town is beyond the bridge, and I finally reach the normalcy of strangers acting out their morning routines. An old woman with a basket stands by a stone doorway. A calico cat leaps onto a flower-lined windowsill beside her. Young Italians glide around corners in every direction, blissfully unaware of the horror in the hills nearby.

An orange bus hisses into the parking lot across the street. I sit down on the sidewalk and try to focus. *Breathe slowly. There is no reason to panic. The fear will not kill you. Just pick something and focus.* I concentrate on the burly driver stepping off the bus. The clip of his silver name badge glints in the strengthening sun as he rests on a bench to light a cigarette. The engine idles in front of him with the doors wide open, a noisy reminder that his workday is just beginning.

My hands are trembling uncontrollably. *This is not really happening.*

Then the image of Kara's lifeless face sears itself into my mind. I push my palms into my eyes until it goes away. A violent force converges inside me, a condensed burning in the base of my throat. I grip my suitcase and stand as the driver tosses his cigarette and steps onto the bus. When he revs a final warning, the consequences of my new reality set in, and the most important things in my life shuffle and reorder themselves, like the sudden successive *tick-tick-tick-tick-ticks* on the enormous schedule board hovering high inside the train station.

Falling Away

My train is headed to Paris. This is all I know.

I don't find out where I am going until I find an empty compartment. I sit on my hands to keep them from shaking. This only causes me to shake all over. I put Kara's backpack and my suitcase in the overhead shelf and step into the hallway where people are smoking impatiently. A man says something to me in Italian and offers me a cigarette. I'm about to wave him off, but my hand won't stop shaking, so I accept. I inhale deeply when he lights it for me. As I cough out smoke, a wave of calm mixes with nausea. *What am I going to do?*

I can't call my dad. He'd be enraged. And then disappointed. The part that scares me most is what would follow: He would be terrified. *What have I done?* He'd feel completely helpless so far away. It would take him days to get here, then— Then what? I try to imagine him talking calmly to Will or Meredith, or even Ben, but I can only see an explosion of chaos that blows up like an atomic bomb.

No. I can fix this myself. I'll go back to the villa and pretend, play dumb. But *Kara*. A terrifying thought slips into my brain: *What if one of them wanted her gone?* No. That's crazy. There has to be an explanation. I throw the cigarette out the window and go back to my compartment. The only known factor triggers the worst realization: Kara *is* gone and no one can bring her back.

My tears blur the moving lights as the train screeches out of the station.

The compartment fills quickly, and there's nothing to do but sit and wait. The other passengers put on headphones or pull out books. I can't take my eyes off Kara's backpack. I can't look through it now with all these people around. I have no idea what's in it. I unzip the front pocket of my bag to pull out my passport and Eurail pass, grateful they're actually there. Kara did the packing. I try to stay calm as I put my bag next to Kara's. My heart is pounding when the conductor finally opens the door. *What if they're looking for me?* I hand over my passport and Eurail with a forced smile. He stamps them without fanfare and hands them back.

As the passengers around me begin to settle in, I try to breathe in and out as quietly as possible. A middle-aged man and woman join hands and look out the window together. The man across from me takes some food out of a paper sack to eat. My stomach gives a slight growl, but I'm too upset to imagine eating anything. My mind won't stop buzzing, like it might even be making a sound. I force myself to look out the window. Fields ripple into the distance and slick rivers snake in and out of sight as the rocking motion of the train soothes my frayed nerves. *Breathe in. Breathe out.*

No one knows me here. It's going to be okay.

At our next stop, the couple pulls down their bags and leaves. When the train rattles out of the station, the other man stands up and wanders off somewhere. I jump to pull the backpack onto the floor by the window. No one even pays attention to this, so I unzip it. I dig through all the way to the bottom, but there's nothing except clothes, her Walkman headphones, an extra pair of shoes, and a Tampax box. I unzip the front pockets to find several 50,000 lire bills. I pull out a photo of Kara standing beside a beautiful woman with short black hair who must be her mother. They're with Will in what looks like an African village. Will's arm is draped around Kara's shoulders like he's proud of her. Kara stares into the camera with a half-smile. Another photo is stuck behind it. I pull them apart. The village appears the same as in the first photo, but this one shows Josh and Kara in an affectionate embrace.

I stare at it, every detail overwhelming me with confusion. I double over and moan as if someone punched me. A thousand questions and explanations come and go, but my sense of dread only intensifies. I snap to and shove the photo back into the backpack just as the door opens behind me. The man returns with a newspaper, oblivious to my inner turmoil.

I force myself to stare at the distorted landscape out the window, so as not to draw attention to myself. The soft curves of hills roll by in a languid blur, but my breathing grows uneven again. *Look at the landscape.* Except for the houses, the countryside almost looks like home. *Home.* I fight back tears.

I will not fall apart.

Growing up, when I used to get seasick, my dad would tell me to look at the horizon. "It's always steady," he'd say. "And no matter where you go, there's never an end to it."

I watch the horizon, desperately hoping for something better beyond it.

I'm shivering under a flimsy youth hostel blanket. The rain outside bounces under the large gap between the bottom of the locked door and the floor of my room in Paris. Herds of squeaky boots periodically cross the opening. Even with the noisy storm, I hear excited chatter, young backpackers eagerly discussing their plans for the day.

This hostel is cheap and rundown, but I don't want to spend too much of what little money I have. I try to imagine the Gulf of Mexico glistening in the sun through the window. The thought causes tears to run down my face. *This is my own fault,* I remind myself. I used to imagine what Paris would be like. This version never occurred to me—cold, rainy, depressing, and under these circumstances.

The rain bleeds under the door and chills the room causing me to shiver again. My hair is still wet. I stare at the empty bottle of hair dye by the sink, which is now stained the same dark brown as my new hair. Walking from the train station, I saw a group of young people wearing smiley face stickers. Part of me wanted to turn around and tell them the truth. Instead, I ran the other way.

A knock at the door sends my heart racing. A large backpack drops outside with a watery thud just before a key scrapes the lock. I can't move. A tall, thin girl pushes open the door and drags her enormous backpack inside. "Sorry," she whispers to me. "I didn't know there was anyone in here. Were you asleep?"

"No," I say.

"Oh good. I'm Freedom. And, yes, it's my real name." I'm not sure if she sees my face, or just continues out of habit. "Hippie parents. *Lots* of drugs." She unzips her backpack and pulls out some dry clothes.

I don't say anything.

"Are you sick?" she asks.

I look away and nod, trying not to cry.

She picks up the empty hair dye container by the sink. "Oh shit. Been there. Done that," she says sympathetically. "I went with red. And it was *not* pretty—literally *or* metaphorically."

I pull the blanket up over my shoulders.

"Listen, I'll be out of your way in a few minutes," she says as she adjusts a blue bandanna over her long straight hair that's so blond it's almost white. She reminds me of an edgier version of my stepsister, but I can't stop staring at the bandanna. My thoughts jump back to the trust games we had in Italy.

"Where'd you get your bandanna?" I ask, trying not to panic.

"From Colorado. It's my Axl Rose look." She laughs, mocking his "Sweet Child o' Mine" swaying dance.

I begin to relax. No one in the Kingdom would ever do that. *Except Kara.* Then the tears rush back.

She eyes me with concern. "Hey. Are you sure you're really okay?"

"No," I say. "I'm really not."

Freedom leaves and returns with some aspirin and McDonald's. The moment I smell the French fries, I realize I'm starving.

"I really hate eating this shit when I'm in freaking Paris, but it's cheap and around the corner, so c'est la vie." She holds up her soda to toast mine. The more she talks and acts like a normal college student, the more I relax.

"So. What's your story?" she asks. "Have you been to Balmer's yet? Oh God. It's *amazing.*"

"Not yet," I say. I smile, only because I'm terrified that she'll figure out my real story if I don't.

"I'm going to Italy next. Trying to hit every country before August."

I try to keep my expression neutral as I take a sip of my Coke.

Freedom stands abruptly as she wads up her McDonald's sack. "Okay. Here's the deal. This room is a real shithole. You're obviously a little bit better. The rain has stopped, and the sun is out. We're in *Paris*, for Christ's sake. Let's go *do* something."

Desperate to avoid giving myself away, I agree.

The sun feels almost unnatural as we walk down impossibly chic Parisian streets. The crowds thicken as we approach the Eiffel Tower. A mime wearing a black-and-white striped shirt and a black beret is pushing against an invisible wall with his white-gloved hands. His face is covered in chalky makeup, his furrowed painted-on eyebrows showing exaggerated frustration. Tourists lining the rows of stone steps clap and cheer in awe. He pounds against the air as if trying to get out. The Eiffel Tower looms behind him as if we somehow stumbled into the pretend Paris—the stock footage that signals where we must be. Sometimes what's really happening is too surreal to believe.

People are moving all around me, and they begin to seem too close. I'm getting dizzy again.

Freedom grabs my arm. "Come on."

I look up at the tower. "Um. I don't do heights," I lie, hoping to have a chance to figure out a plan while waiting for Freedom to return.

"Okay, fine, but will you take my picture?" She hands me her camera and stands in the foreground with her arms out in a *ta-da* pose. I take it and give back the camera, and she disappears underneath the metal arches on her way up.

A young American couple asks me to take their photo. I count to "three" and they kiss as I snap the button. The wife thanks me when I hand back their camera. Her diamond necklace glitters in the sun. A sudden realization catches in my throat as my hand touches my bare neck. *My necklace.*

By the time Freedom gets back, I'm sick with panic.

"What's wrong?" she asks.

"I have to get back to the hostel." Nausea overtakes me again.

When we finally get back, I tear through every item in my bag. I open Kara's Tampax box where she hid things she didn't want the others to find. My heart sinks when I see it's only full of her mix tapes. I check the front zippers. Nothing. The growing sense of regret takes over like a sudden virus. I try to remember when I took it off. Everything in Italy seems jumbled and blurred. I can't even remember the last time I saw it.

"What in the world are you looking for?" Freedom asks.

"I lost something. I mean I think I left something in Italy."

"That sucks," Freedom says. "Do you remember exactly where? Maybe it's still there. Most of the hostels have a lost and found."

"I wasn't in a hostel."

"I'm meeting up with some friends in Florence in a few days. Why don't you come with us?"

The idea of returning to Florence is way too risky. I don't even know if anyone is still there. *Or if anyone there is looking for me.* Maybe I was out of my mind when I found Kara. Maybe I imagined everything—*no.* I know what I saw. My mind flashes to Josh, how he protected me from Shannon and the others that night. *But why did he lie about Kara?* My memories of what happened are splintered. Josh is the only one who would have helped me get away. How else was I able to get out of that room and run? *Until Ben caught up.* . . . I shudder and rub my temples. "I can't go back to Florence," I blurt out, and immediately realize how weird that must sound.

Freedom waits for my explanation while loudly crunching an apple she pulled out of her backpack.

"I mean . . ." I level my voice, glancing at the stack of travel maps on her bed. "I already made other travel plans."

Freedom stares at me in supportive contemplation. She's been problem-solving her way across Europe for months on her own. Of course she'd try to help me. "Hmm. Who were you traveling with when you were there? Maybe they found it and held on to it for you," she says.

Her words make sense, even under my disturbing circumstances. A glimmer of an idea sparks hope. Someone like Freedom could get a message to Josh if I tell her exactly where to go and what to say. I could meet him at a neutral train station. I look at Freedom, who is so confident and carefree. If anyone could pull this off, it's her.

"I need you to do me the biggest favor I've ever asked of anyone."

I Am (Not) Her

I wait in the Milan train station with as much optimism as I can conjure.

Freedom promised to hand Josh my note after I told her where they recruit in Florence. The note stated this specific date and time based on the train schedule to Milan, which seemed like neutral ground and only two hours from Florence. All of the unknown variables heighten my anxiety. He would have to be alone. He would have to keep it a secret. He would have to find the necklace and somehow get his train pass. He would have to lie convincingly enough to get away from the group for a few hours. *Just please come to Milan with my mother's necklace*, I wrote. *I have money.*

I hoped after everything we'd been through that he'd

want to help me, but I'm just not sure. If there was even a 1-percent chance, though, then I had to try. My mother's necklace is the most important tangible thing I have from her, and I refuse to leave without trying to get it back. I think about the last time I was alone with him, how I would have done anything to get him to leave with me. And I'm almost certain he pushed Shannon out of my way when I ran. His voice is the last one that echoes in my head from that horrible night—the last thing I heard before getting out of that locked room.

The station is packed with travelers: backpackers and locals and tourists rolling bags in every direction. I find a spot with a clear view of his track just before the arrival time. When I see him walk across the platform, my legs go numb. I'm relieved he's here in person, yet I can't believe he showed up. I move behind a column where he can't see me. I didn't have a plan for this. What was I thinking? Josh looks around. I'm not sure how to read his expression. His hands are holding the straps to his backpack and fidgeting with the adjustable clip. I scan the train station for anyone else from the Kingdom but see no one. I rush toward him.

He looks shocked to see me. Then a deep sadness clouds over his features. The photo I found of Kara and Josh flashes through my thoughts. I touch my darker hair and wonder if for a split second he thought I was Kara. My heart sinks as I realize why he looks so disappointed. *I am not her.*

Announcements blare in Italian over the loudspeakers

as the train schedule spins its endless changes—new times, different cities—in rapid clicks and swooshes. It feels like years since I last saw Josh. His eyes are red and swollen. I've never seen him this out of sorts.

My own eyes well with tears. "Is she really gone?" I ask.

He looks around, still fidgeting with the straps on his backpack. He puts his arm around my shoulder and leads me farther down the platform, away from the main area full of people. His hand is trembling. He touches my hair as if confused by its new color. He doesn't say anything, but it's clear enough by the pain in his eyes he doesn't want to answer my question.

An intense pain explodes inside my chest, that same ache tearing through me all over again. "You know, I didn't— I was just so scared. . . ." We stop by the column where I was hiding before.

"No one blames you, Emily. It was an accident." He won't look at me when he says it. I follow his stare down to an orange Fanta can on the ground. Anything to avoid talking about what happened at the villa.

But the image always reappears, ignoring my wishes. New details emerge in my memory every time. Kara's body. Her wet hair. Her swollen arm. Just left there alone. By me. Shame and regret overwhelm me.

"I just don't understand," I say, pressing my palms into my eyes.

"She drowned. It was an accident. She was drunk." He

says it like he's reciting lines he memorized. It reminds me way too much of Lily's weird behavior that day with Shannon.

I desperately want to believe him, but I know what I saw. Kara was beside the pool, not *in* it. And no one else was around. Or at least I didn't see— Chills spread across my arms as a train squeals into the track beside us. As people flow down the steps with their luggage, I have to fight the sudden urge to take off with them. To follow someone else on a carefully planned journey through Italy's landmarks and museums. I would do anything to get out of this nightmare.

He tries to take me in his arms, but I pull away. "No, Josh. I *saw her*. That's not what happened. Someone is lying to you."

Josh gives me a look I don't recognize. There's some-thing else behind his hollow eyes—something like rage. He looks around the train station one last time, pensive.

"Do you have your Eurail pass?" he asks.

"Yes."

"Let's get the hell out of here," he says.

I'm surprised by his surety. "Don't you have to go back?"

"I think we both know there's no going back now."

He glances at my bag, confused. "You just have one?"

"Yeah." I don't tell him I left Kara's backpack in a Paris trash can, that I consolidated her stuff and packed it into my own bag to lighten my load.

But none of this matters because we're finally leaving.

"How does Germany sound?" he says nonchalantly as he studies the train signs. Under normal circumstances, I would laugh. Maybe even question him, or at least want to talk through a plan. But circumstances aren't normal, so I silently follow him onto a train and into an empty compartment. Josh shuts the door, locks it, and sets his backpack on the floor.

I stare at his backpack with a jolt of hope. "Did you find my necklace?" Seeing him in person had yanked Kara's death to the forefront, overshadowing everything else. I was counting on him to save the one thing I have left of my mother. By his sad expression, I already know what he's going to tell me.

"I couldn't find it." Josh hangs his head and stares at the floor. "I'm so sorry, Em. I looked all over your room. All the drawers were empty."

A dull pain radiates in my chest. I know it's just an object, but right now it feels like I've lost *everything*. I picture the room, racking my brain over where I could have left it. Then that horrible night creeps back into my mind all over again. "Josh, what happened to us? I mean, that night. What did Ben do to me? I woke up in a vineyard, and that's when I found . . . her." My voice is so shaky I barely make sense.

Josh unzips his backpack. He pulls out a fifth of bourbon, unscrews the lid, and tilts back the bottle, which is already half gone. People bustle through the hallway still searching for a place to settle, even after the train pulls away. The conductor pounds on our door until I unlock it. He inspects our Eurail passes and passports and shuts it again, but not before shooting us a disapproving glare. I've seen this look before when I shared a compartment with a group of rowdy backpackers on the way to Italy. Conductors must see this a thousand times, every day: American kids getting drunk on a train, as if being in another country full of sounds they can't interpret makes them invisible to everyone around them. It doesn't stop Josh from taking another long swig.

"Josh. Please tell me what happened." The memory of the needle beside Kara's body flashes through my mind. "Do you think Kara was on drugs?"

"Drugs?" He looks at me like I'm crazy. "No way. Not Kara."

I can't help but visualize them together in the photograph where he clearly knew her very well. *Stop*. Focus on what happened to Kara. The needle just doesn't make sense. Kara never once seemed high or strung out like Sadie or Christina always did. "Are you sure? I saw—"

"I really don't want to talk about Kara anymore," Josh says, lifting his hand in a definitive gesture. "It was an accident. She drowned. The Americans checked out the day before. Case closed." He takes another deep swig but doesn't flinch. His eyes are more and more hollow, darkened out. He talks in random gusts, as if the entire story is replaying a loop in his mind and he's just waiting for the parts he's willing to reveal out loud. "Here's what matters. I knew I had to leave. They all said you'd abandoned the church and God, and that you'd fallen away. They said you have sin in your life and couldn't handle God's plan for Kara. That you would never be in the Kingdom and that we could never have any contact with you again. When that girl gave me your message, I took it as a sign."

My breath gets ragged listening to him talk. *God's plan*.

"We need to get out of this place—get back home. To our real families. Screw the consequences. I couldn't take those people for another day. They made me feel like I was crazy." His voice quivers a little, tripping over the last *A* sound.

Our uneven breaths fill the space between us. I break the silence with a near whisper: "What did Ben give me that night?"

"Venom. And other stuff."

"*Venom?* From *what*?"

"A snake."

Chills run up and down my entire body as I think about the snake left in my and Kara's room. "*What?* Why would—?"

"To 'eradicate the sin,' so they say." Bitter sarcasm laces his slurred words. "I'd done it before, so I knew to throw up right after. Weakens the effects."

"You'd—what? Where? In Boston?" I pause. "Or Africa? Or maybe even Florida?"

Josh looks stunned. I'd be lying if I said I didn't enjoy catching him off guard.

"Kara told me all about it," I lie. "I've known since we got here."

He looks so lost, his eyes brimming with sadness. I take the bottle out of his hand and swallow a mouthful of bourbon. It sears my throat and burns deep into my stomach, but I keep drinking. After the third tilt, an invisible cocoon radiates warmth all around me, and for the first time since I got to Italy—maybe even before then—I feel in control.

"Did you love her?" I ask.

"No." He says it too quickly.

"I don't believe you."

Josh moans, running his hands down his face. "We were on a mission together, Emily. Things got really crazy. Out of control. We were in the middle of *nowhere*. She's the only person in the world who understands what all I've been through."

"Under-*stood*. Past tense. She's *gone*." My fear and sadness shift to a focused bitterness. Then the first tear drops. When Josh starts crying, my own emotions waver as he sobs into my shoulder. I stroke his hair with my hand. But this isn't over. I have to get him to tell me what happened.

"Josh," I say gently, continuing to stroke his hair. "I need to understand what happened. Why would Ben give us venom?" I cringe at the memory of his finger pushing around in my mouth. I squeeze my eyes shut to block it out. "Has this been going on all along? Was Heather doing this too? The whole Kingdom?"

He sits up and takes a breath. He wipes his eyes with his T-shirt and looks out the window. "No. This is something else."

"What do you mean?"

"It isn't like in Boston. It's something Boston doesn't like to talk about. More and more people were practicing after the Africa mission. Some saw it as a miracle."

"Practicing what?"

"The rituals. Those who practice them are part of what they call the Remnant."

I search his face for answers, but now I'm not even sure I want to know. A strange sensation is taking over, like that feeling in a lucid dream when you suddenly become aware you're dreaming yet you're still stuck in that world, trapped in your own imagination. I stand to pace. *Rituals? The Remnant? What in the hell is he talking about?*

"I think it started in Florida. When we all came back to the United States, Will spent the entire summer there under medical care and worked with the church where Ben grew up. The one where the Kingdom first started."

"Did Ben know Kara?" I ask, turning to see his reaction. Josh's eyes flinch when I say her name out loud. Our new reality repeats in my head: *Josh was with Kara. They both kept it from me. Kara is gone.*

"They grew up together, but they've always hated each other." Josh drinks again.

"Why?"

"I've never gotten a straight answer on that. I know Kara's mom left the church for a while after Africa. She was re-baptized by Will in Florida and he convinced her to let Kara come to Italy."

I sit quietly. Of course he was close enough to Kara to know this fact firsthand. Did she let Josh tell her what to do? I listen to him babble while playing the kind friend, trying to measure his words against what Kara told me. I take the bottle out of his hand and tilt back another drink. The bourbon doesn't even burn this time.

"Meredith stayed in Boston to coordinate the missions, but Will wanted to stay behind in Florida. As far as I can tell, she actually ran everything. When he finally came back to Boston, something changed. They were always with their disciples, separately. It's almost as if they were training them for different missions."

Meredith had seemed so far away that day at the volleyball game, like she was sad just talking about how they met.

"Do you think they were having problems?"

"I've heard things. I have no idea if they were actually true."

"What things?"

"I heard she wanted a divorce, and I think he did too, but the Leader wouldn't allow it."

"Why?"

"Divorce is against the Kingdom's strict policy. And even if it wasn't, they would never do anything to jeopardize their position in the Kingdom. Plus, she wouldn't be allowed to lead without him. Women can't be sector leaders without a husband."

I think of Meredith's friendliness at the Castle and her confident mission speech after church when Will couldn't be there. Students were so drawn to her. She had so much more charisma than Will, who just seemed angry and erratic, especially here.

"I got the sense the Leader's attitude toward Will shifted after the incident in Africa. Will came back from Africa completely changed. As if nothing could touch him. Like *he* was the one chosen to lead. But he was also very sick. He had to have continual blood transfusions due to the snake bite. And I also heard . . ." Josh's voice trails off. He takes another drink of bourbon and looks out the window, where the sun sinks into the horizon. It casts a warm glow over the picturesque landscape, a stark contrast to the ugly nightmare we're both trapped inside.

I watch Josh stare out the window. I want to scream, to demand an immediate explanation. I can hear the edge in my voice, even though I'm trying to sound calm. "Heard what?"

Josh's eyes don't leave the window. *Why won't he look at me?* "I heard he was keeping venomous snakes in their house," he finally says.

"What?" My mouth falls open. Poisonous snakes are the last things I'd ever imagine finding in their pristine home.

"That was where Meredith drew the line," he continues. "She said she would not allow anyone to put her life in danger, or Rachel's life, not even him. But the Leader somehow convinced her it would be okay."

"Why in the world would he do that?" Now I'm the one staring outside, grasping for normalcy, desperate to make sense of this bizarre information.

But nothing makes sense anymore. And I'm terrified it never will.

"The Leader claims he laid hands on Will in Africa, and the locals thought it was a miracle. No one there had ever heard of a survivor after a black mamba bite," Josh explains. "Kara's mother was a nurse and knew otherwise—antivenom, meds, even blood transfusions, all the things they kept secret behind the scenes. After that their ministry multiplied faster than all of the other ministries put together, and Will came to believe *he* was chosen to survive, chosen directly by God. Not healed by the Leader."

My rational thoughts spin off into the ether—far beyond anything I can grasp as reality. I look at Josh's bottle, which is almost gone. His eyes are swollen and his hair completely disheveled, but I can still see the charming boy that interrupted my reading of Henry James that first day. "You realize how completely crazy this all sounds," I say.

Josh looks at me and I want to curl up in his arms, as if that would somehow make this all okay. *I cannot let myself feel this way about him.* "Why would anyone stay with a church that believes drinking venom is part of God's plan?" I ask, looking at him for a plausible answer.

He looks into my eyes with a tormented expression. "It eradicates the sin. Like a cure."

And that's when the flow of information shuts down. He looks so distraught, and all I want to do is make things right for both of us. None of this matters anymore because we are leaving on this train hurling us far away from these people. "What were we thinking?" I ask, sitting beside him in shock. "What was *I* thinking?"

Josh moves closer and wraps his arms around me. I'm overcome with a sudden sense of calm until I look into his eyes. They have that same unfamiliar look from that first moment when he saw me on the platform, almost like he doesn't recognize me. His fingers slide into my hair just above the back of my neck. I start to pull away, but I don't want to.

"It's gonna be okay. This is all my fault. And I'm going to get you away from them. Trust me," he murmurs, just before his mouth covers mine.

The weight of his torso feels inevitable and somehow comforting, even though I'm pinned underneath him. I shouldn't be kissing him after everything that's happened, but it just feels so damn good to do something normal. *But I am not her.*

"Josh . . ."

His mouth is on my ear, down my neck, over my mouth

scary, Em, but I have to know your exact sins in order to help determine your spiritual weaknesses and assist you on the path to righteousness." Pause. "Emily? You are going to have to be *completely* honest with me here. I have to know *specifically* what you've struggled with so you can come to grips with your sins. It's the only way to become closer to God."

"Okay."

I cringe at the sound of my voice. *What is this?*

"On number three, for example—"

Josh taps my shoulder, and I jump out of my seat. He's holding a croissant and a cup. I hit the stop button.

"Hey, watch the coffee," he says. "What're you listening to?" He leans in and kisses my cheek as he hands me the hot cup, then steps back to look at me. "Is something wrong?"

"You just scared me," I whisper. Trying to think fast, I hand the coffee back to him. I try to clear my throat. "Would you mind getting me some water? I don't feel so good."

"Sure," he says. "I'll be right back." He looks at me with concern one more time before going down the hall. I watch as he disappears into the next train car.

I eject the Walkman. The tape is labeled *SL EG*. I cram the headphones into my bag and rip open the box of other tapes. One labeled *SL* with other interns' initials. A chill runs through me when I see it: *SL JS*. People are flooding the narrow train, and without even thinking I grab my bag, wake the travelers, and run down the metal steps, nearly again, refusing to disconnect. Nothing matters to me any-more except this. One hand tugs at the buttons on my shorts while the other is in my hair, pulling with an urgency, as if grabbing hold of something he can never get back.

"I'm not her." I say it out loud.

He raises himself up on his elbow and traces my face with his finger. "I know," he says. I'm the one crying now. He backs away and settles beside me, his arm around m waist as if making sure nothing could pull me away f him until we both fall asleep.

I wake up to an empty compartment. The train As I sit up, a wave of nausea hits. The stale b up my throat; I will it back down. I yank th closed and collapse across the row of seat Then I see Josh's green backpack we *He's coming back*.

I lock the door to change clot out as I'm grabbing a T-shirt fr myself to listen to it in Paris, away. Her mix tapes were in the Tampax box—her Kingdom. I throw or press play. A roarir distant voice star

My heart lu

"This is it. Your

tripping on my way down. I hear the loud *ding-dong* signaling a departure followed by announcements in Italian just as I move into the safety of the crowd on the platform.

When I turn to look back, Josh's train is leaving the station.

I run to the schedule board to find the next train to Florence.

Like Mother,
Like Daughter

The villa is dark and still.

I can hear my own breath as I wait and watch the door and the closed window for signs of movement. I let time pass as the stars move and the sky seems to expand into a vast unknown and scary place. A sudden wave of homesickness hits me. I long for my bedroom back home. For Tamara's music in the next room. For Patti's voice that mingles with my dad's at the foot of the stairs in our kitchen. I want to crawl into the back of my closet and hug my knees and close out the rest of the world, but the idea seems like an impossibility under this ominous sky.

As soon as I hear them singing in the main villa, I stand up and quickly rush to the door. I slowly turn the knob and my heart leaps into my throat when it opens without any further effort. I decide against turning on the light, just in case someone looks out the window at the villa. I hold my hands out, pressing into the darkness for familiar objects. The bunk beds must have been moved. I can still hear the interns singing in the villa and my eyes begin to well as I remember the feeling I used to get when I was with them in the circle, all of us singing together. *Lifting up our voices*.

"Looking for this?" Meredith says as she flips on the light.

I gasp so hard that it feels like my heart has stopped.

I turn to look at her, her friendly expression catching me off guard.

"Oh, sweetie. We've been so worried about you," Meredith says, tilting her head. She sounds genuinely concerned. *Maybe I can still play this off.*

"I'm sorry about running off. I just . . . wanted to make things right," I finally choke out. I glance around the room where the beds have been pushed to one side against the closed window. Boxes and bags and stacks of papers are strewn in the corners and on the bunk beds, as if someone moved the entire office into this building.

"Josh has been beside himself with worry," she says.

"Josh is here?" I blurt out.

Meredith's smile doesn't falter. "Of course he is. Right up there." She motions to the villa. "Where else would he be? He and Ben have taken over to lead the mission in a new direction, since my husband became *ill*. And Josh just knew you'd come back. He said you seem truly broken. I knew Kara's sins had nothing to do with you."

She steps toward me, and I step back instinctively, positioning myself closer to the door. There is no way possible way that Josh could have beat me back here. *She's lying.*

"Emily," she says, her brow furrowing in overacted concern. "Why are you upset with me? I've always been one of the few people to care about you. Heather would have stabbed you in the back in a heartbeat if it had meant she could be here on this mission. Too many students take the competitive road in Boston, and it makes our groups no different than a nest of angry hornets. You were always my favorite disciple—always so sweet and kind to others."

Her button-down blouse shifts as she reaches out to touch my shoulder, and I see my mother's necklace glinting from her collarbone.

My entire arm goes limp. "Where did you get that?"

Tracing the charms with her fingers, she says, "They found it the night you left. I recognized it and was keeping it safe for you. I knew you'd come back."

"That's my mother's," I growl. My fists clench at my sides. The Kingdom has already taken so much from me; I won't let them have anything else. Meredith reaches behind her neck and unlatches it. "Here," she says, holding it in front of her. "Turn around. I'll clasp it for you."

I hesitate. The necklace dangles between us. Could it

really be this easy? Meredith was never a part of this mess. She just got here. Maybe . . . maybe she's actually here to help. A mixture of desperation and confusion prompts me to follow her suggestion.

"Oh, sweetheart." She brushes my hair to the side in a maternal gesture. "I know you must miss her so much, even after all these years." This time I catch it—the lack of sympathy that doesn't match her comforting words. And as I realize I've never spoken to Meredith about my mother, a surge of anger overrides any other emotion.

The second the necklace is secured around my neck I step away and face her. "Did Heather talk to you about my mother?"

"Honey, Heather talked to me about everything."

"That doesn't mean you know anything. Not really. You know nothing about me."

Meredith stands casually, making no move to stop me. "That actually couldn't be further from the truth," she says. "It's amazing what a little digging can do."

I take a step away from her, jabbing my fingernails into my palms so hard it hurts.

"I also found out the truth about your mother." Her tone is casual. "And I know she didn't drown *accidentally*."

My feet feel concreted into this spot. My heart constricts.

Meredith closes the space between us and touches my arm.

"I'm sure you've had the same thoughts about killing yourself, and your friend Kara must have too, considering.

Poor thing. You must have that effect on people."

Her words are a punch to the gut.

"Or maybe *you* got upset with Kara . . . ," she trails off. "You know I heard Josh used to be very fond of her. Even with her questionable upbringing. Like mother, like daughter, as they say."

My hands are shaking uncontrollably. My mind won't stop reliving the moment I found Kara. This time, I see a person at the edge of the pool. Was it that night? It was so dark. Someone sitting on a pool chair staring into the water, but the pool lights weren't on. Maybe I didn't find her until the next morning. Maybe I was hallucinating. Could the snake venom they gave me do that? My thoughts spin. I can't tell which way is up, what was real and imagined.

"There's only one thing I know for sure," Meredith says right up in my face. "Your mother isn't in heaven because those who commit suicide can only burn in the flames of hell."

In an instant my confusion disappears, leaving a distilled rage. It materializes through my entire body as I push myself into her as hard as I can. She falls back and her head hits the corner of the bunk bed so hard I can hear the crack. The sound of her groan disappears into the night as I race out the door and into the vineyard, and I run and run until I get to the safety of town, to the train station, to the locker with my bag, on another train away from here.

Sacred Confession

Tamara answers the phone: "Emily. Where in the hell are you?"

"I have to talk to Dad."

"He isn't here," she says. "But he wants to talk to you. He's really pissed off, Em."

My entire body tenses with frustration.

"Tamara, I need you to find him."

"He isn't here. They're out and about, so he'll have to call you back. What's your number there?"

"I don't know. I'm traveling," I say, looking around at the train station, not even sure where I am. As soon as I reached a safe distance from Florence, I jumped off during a stop to use a pay phone.

"He's been really angry about not having a contact number that works. No one ever answers the number the director gave him," Tamara says.

Director? He spoke to Will?

"Then we tried to ask your school contact about it, and they said the phone lines are unreliable."

"School contact?" My grip on the phone tightens.

"Yeah. They came by the house earlier this week. Mom spoke to them."

Holy shit. "They came to the house? What did they say?"

"I don't know, but they were best friends with Patti by the end. She was excited about all the museums you're seeing."

"What were their names?"

"I don't know. Listen. Dad can tell you. He should be back any minute." Her tone shifts to concern. "Emily?" She pauses. "Is everything okay? What's going on?"

"Nothing. Everything—"

Tamara cuts me off. "Dad just walked in."

"Emily!" The sound of his voice makes my heart leap, but I immediately recognize the questioning tone. I wish he were here so I could explain. "Give me just a second so I can pick up on the other line." I hear mumbling, a succession of clicks, and then his voice. "Where are you right now? I need a better way to reach you, hon. That damn phone number you gave us never connects."

I desperately want to tell him everything, but the

moment I hear his concerned tone from so far away, I know that I can't. He would be sick with worry. It would kill him.

I take a deep breath and try to sound like nothing is wrong. "I'm so sorry I haven't called. We've just been so . . . busy. But I have some, uh, free time now and wanted to visit Deborah in Zurich. It's just . . . I lost her number. Do you think she'll know who I am?"

His voice brightens. "Deborah? Well, I should hope your godmother would know who you are. I can give her a call to let her know you're coming. Do you have a pen?"

I'm so nervous that I can barely write. I manage to sound normal when I tell him I love him.

To be in motion is such a relief. As I look out the window, I can't help but imagine how Josh must have reacted when he returned with my water to an empty compartment. Fear and regret burn like acid in my stomach. Kara was right all along; I can't trust him. *They're all liars.*

What if he was looking for the Sin List tapes in my room the night he kissed me? If he was lying about that, then what else was he hiding? What if Kara's death wasn't an accident? I know the answers could be in the Sin List tapes. My face flames just remembering what I said to Heather, what she promised was only between the two of us.

A sacred confession.

A hollowed-out numbness takes over. I welcome the change, and by the time I switch trains in the hectic bustle of the Milan station, I'm almost like a tourist—just another backpacking student traveling across Europe.

Except the tapes are like carrying live ammunition with me everywhere I go.

I try to focus on the moving scenery out my window: the pine-covered mountains, the stone-arched bridges, the curving tracks. I look down at an enormous expanse of lake. *What if I threw the tapes out the window?* I imagine them shattering the glassy surface of the water and disappearing forever. It's enough to make me release a bitter laugh.

Even as I stare down at my bag, knowing how easy it would be to get rid of them, I can't. What if they hold the truth?

As we get closer to Zurich, the mountains are patched with snow, even in summer. The high pitch of the brakes makes my heart race every time we stop. I scan even the tiniest train stations for anyone who might be looking for me. Each time, I hold my breath until I hear the sporadic rattling of the train moving forward again.

Deborah Klein isn't in her office, but there's a couch down the hall where I crash in exhaustion. A small man with thick round glasses walks by and speaks to me in German. I say her name like a question, and he goes in an office and rattles off more German to someone else, then I hear someone make a phone call. I have no idea what Deborah looks like, or anything else about her except that my dad knows her and she is my godmother, even though she hasn't seen me since I was a baby.

A woman with unruly brown hair rushes toward me in a flurry. "Emily! I'm so happy you came by! You know, your sister was supposed to call me when she was over here but was apparently too busy." I stand up and she embraces me in a huge hug. "I've got you set up in a fabulous hotel. I'm so glad you—" She steps back, straightens her glasses, and looks at me with an odd expression. "My *God*, you look just like your mother."

Then she really takes me in—my greasy hair, sallow skin, bloodshot eyes—and seems to register my physical and emotional state. I can't remember the last time I had a proper meal and a shower. The thought of it is enough to make me fall apart right in front of this practical stranger. Deborah gets her keys and opens her office door. "Let me grab my stuff and we'll head out. You're staying with me tonight."

It's a short drive to Deborah's house, and she quickly ushers me into a tiny guest bedroom. I take the hottest shower I can stand and dig through my bag to find the least dirty outfit. I almost feel normal again. I walk into her kitchen to find her with her arms full of bags.

"I ran out for food. And wine. You look like you could use a glass."

Deborah arranges our food at a small table by the window, which overlooks a twinkling bridge arching over a canal. I can't stop staring out into the night. "This city is so beautiful. It almost doesn't even seem real," I say. And as soon as I say it, the dark flood of memories creeps into my thoughts. My heart quickens and I can't catch my breath. I take a sip of the red wine she just poured and try to focus on the view.

Deborah sits across from me and arranges the food. "I wasn't sure what you like, so I got a bit of everything." Starving, I take a giant bite of a flaky pastry. Then a wave of nausea hits, and I have to force myself to swallow. Deborah looks on expectedly. I pile my plate with meats and cheeses to be polite, but barely nibble at them, hoping she won't notice. "So tell me about your exciting travels," she says cheerfully. "Oh to be young again . . ."

I drop my fork and lean forward. "I need your help." Even as I'm blurting it out, I realize how desperate it sounds.

"With?" Deborah takes a careful sip of her wine and waits for me to continue.

"But please don't call my dad," I say. "I mean, yet. I need to talk about something that cannot go past us."

"That's what I do for a living, honey. You just let me know how I can help you. Now tell me again why we can't involve your dad?"

I take a deep breath. "My friend died. In Tuscany. I found her body actually, and—I—I . . ." The tears are falling, but I try to stay focused. "I ran."

"Whoa. Whoa. Whoa. Slow down. Ran where?"

"Here," I say.

"Have the Italian authorities been notified?" Deborah's lawyer voice reminds me so much of my dad's I simultaneously relax and almost start to sob.

"I honestly don't even know. They said she drowned by accident. Or maybe committed suicide. That the case was closed."

"Who is *they*? And how do you know this if you left Italy?"

"I went back. To meet the guy I followed here. I mean there. And he told me. Then I left him on a train because I wasn't sure if I could actually trust him, because I saw a picture of him with my friend—the one who died. And *they* are the people in the Kingdom."

Deborah is already across the room frantically digging through her bag. "Jesus H. Christ. You are going to need to start from the beginning." She pulls out a pen. "Shit," she says. She trips over something on the floor and swipes a notepad from the kitchen counter before sitting down at the table.

"Okay," she says. "Start from the very beginning. I thought your dad said you were here on a college internship. What is the Kingdom?"

I start to explain everything, but Deborah stops me. "Okay. Sweetheart?" She scoops my hands into her own. "Let's just sit quietly and think about that time line for a second. And don't be alarmed, but I need to make a phone call."

I grab her arm. "*Please* don't call my dad," I plead.

Deborah rubs her hand over mine. "Sweetie. I'm going to help you. But in order to do so, I must call my travel agent."

"Travel agent?"

She rushes across the room and punches numbers into the phone. "You need to answer all of these questions in the United States of America," she says. She flashes a worried expression at me and quickly regains her composure. "Everything is going to be completely fine. I promise I will personally put you on that plane." She looks back at me again. Something flickers across her face, like a memory. *My God, you look just like your mother.*

"Or, better yet, I'll come with you. I haven't seen your family in way too long." As she eyes me with familial concern, I realize she's putting on a calm and collected front for me while her mind is probably spinning with a million tasks.

I also realize with enormous relief that no one could stop her from getting me home.

In Africa, they call its bite the kiss of death.

"Do you have one here?" I look at the crates again, accounting for every closed lock on each separate lid.

"No. I would never keep a snake like that here without a specific request," he says. "But here's the weird part.

"He asked if he could take the mamba out of the box here, I thought maybe to inspect it. I asked him repeatedly if he was an experienced handler, and he said yes. I was still hesitant. Something about him seemed a little off. I finally agreed only if I could watch through the garage window from the outside with the door shut." Cory points to a small window over the sink.

When asked why he trusts a stranger to be alone in his shop, Cory says, "I wasn't taking any chances, man. That snake was 6 feet long, and it's the fastest snake in the world. Black mambas are slender, but they can be mean motherfuckers when you try and handle them."

According to Cory, the man grabbed it just behind the head with one hand and lifted its body with the other with zero fear, "like it was just a movie prop or something. He had total control. Even with its body writhing around trying to break free, he held its head up to his face as if inspecting it until the snake opened its mouth."

The inside of the snake's mouth was as black as ink. That's where black mambas get their name.

Cory pauses and stares at the window where he was standing that day, as if he isn't sure how to explain the rest.

(continued)

On August 8, 1994, Cory Daniel says a man contacted him after seeing an ad in the back of a local magazine for Florida events. When I show Cory the three photos I have, he frowns with comprehension. "Yes. That was him."

"Did he have a permit?"

Cory doesn't look at me, but continues to rinse trays in an oversized utility sink. He sets them aside to dry out. "He was a regular client. But he started with just the venom."

"Why would a regular person want to purchase snake venom?"

"You'd be surprised the crazy shit people will do with it. I've heard some people say it can cure any illness, and even that it holds the key to eternal life. But I really don't ask any questions when they pay me double what the scientists pay."

Eventually, the man inquired about a black mamba, which was difficult to procure even with the reliable suppliers. "Mambas are pretty hard to come by, but he offered the right price and showed me his paperwork, which opened up new options."

I ask how fast a black mamba bite would kill an adult male, and the answer is in about 20 minutes flat, sometimes less.

"So what happened?" I prod.

"Then he took its head and held it right over his forearm. And I watched him place its fangs into his own skin. On purpose. He barely even flinched, even though his arm was bleeding. Then he calmly placed the snake back into the container and secured the lid like nothing happened."

Cory's eyes are animated, like it just happened all over again.

"I totally freaked, man. I had no idea what to do. I couldn't let some guy drop dead in my garage. My wife would have flipped out. I was about to run inside and call 911, but the man looked right at me through the window and waved me off as if to say he's okay. Other than the fact he was sweating like crazy, he was just so . . . calm."

When Cory opened the door and rushed to help the man, he told Cory not to worry and that he was fine.

"Then he said something weird," Cory remembers. "He said, 'Don't worry. I can't die.'"

And, somehow, he didn't.

He sat there for about 30 more minutes, sweating profusely. Then he got up. He paid Cory. He carried the container with the mamba to the backseat of his car. And he drove away.

• • •

INTERVIEWS FOR EMILY X—

Article by Julia O. James

LILY: When my brother died, they actually blamed me—
and my sins—for his death, and then they told me I would
burn in hell with him if I left the mission. Can you believe
that? Just because I called home to check on him.

They said I would be like a dog returning to its own
vomit. And then they described hell, like what it actually
would feel like. They told me in great detail what my
brother was experiencing every second of every day
while his flesh burns and sizzles and rots for all of eter-
nity. They said the same thing would happen to me.

I remember sitting there so helpless. I couldn't stop
crying. But then something clicked inside of me. Something scary. And I remember thinking if what they're
telling me is true, then I hope they all burn in hell with us
for being such horrible human beings.

DAVID: I had no idea what was going on. We checked
out and left the villa the day before, so she must have
gone back there after we left. I actually didn't know what
happened until Ms. Klein contacted me. It's devastating.

MEREDITH: The authorities said the poor girl must not
have known how to swim. She must have been alone
when she jumped into the deep end with no way to get
to the side. One thing we all have to come to terms with
is the fact that God can't protect those who choose to
turn their back on Him.

PATTI, EMILY'S STEPMOM: I've never seen her eyes so vacant, almost hollow, as if something had blown the light out of them. That look in her eyes when she walked off the plane still haunts me.

PART FOUR

Oceanview, Mississippi, August 1994

"*For whatever we lose (like a you or a me)
it's always ourselves we find in the sea.*"

—E. E. CUMMINGS

This is exactly how it happens each time.

I'm diving into the deep end of a pool, just like in swimming lessons when they throw the colorful rings into the water. The rings begin to sink, and I grab them one by one before they hit the bottom. As I'm coming up, Kara is there. She tries to talk, but bubbles spill out of her mouth in wordless glubs. Her eyes are calm, like she's simply trying to tell me something, like she doesn't even know she's underwater. She's wearing the bikini I last saw her in, but her tattoo is missing. I hold my breath as long as I can until I know I have to get to the surface. When I get there, it's covered with a clear solid sheet of glass. The interns stare into the water from the edge of the pool. I'm pounding to get their attention to let me out. They can't see or hear me. They smile at one another. They join hands and sing. When I look down, Kara is gone. When I look up, a long slender snake slips across the top of the surface. And that isn't even the scariest part. At the surface, I can see myself leaning over the edge to peer down into the water, serene and calm, watching the underwater me drown. And just before my last exhale, I wake up.

This time, I'm so sweaty that it feels like I actually slept in a pool. I rip the covers away and slip my feet onto the thick carpet. The ceiling fan undulates above me.

I'm home now. I'm going to be okay.

It's one thing to say it to myself. It's another to actually believe it's true.

Things You May Feel: Isolation. Nightmares. Feeling "out of it." These after-effects will get better as you heal. Don't push yourself. Rest is an important part of recovery.

Ghost of Me

My reflection startles me as I pass my bedroom mirror.

That isn't me. It's like I'm the person in a movie who realizes they're being watched because they glimpse someone else in a mirror. Except it *is* me. The dark hair. The gaunt face. Even Tamara was shocked by my appearance when I first walked into our house. "Jesus, Em." She hugged me and pulled away with a look of actual concern. "The waif look really doesn't become you."

When Deborah and I got off the plane, Patti and Dad were pacing at the airport gate. Patti's eyes were swollen with tears when her gaze caught mine. Dad immediately rushed to smother me in a hug, pressing my head against his chest. His relief to see me in person abruptly shifted to the tension of not yet knowing the full story. *My* story. Dread bloomed inside me like a rotten flower. I gravitated to Deborah, like she could protect me from the barrage of questions I'm not ready to face.

"Let's get her home to rest," Deborah said to Dad and Patti in a reassuring yet authoritative tone, putting her arm around my shoulder for emphasis. "She's been through one hell of a trip."

Somehow they listened, and when we finally got home, I basically slept for what felt like days, intermittently waking to the muffled sounds of them talking downstairs. This time, I've woken up to my window framing darkness outside. My body feels like it doesn't know which way is up.

The sound of a cork pops downstairs, and I hear Dad laughing at something while Deborah and Patti sound like two old friends chatting. Tamara laughs at something Deborah says.

I'm finally home.

So why am I crying? I swipe at my face with my T-shirt.

I stand at my bedroom door, my hand on the knob, yet I can't bring myself to turn it. Even though everyone sounds happy down in the kitchen, I'm filled with fear. The idea of leaving my bedroom is terrifying, but I promised to answer more questions as soon as I felt rested. Everything feels so heavy that I'm beginning to think rest is a thing that won't ever happen. With one last grimace at myself in the mirror, I wipe my eyes and stumble downstairs. Deborah is sitting on a kitchen barstool like she's been in our house for years.

Everyone has a wineglass, except Tamara, who is chugging a Diet Coke out of a can.

Patti sees me first. "Em!" A huge smile spreads across her face, but I see her quick glance at Dad. Patti turns to Tamara. "Come on, T. Let's go see what's on." Tamara rolls her eyes, then reluctantly follows Patti into the living room to watch TV.

Deborah stands and touches my arm. "Okay, sweetie," she says in a gentle voice. "I know this is really difficult, but are you ready to talk us through it one more time, just like you did with me in Zurich? We need to try to put a few things together as soon as we can."

I nod my head yes.

I follow Deborah and Dad into his office where papers are strewn across his desk. I look at the clock. It's almost midnight. *Shit.* I don't even know what day it is. My brain feels upside down. I'm too exhausted to be afraid of talking about what happened.

Just get it over with.

I start with meeting Josh in Boston, then Heather, then Will and Meredith and everything that happened in Italy. Well. Almost everything. My story gets fuzzy around finding Kara's body. How they ruled it an accident.

Dad stares at me the entire time, like he's looking at someone else—anyone but the girl he raised. A sadness fills my chest as he turns to Deborah. "Did you reach any of the Americans from California?"

"I already spoke to someone named David in Los Angeles," she says. "He was very distraught but probably more about the possibility of a scandal in the press than anything else. Understandably so." She mumbles the last part and glances at me with a worried look. "He said you told him you were backpacking after a Peace Corps stint."

Dad looks at me for confirmation.

"Yes. Kara told him that," I say. My mind flashes back to Kara that night casually drinking wine in a bikini like she'd known those strangers for years. How adventurously and fearlessly she lived her life. *Lived. Past tense.* I'm surprised when tears don't follow the memory, but my eyes are dry and numb. My whole body is numb.

Deborah writes something on her notepad. "He clearly had no idea that she died. And I honestly don't think he, or the others, had any clue as to what was going on with the cult."

Cult.

I keep hearing this word bounced around, but it doesn't make any sense. I didn't *join a cult*. I shake the word out of my head.

Dad is staring at me, his eyes pained. He must see I'm getting upset because he says, "Honey, why don't you go get some more rest. Let us sort through this." He turns back to Deborah as if seeking guidance, and she gives him a subtle approving gesture. As they fall back into deep conversation, I walk out of the room and click the door shut.

The glass doors across the back of our house glitter

against the bright kitchen lights. I open one into the dark humidity, the swell of insects screeching through the night. *Home*. I curl up in a chaise and stare out at the dark tree-tops. A normal person would feel safe right now, completely relieved. But the tangible baggage I brought with me—the box of tapes I carefully hid in the back of my closet—will never allow for peace.

I can't tell anyone about the tapes. The thought makes me nauseated. When I think about what was on my Sin List, tears fill my eyes. I can't bring myself to listen to the other Sin Lists, even now when I wake up with nightmares and can't go back to sleep. I don't even want to know. After hearing my own voice on a tape that who knows how many people heard, it would just be . . . wrong.

Knowing someone's darkest secrets is a burden no one should have.

I long for peace.

For a full night's sleep without nightmares.

For no memories of Europe.

Or Boston.

For a town where I can be completely anonymous.

For a brand-new life.

I wake to the sound of gentle knocking on my door. "I'm up," I say, assuming it's Patti, but to my surprise, Deborah pops her head in.

"Are you sure?" she says with a friendly smile.

I sit up in my bed. "Yes, of course."

She steps into my room, dressed in a sleek pantsuit with her purse over her shoulder. She stands near the door, as if careful to respect my space. "So I'm flying out today, but I wanted to say a proper good-bye."

My sadness at her announcement takes me by surprise. After all, I barely know her. But Deborah had taken over in Zurich and made me feel safe when I didn't know where else to turn. And now she's leaving. I try not to cry as she stands in my doorway.

"Please," I say. "Sit down." I point to the end of my bed. "I don't even know how to say this, but . . . thank you for . . ." Tears smear my room into a giant blur. "I was so scared, and you—"

"No, no, no." Deborah waves her hand around as she moves to my bed. "Please don't cry. I've already spoken to your dad about planning our next visit. We'll meet up very soon, maybe in New York. I really want to get to know you, Em. If only to hear about the crazy shit your stepsister gets into," she jokes, already knowing how to make me laugh.

And I do laugh through my tears. Yet we both know the unspoken obvious: My situation is the new handful.

Deborah presses her hand into the bed and stares at it before looking up at me. "Listen. I know you don't like to talk about your mom. Patti filled me in. But if you ever want to, I'm here. Even in Zurich through that thing called a phone line."

I sit still and silent, grasping the necklace I hadn't taken off for a second since I left Italy.

She briefly glances at my mother's necklace and then directly at me with a serious expression. "She was an amazing woman, you know . . . and so much like you. One thing about your mom: She was the kindest soul, and she always embodied that saying about people taking on the weight of the world." Deborah smiles tightly. "Sometimes the world burns you for that, but your mother . . . even then, she never closed her heart to others."

I can't help a small smile. It disappears just as quickly. "I barely remember her, but I've missed her for . . . so long," I whisper.

"She's with you. I know it. And I'm sure you can feel it," she says, standing to lean toward me and take my hand into hers. "She's *always* been with you."

It's something people have said to me my whole life, yet right now with Deborah, I actually believe it.

Disassociation. Floating. In some ways it will feel like your old self is dead. Specific memories may hit you unexpectedly. Acknowledge them and let them pass. Don't give these memories too much power.

Shattered Pieces

My best friend, Summer, lives in a tree house.

Well, not an actual tree house, but it feels like one when you're sitting in her bedroom looking out the window at the dense green canopy of limbs. I can hear her mother's wind chimes even through her closed window. A storm front is stirring them into an erratic urgency.

I haven't seen Summer since Christmas, and even then we had only a few random days in between her work hours, but Patti is the one who suggested I visit her. "It'll make you feel better to see her," she said. And as usual, Patti was right. Just being in Summer's house is a huge comfort. Hanging out with her feels as much like home as my own house— like no time has ever passed between last year and now.

When I appeared at her door, she took me into a giant

hug, one that felt like it would never end. She quickly ush-
ered me up to her room, where we've been sitting in near
silence. Summer plops onto the floor to rummage through
a box of CDs as if searching for the right soundtrack for
this awkward moment. She's the kind of friend who can just
hang out while leaving things unspoken. She's always been
a listener, but this time everything is way too heavy and I
don't know what to say, so she finally turns to me and breaks
the silence. "Do you want to talk about what happened, like,
even at all?"

Of course I want to tell her, but the idea of reliving everything all over again is too scary, even though Summer has been
my best friend for as long as I can remember. It terrifies me to
think that she wouldn't understand this. Plus, I have no idea
how to explain something that still doesn't feel like it's over.

"Hey, it's fine. Really. I get it," Summer says with a
soft smile and goes back to rummaging through the music
choices, each plastic square clicking against the hardwood
floor in quick succession.

My heart swells. I remember how Heather would beat
information out of me until she was satisfied she had enough
for the Kingdom to manipulate me with. She was never a
real friend. Summer will be around to listen the moment
I'm ready to talk. *Of course she will be*. "Tell me something
happy and exciting," I say.

Summer glances up at me. "Well, I got a new job."

"No way. You quit the restaurant?"

"Yep."

"So what's the new job?" A glimmer of normalcy illuminates our conversation.

"It's at a resort." She pauses. A worried look crosses her face. "In Pensacola."

I pause. "You're *moving*?" I try to hide my disappointment. All I want is for things to go back to the way they were before, but life is still moving on without me. The Kingdom took so much away from me in ways I'm just beginning to understand.

"Just temporarily. It's only for a month. Or so . . ."

I stare out the window at the trees rustling under a bright sun bearing down between clouds. I guess this is the phase of life everyone talks about—when our paths and plans shift and U-turn into random directions without warning. I always looked forward to this time, but I never thought about it being sad . . . or scary.

"Em! You can come visit me! I actually think it would be good for you. I mean, to get away from—"

"The rumors?" I say what we're both thinking.

Summer laughs. "Oceanview gossip. It's better than the tabloids." Tamara was always the gossip magnet in my family. I was always . . . well, the boring one. That changed when I got home and everyone got word of what had happened.

Summer's expression turns serious. "Em? I know things are weird right now, but I need to say something." She opens and closes a CD case nervously. "I'm . . . *so* sorry. I mean, I kept talking about coming to visit you, and I just . . . I feel like I should have been there for you. That I could have—"

"Stop." I hold up my hand. "Seriously. Nothing about my personal disaster was in any way your fault. I was . . . Well, I was an *idiot*." I know I was manipulated, that much is clear now even if so much still isn't. But I can't believe I didn't see the signs.

"What about . . . the guy?" Summer gives me a tentative look, like she's afraid to ask too many questions beyond that.

"Josh," I say matter-of-factly. I fidget with a pillow in my lap. "What can I say? I was a *lonely* idiot." I let out a sarcastic laugh. My analytical brain confirms it, but my heart still wants to know what happened to him—if he actually left the Kingdom for good, or if he never will and was playing me all along.

Summer goes back to her CD search. "Aha!" She holds one up with a giant smile. "I found the perfect song." Summer always knew when to change the subject. It's one of the many things I love about her.

The intro to Deee-Lite's "Groove Is in the Heart" prompts me to laugh as Summer starts dancing spastically. "Come on," she says. She grabs my arm. She swings her arms around, and I do the same thing, spinning and spinning until I have to flop on her bed. The jet lag still pulls at me like a drug that won't leave my system. "Okay. Okay." She rolls onto the floor to flip through more CDs. I stare out the window again, thinking this is just the same view I spent my entire childhood looking at while talking to Summer about everything I've ever wondered. Talking about the horrors in Italy would infect such a special place with negativity and regret. I won't do that. I'd rather keep it locked inside, where at least I'm the only one affected by it.

A loud crash echoes outside. I sit up. "What was—" Then another even louder crash sounds, like something shattered. I stand up, but Summer seems unconcerned as she flips through CDs again.

"Did you hear that?" I ask.

"Oh, that's just Jo."

Summer has always called her mother Jo, instead of Joellen (her full name) or Mom. And they've always been more like partners in crime than mother and daughter. Jo always treated both of us like "little adults," a term she used for us. Summer's mom is an artist who sells her work at local festivals and galleries, and growing up, there were never rules about which parts of the house we were allowed to eat food in or work on our own creative projects. Every room holds works in progress in various stages of completion, sculptures surrounded by objects that haven't made the cut yet. My favorite thing about Summer's house is every window frames a view of the treetops; there are so many trees that they block the view of the bayou just behind them. Staring out the window now at the movement of leaves, I'm mesmerized by how they sway collectively by one outside force, like something being shaken to life.

"What in the world is she doing?" I ask.

Summer gets up to look out the window. She turns back

to me, her brown eyes sparkling with the same playful curiosity she's had since we were kids. "Wanna go see?"

We stumble down the spiral staircase to the ground-level room that is Jo's studio. Mr. Kitty, their giant black cat, is sprawled out on a rug by the sliding glass door. Summer yanks the door to the side with a loud rumble, revealing Jo in the backyard, standing over a wooden table stacked with mismatched plates and colorful squares of tile. She picks up a hammer and brings it down on a piece of tile.

"Jo!" Summer yells. "You are disturbing the peace!"

Jo turns around and pulls the clear, plastic eye protector onto her forehead. Her face lights up when she sees me. Her ash-brown hair has grown so long, it's almost to her waist. A tiny braid wrapped in colorful yarn hangs even longer, a few inches past the overall length. Jo was always the cool, artsy mom.

"Emily! Look at you!" I can tell she's taking in my appearance, and I'm embarrassed. Even with Patti's home cooking and all the comfort food I could want, I still look gaunt and pale. Jo's expression isn't judgmental. It's more like she's looking at something she wants to fix.

"She's finally home," Summer says, as if explaining something she can't say another way out loud, but Jo stays in the moment, which is totally her. Summer and I once watched her painting a canvas in the backyard when a mid-sized alligator slipped out of the marsh grass and watched her from the edge of their yard. She never stopped painting but periodically acknowledged it by saying things like, "I see you there," until it finally turned around and slid back into the water.

"We're glad you're home," Jo says to me with a genuine smile. "Now"—she glances at Summer—"go find something to put on your feet other than flip-flops so you two can help me with this." She pulls the protective glasses back over her eyes and turns her attention to the table.

Summer squeals and takes off running up the stairs. I go inside and sit on the floor with the cat until Summer comes down with a pair of Doc Martens and rainbow-striped socks.

"Seriously?"

She laughs. "Sorry, Rainbow Brite. Laundry isn't really Jo's thing when she's in the middle of a creative project. Just pretend you're an artist."

I slip off my sandals and put on the socks and boots. I stand up and tug at my khaki shorts, as if that will help with this ridiculous ensemble. When I pull the door open, a blinding patch of sun gleams across the blue tile floor, triggering a sudden anxiety.

The floor morphs into the flash of sun on the swimming pool in Italy. *Kara*. I see her arm, her face. *No. No. No. No.* I try to stop the flashback by stomping on the tile with Summer's boots. I even tap my heels together. "There's no place like home," I say in my best Judy Garland voice to Summer. We both giggle, even though I have to force myself to speak and to laugh. And even as my anxiety fades into the background, I can't take too much comfort in that—its undercurrent never completely disappears. Panic is like a permanent live wire I'm learning to step around.

Jo shuffles through the plates on the table. She picks up a blue one that has a year and a building printed on it. She hands it to me.

"Why would you break this?" I ask.

"Because it was twenty-five cents at Goodwill, and I need that shade of blue for my sky."

"But this belonged to someone who wanted to remember this building in 1978."

She ignores my comment as she places the protective glasses over my eyes. "All right, Emily Dickinson." This is what Jo and Summer always called me when I would say things that seemed too serious.

I put the plate on the wooden table full of gouges and pockmarks. The wind blows my hair into my face. I take a deep breath and let myself feel it stirring before brushing my hair back. I notice the birds and squirrels moving through the periphery of trees. My heart races as I lift the hammer. I adjust my grip. I squeeze my eyes shut and my Sin List tape pops into my head.

The world around me goes completely blank until I hear the loud, satisfying *crack* of intentional force.

Anxiety when faced with choices. Inability to make decisions. It's okay to let someone else help you make decisions while you find your bearings. Take baby steps.

Surfing for Sanity

My toenails are pink.
This is what I'm thinking as I watch the surfers glide across the waves. I burrow my feet into the sand and lean into the warm breeze, where the smell of beer and cigarettes mingles with traces of coconut from our oily Banana Boat bottles. I lift my toes up one at a time, let the sand fall away, then bury them back under.

I didn't pick out this toenail color, but this is the sort of thing that happens when Patti takes control. I followed her around the salon in silence. When they sent me to pick the color, Patti found me twenty minutes later blanked out in front of a cheerful display of bottles.

Ever since I returned from Italy, even the easiest decision can cause me to freeze. And then the trembling follows, like a personal earthquake, the fault line always under my feet. Patti was in her element, though. She even directed the hairdresser. "Just lighten it up as much as you can," she said with a wave of desperation. Her thin silver bangles jangled too close to my ear, causing my skin to prickle. I looked up and caught her extended glance at my stringy locks. I knew she was cringing at the idea of where my hair had been, what the dead ends may have brushed up against. "And cut off at least two inches," Patti added before clicking away in her open-toe heels.

My new therapist—the "expert" Dad found who "has experience with cases similar to mine"—told me this will get better. She said I'll begin to feel things again as I gain control over my life. I didn't respond to her promise but sat there studying her antique cypress mantel that held an exotic collection of lit candles.

After our first session, she gave me an article that outlines how I'm supposed to feel at this point. She said many people who choose to leave a "high-demand" group struggle with the same feelings, even though the groups are very different. She told us about a facility in Oklahoma, but Dad said there was no way in hell he was sending me off to another state after all of this.

He did make an exception for me to visit Summer in Pensacola. When I first mentioned the idea of meeting up with friends in Florida, Dad hesitated, but Patti fell over herself to say I should absolutely go enjoy some time with Summer. "Oh, honey, it's only a few hours away," Patti argued, placing her hand on Dad's arm. The therapist told us the sooner I can assimilate back into the normalcy of my old life with my pre-cult relationships, the better. I know Patti must have reminded Dad about this as soon as I left the room.

All because she insisted, I'm sitting beside Summer watching the surfers, just like old times. Except now my toenails are bright pink, my hair is full of honey-blond streaks, and I don't even recognize myself anymore—inside or out. But the last part really isn't Patti's fault—she's always just tried to help. And on days like this when the atmosphere is charged with something ominous, something more powerful than me, it doesn't seem to matter. I turn myself over to the intensity of the weather, the raging Gulf, the rippling red flags—the same way the surfers give themselves to the whims of the water and the dangerous riptide.

While our other girlfriends chat and laugh and sip their beer, I study the ocean, my ears tuned to the rhythm of incoming waves. I watch the way the surfers brace their boards, crouching in position to maintain balance as they continue forward, how they fall into the turbulent water with pure abandon, and climb back up without hesitation to go at it again.

There's one guy in particular I don't recognize. He's wading toward the beach with a worn surfboard tucked under his arm. When he turns back to face the water, I have a fleeting realization that the Ultimate Creator must have been a woman—one with a careful touch and an artist's eye. I imagine Her gliding a steady thumb firmly down the middle of his back, molding the perfect indent between his muscles like ripe clay. Then I remember I'm not supposed to think about God. The therapist says that's something we'll work up to as I distance myself from what happened. I focus on the "now," as she suggested, and on the beads of water sparkling across his skin.

"Who's he?" I ask Summer.

She's digging a cigarette out of a crinkled pack of Marlboro Lights when she answers as if she's been waiting for this exact question. "That's Alex. He just moved to our beloved town of Oceanview for the marine lab program." Summer smiles knowingly. "Paul brought him over today to surf and hang out with us." I note the hushed exchanges between the other girls, the sudden break in their banter to gauge my response. I can tell my friends are worried about me. Well, Summer, at least. The others eye me like a time bomb, wary of the invisible triggers.

I stand up and trudge through the sand toward the edge of the water. The red flags ripple in the wind like silent alarms, but this is the only time the surfers come out. There isn't much in the way of surfable waves around here other-wise.

The water sweeps over my feet, then another wave just

behind it swooshes through my legs. I balance myself as the tide pulls it back to the horizon. I'm cemented into the wet sand, its great expanse pocked with half-buried sea life— once whole but now shattered into fragments. On the horizon, I can see numerous bodies gliding across the water.

Alex is already paddling back out to mount another wave, his short hair glistening in the sun. His arms stretch out for balance and his abdominal muscles tighten as he slides in front of the crest of water. And for the first time since I returned home, something cuts through the numbness.

That night at the bonfire, Summer sits down beside me. I don't even realize I'm no longer sitting by myself until I look up. "Hey. Emily Dickinson. I want you to meet someone," she says. Then she leans back and introduces me to Alex.

I've been staring into the fire, so it takes me a few seconds to shake the burnout vision. As the bright splotches fade, his face could be anyone's. In those brief moments, I have to block out the faces of the other students from the Kingdom's mission. Or "cult," as my therapist carefully referred to it as she leaned forward with her rectangular glasses dangling from her hand. I had to fight the urge to grab her spectacles and put them on my own face. As in: *Maybe if I could see what you see, then it would all make sense.*

"Emily," I say to Alex as Summer slips away.

"I know," he says. "But I can't get anyone to tell me anything about you. What did you do . . . rob a bank, or something?"

I surprise myself with a genuine laugh.

This must have been easier for Tamara when she returned from rehab a few years before. After the initial gossip waned, people didn't care. Maybe it's because, with her, they can easily categorize it. *Oh, that.* Then it's on to her next screw up. But with me, no one seems to know what to say. I definitely would have been the least likely of my friends to end up in some sort of trouble. But I'm learning that what happened to me triggers a specific fear in other people—the idea that something could drag one of their loved ones away from their own religious beliefs, traditions, social circles, or worse, familial grasp. In the South, it's the scariest thing anyone could imagine.

"I have an idea," I say to Alex, surprised my voice doesn't sound as shaky as I feel. "Why don't we just start with yesterday."

He squints at me as if unsure of how to respond.

"So, Alex. What did *you* do yesterday?" I prompt.

"This," he says, gesturing to the ocean without hesitation.

"And where did you learn to do *this* so well?" I say, copying his gesture.

His smile is stirring something buried deep, but it's still a vague sensation.

"San Diego."

"*California*. I've always wanted to go there. Tell me about San Diego."

"No. Nuh-uh. It's your turn."

I smile at him, but I know I'm forcing it. After three weeks, I desperately want to feel something again, but I can't forget that falling for a guy was the start of how everything went wrong. Because of that, the newness of Alex is unpredictable and scary.

"Oh, wait. Sorry, I forgot. What did you do yesterday, Emily?" He mimics my pretending-to-be-friendly voice.

"I got my nails done," I say, wiggling my toes for full effect.

If only our past could always start with yesterday.

He looks down at my feet through the golden glow of the bonfire. "Nice," he says. "But you don't really strike me as a hot pink kind of girl."

"And how would *you* know? I thought you said you didn't know anything about me."

He's silent for a few seconds before answering carefully. "I know you're not like those girls," he says, glancing at Summer's crew. They're huddled in a semicircle on the other side of the bonfire, probably sharing a joint, from the sound of their unguarded bursts of laughter. "I know you're quiet. I know your thoughts are far away from this place right now."

My nerves fray with the urge to contradict him. "See, that's where you're wrong. I happen to like my pink toe-my underlying

oulders-first

seconds. He

vay a swimming

n. The water

his is how I t

ear as the

ion of the

e pulls me deeper into th

se my eyes, and feel my initial trembling giv

ning force of the ocean.

nails. An recently ma

the momt," I say

somethingmy th

ably verbaim

her linen

giving

Alex

...de a consc...

...knowing full...

...rapist said to me...

...I imagine her sittin...

...op with chunky beads...

...e a thumbs up. This mak...

...still looks serious.

He takes my hand and gentl...
others are staring at us as he lea...
care. And I don't resist him.

It's so nice to be led.

He lets go of my hand to...
tosses it in the dry part of the...

"Are you coming with me...
darkening Gulf.

My bathing suit is almos...
want to follow him. Then I f...
line threatening to shift.

"Come on," he challeng...

I like that he isn't afr...
care what the others think...
though, is the fact that...
between me a year ago...
right now. The dark wav...
every direction, and pul...

I yank my sweater o...
to shiver. My teeth are...

cold...

rush...

within...

same...

a lesson...

"Th...
into my...
the mot...

As h...
ders, clo...
the chur...

Panic disproportionate to an ordinary situation. Loss of control. You will have a moment. And it will throw you off. Prepare for it so it doesn't wreck everything you've accomplished. Remember these "moments" are temporary.

Home Is Where the Water Is

Back in Oceanview, Alex and I continue our surfing lessons on weekends.

We just throw his surfboards into his old beat-up truck and drive down to Dauphin Island, the nearest spot Alex knows with good waves. We've been hanging out a lot, just as friends, even though I know what people are thinking when they see us together: A guy led me into a cult, yet here I am already attaching myself to a new one.

Whatever. They never knew me anyway, I rationalize.

When Alex and I ran into Patti's tennis partner at the grocery store, her eyes glanced back and forth at us before she managed an awkward hello, grabbed something random to throw into her cart, and practically sprinted in the other direction. Patti just laughed it off when I told her about it later. "Emily?" Patti always says my name like a question before offering advice. "The sooner you quit worrying about what other people think, the better off you'll be. Trust me on that. And when you're ready for us to meet Alex—or not—just say the word. We only care about you being happy again."

I appreciate Patti's support, but I have no intention of bringing Alex to meet them—now or maybe ever. The beautiful thing about Alex is he doesn't know my past or what I've gone through. He's also graduating next year and already applying to grad schools all over the country. When I'm with him, I'm not thinking about the past, or looking ahead. Hell, I'm barely even thinking at all.

"Have you ever seen an elephant?" Alex asks me one afternoon. *See? No thinking involved.* "And zoos don't count." His smile reveals tiny teeth with a slight gap between the front two. He's asking the questions in a game he learned from growing up in so many different places, a contrived way to get to know people as quickly as possible.

"No." I sweep my hair behind my shoulders and pretend to take this initiation very seriously. His playful mood is contagious. My mind is buzzing from the newness of what's happening between us. We're sitting on the hardwood floor of his living room. I don't want to go home and risk losing that blooming intensity that floods through me like a soothing tonic.

He leans in nearly close enough to kiss me. "An alligator?"

I laugh, breaking the mood. "Um, hello? Look where I grew up."

"Okay, stupid question." He leans back, feigning a dramatic thought. "Enough with the animals. How about a . . . castle?"

"Yep." I smile as I remember my first train ride to Italy. I don't share this with Alex, but instead let the memory burn out and fall away, leaving its familiar aching trail.

"What about a volcano?"

I think about it for a second. "No."

"A movie star?"

"I don't think so. Wait, no, once in New York."

"Really? Who?"

"Al Pacino. He was having lunch at an outdoor café in SoHo. My stepsister made me walk by his table twice, and the second time around he looked straight at Tamara, raised his eyebrows, and said, 'Hey, baby.'" I laugh at my own gravelly voiced Pacino imitation. It's a relief to reveal an emotionally neutral memory.

"No shit. That's a good story," he says, impressed. "Okay, then. Hmmm. What about a king cobra?" he asks.

It's a totally innocent question.

Yet my frazzled mind jumps to the snake on my bed in Italy. Kara's tattoo. Josh's talk about the venom. That night Ben chased me down . . . My body turns to pins and needles as the image of Kara's lifeless body appears in flashes, like a horror movie burned into my memory—legs at odd angles, a bloated arm, her long hair swept over the top of her face.

A solid knot expands in my throat, making it difficult to swallow, and then impossible to breathe. Alex's hands are on my shoulders, but I can't see anything. My vision is already closing in, narrowing itself down to a distorted tunnel. I try to talk myself out of panicking. *What is wrong with you? He just asked about a stupid cobra. It isn't even the same snake as—*

"Oh, God. What's wrong?" Alex is at my side, his arms around me protectively.

"No . . . it's okay." I hear myself say it, but my voice sounds unfamiliar, like a disembodied whisper. Losing Kara hits me with fresh pain, the memory just as intense and surreal as the day I found her.

"Emily? Emily . . ." Alex is a blur in front of me, his voice a distant buoy in a sea of panic. His arms close around me as he smooths my hair down my back with his hand. "It's okay. It's okay." He says it over and over.

I remember two things after taking a pill from the brand-new prescription in my purse: my teeth chattering as if I'm half-clothed in the middle of Antarctica, and the strength of Alex's arms still wrapped around me when I wake up on his couch in the middle of the night.

I surface to consciousness a little too quickly, so fast that I imagine that suctioning noise on TV shows when someone is either leaving or entering a flashback. The Xanax haze has worn itself thin, yet it still offers the blessed illusion that nothing scary ever happened—nothing but a neutral fatigue. The warmness of Alex surrounds me, and for the first time in months I feel like an ordinary college student making spontaneously questionable decisions just like the other girls from my dorm.

I touch his face until his legs begin stirring. I kiss him gently. His hands press into my back as he pulls me closer. Our kissing becomes more forceful, the kind that completely shuts down an otherwise rational mind. I don't want to think anymore, *just feel*. Through the silent darkness, I feel a mouth on my ear, his weight shifting on top of me, hands moving everywhere at once, the tandem rise and fall of breath. His finger gently slips its way inside of me, then out and away, leaving me with an irrepressible desire to lead it back. *"Are you sure?"* I can only answer by matching his urgency, by tugging at clothes, by legs twining legs into place. I never fully open my eyes until we're both tangled and naked and pushing through the numbness. The intensity of every movement forces me to stay with him in those tangible moments, leaving Kara's memory behind in a distant wake.

When I open my eyes, it's daylight, but Alex is still asleep. I reach around the floor until I find a T-shirt. At first, the absence of regret surprises me. What happened felt natural in the moment, even inevitable. And now, I'm just another ordinary adult waking up with someone I like very much and in desperate need of coffee.

It's all so normal I could cry.

Alex's kitchen is in a tiny hallway at the back of the house. The long window overlooks a patio with a wooden picnic table. He told me this had been a vacation rental cottage, but he worked out a long-term lease with the owners. Just as I find a coffee filter, his phone rings. I freeze, unsure of what to do. I've never stayed the night with anyone before, and I hadn't thought to call someone to say where I was. I hear the machine pick it up, and Tamara's voice begins talking.

"Hey, Alex, Emily's *friend*, can you pick up, please?"

There's a long pause.

"Um. Okay. Is Emily there? Emily, are you there?"

Shit. I grab the phone and push the talk button.

"Shhhhhh," I whisper. "Tamara? How did you know I was here?"

"What the *hell*, Em," Tamara mock-scolds. "This is so not like you, shacking up. I wonder what Dad would say. . . ."

"Stop it. I just fell asleep, okay? How did you get his number?"

"Dude. Summer is my source for everything Em-related. You of all people should know that. Anyway, don't worry. I told Mom you were at a friend's house. And Dad left early to go to the office before we were up, but that's not why I'm calling."

I stand there quietly watching the neighbor's gray cat slink under the picnic table. It crouches at the edge of a shadow as if stalking something. My focus shifts as I catch my own reflection in the window. My hair looks wavy and disheveled, almost sexy. I notice the small image of a jumping fish on Alex's T-shirt and feel a straightforward surge of happiness that has escaped me for months.

"Some lady's here to see you," Tamara whispers into the phone. "She says she's a journalist and drove over from Florida."

"Florida?" I stare into the sink wishing Tamara had never called. "Who is she?"

"I. Don't. Know." Tamara pronounces each word slowly, as if talking to a child.

"That is why I am trying to track you down before Mom gets back from the store."

"Why does she want to talk to me?"

"She said she wants to ask you some questions. Something about an incident with a preacher in Gainesville." The word Gainesville makes my stomach turn. I try to block visions of Will and Meredith. And especially Kara.

"Tell her to meet me at the harbor park. I can be there in twenty minutes," I say without even thinking through what it means to agree to meet with her. "Just *please* get her out of the house before anyone gets home."

"Okaaaay," Tamara says, her tone signaling she'll help me with this situation.

I hear Alex stirring in the other room. A wave of dizziness causes me to lean against the counter. An intense fear overrides any curiosity I would otherwise have about news from Gainesville.

Guilt. Shame. It's natural to wonder how you didn't realize what was going on at the time, but don't obsess. Focus on how you can live an authentic life now and in the future.

A Journalist Named Julia

The bank sign says 102 degrees.

The park is empty except for a man fishing from the bridge, and I spot the journalist pacing around the enormous gazebo at the top of the hill.

I know I could have stood her up, or let her come back to the house to face Dad, who undoubtedly would send her scurrying away for good. But when I started the engine of my car to leave Alex's house, something clicked in my mind. As much as I thought being at home and sleeping in my own bed far away from the Kingdom would solve everything, it hasn't. *At. All.* The entire situation still feels so unsettled. *Unresolved.* What if she had information that could help me process this mess?

When I walk up to her, she immediately sticks out her hand. "Emily? I'm Julia James. A reporter working on an article about an incident that happened down near Gainesville."

I shake her hand and we sit down at a rickety picnic table. The vague squeal of children echoes from the playground through the massive oak trees; it's a sound requiring constant intonation to decipher amusement from possible terror. I sit silently, watching her put a notebook on the table and rest her hands on it. "Oh. Here's my card." She hands it to me, and I stare at it while she's talking. "I'm so sorry to contact you out of nowhere, but I'm covering a story that you may know something about. Did you know a couple from Nashville who moved to Boston to manage a church called the Kingdom? They went by the names Meredith and Will."

I look up, but don't say anything. I sit quiet and still until she starts in again, hoping she will answer the questions I've had since leaving Italy without requiring much from me in return.

"Will was found dead in his car." Julia stops talking just as my face goes numb.

My stomach lurches.

"Are you okay?" she asks in a concerned tone.

"I'm fine," I say calmly, looking her in the eye. From her expression, it's clear that I most certainly do not appear to be fine. "Go ahead," I say, pushing my fingertips into my forehead. My eyes burn, but not with tears—it's more like an escalating headache.

"A large crate containing exotic snakes was found more than sixty feet from the vehicle, which is odd because no one else was at the scene. One of the snakes, a five-foot black mamba, was found loose inside the car with him. He also had a glove compartment full of sterile syringes. Did you hear about this in the news?"

"No," I say. All I can think about is how sick Will looked the last time I saw him and what Josh had told me about the Remnant.

"Okay. Did you know a college student named Josh?"

What? I try not to give a reaction, but I can tell she knows she's onto something. Beads of sweat begin dripping down my back. "Yes," I whisper, staring at the graffiti on the picnic table.

"He's actually the one who gave me your name." She shifts her notebook deliberately and watches for my reaction.

My eyes widen in shock. "What?" I say it out loud this time. The entire world spins. *Josh gave her my name?* "Why would he—" I press my lips together. *Don't say anything else.* I take a deep breath and stare off at the bayou. A pelican calls overhead and lands on a nearby post in the water. It tucks its beak down into its chest as if protecting its heart.

"I know it must be scary to talk about an experience like this, but sometimes it can help with recovery," she says.

Her gentle tone softens my resolve. Still, I don't say anything.

She writes something in her notebook and flips to another page. "Your friend Josh was hoping to find you but didn't know where you were. He said you both were in the cult—"

I stand abruptly, my mind reeling. "I'm so sorry, but I have to go." I don't even let her respond before I take off for my car.

I'm already halfway to the parking lot when she calls out behind me. "I know about Italy. And your friend Kara."

That stops me in my tracks.

Anger and fear burn through me, causing my hands to shake. Waves of heat radiate from the black asphalt of the parking lot. I fight an overwhelming surge of nausea. I'm not even sure I can make it to my car.

Julia calmly continues as if giving me mundane information I could take or leave while catching up with me. "Kara's story is key to figuring out what happened—to stop it from happening again. I think we could put some pieces together," she says, now within hand-shaking distance.

"What did Josh say?" I ask quietly.

"One thing he said is that he really wants to talk to *you*." She lowers her voice. "Look. I know this must be extremely difficult for you. But I write about the aftermath of the most horrific situations for a living, so I also know closure can be a powerful thing."

Closure is all I want. But I don't trust anyone to give me what I need.

I calmly make it to my car, slam the door, and drive away. My hands shake violently the entire drive home. The house is empty. I bolt straight up to my room and lock the door before allowing myself to sob uncontrollably.

I try my best to forget about Julia, but I can't stop thinking about our conversation. . . . *To stop it from happening again.*

I did not mention any of this to Dad. He would have a fit, as it took weeks of irate phone calls and angry lawyer letters to finally get my stuff shipped here from Boston. They tried to say I signed some sort of contract, but by the time Dad was through with them, they actually had my car specially driven all the way to the end of Mississippi. (Free of charge.)

I decide to go to the library to verify Julia's story about Will and the black mamba snake. It's all there in print. And it's all true.

Will is dead.

I fall against the back of a wooden library chair. I feel . . . I don't know how I feel. Knowing for sure doesn't make me sad, yet it isn't cathartic, either. Since returning home, it feels like the Kingdom had opened up a hidden corner of my heart that's now torn apart and exposed—like having surgery without being sewn back together. And if knowing Will is gone forever doesn't make it better, then what if it's impossible to ever fully heal? Someone else has probably already taken his place to yell at brand-new disciples—to tear their hearts apart. The thought sickens me.

Maybe helping Julia get justice for Kara could work. Maybe it could even stop the entire Kingdom.

While the idea scares me, I can't bring myself to dismiss it. So I study the details in the article, which explains how the snakes were shipped through a commercial airline. Will picked them up and signed for them himself. But that doesn't explain why one was loose in his car, yet the crate holding the other snakes was a good distance away. It also doesn't explain why he had syringes in his glove compartment.

My mind flashes to Kara's snake tattoo, to the syringe by her body. The fact that Josh insisted she didn't do drugs, and I never saw signs of that either.

Kara, what happened to you?

The news story hints that someone else must have been involved in Will's death, but the local authorities have no leads. It also says snake venom is nearly impossible to pinpoint as a primary cause of death, because of the way the venom breaks down in a body.

Julia James is onto something with this. The tapes haunt my thoughts like something dark and unspeakable. I wish I'd dumped them in a train station trash can when I had the chance.

But what if they hold the answers . . . ?

you are. And that you have no shame for those sins."

"Please . . . *Please* don't tell anyone!" Andrew begs. "I'm so sorry. It will never happen again. Please don't say anything."

There's a long pause. Then Will speaks very low, almost in a whisper. "Your parents may understand, but voters won't."

Andrew is sobbing. "Please just tell me what to do to make things right."

"There is something. Something very powerful that eradicates the sin." There's a long pause. "Are you willing to try it?"

"Yes," Andrew says, his voice cracking.

My hands are shaking violently when I press stop. My heart races. I remember Andrew's face the last time I saw him. How afraid he looked when I told him about the snake in my room. Andrew knew about the Remnant. Will must have been poisoning him with the promise of eradicating his "sins." I pull the tape out, stick it back in its case, and shove everything in the box. It sits in front of me like a loaded gun.

I'm sobbing as I shove it back into the darkness of my closet.

Soon after, Dad starts pounding insistently on my door. I let him in and collapse in his arms. We sit on the floor together, and I cry hysterically until I'm too exhausted to move. He gently smooths my hair with his hand. *Shhhhhhhh*. He says it over and over. And when I'm almost asleep, he carries me like a child and pulls the covers over my shoulders.

Back home, I open my closet door, my heart racing inside my chest. Kara's Walkman is on top of the box of tapes. A wave of nervousness hits me as I open a tape at random and click it into the Walkman. I press play and watch the small-toothed circles spin for a few seconds before putting the headphones over my ears.

It's Andrew's voice. When I hear the level of fear and sadness in his tone, I immediately start crying. Will is asking questions. "How many times were you with him?" he asks.

"Three," Andrew says. I hear him sniffling. He's crying.

"Did you know it was a sin the first time?"

"Yes," Andrew whispers.

"Then how could you go back to that sin, not just once, but *twice*?"

Andrew doesn't answer, and I hear Will sigh in frustration. This must be what they call a breaking session.

"You know that homosexual behavior will keep you from the Kingdom of God. Do you not?"

"Yes." Andrew sounds like he's trying to hold it together.

Will starts yelling. "Then why would you go back to that sin like a dog returning to its vomit?! Do you not know tha the Lord detests sinners? And that you will *never* be able t enter into the Kingdom of heaven?"

Andrew is crying again. There's a long, silent pause.

"I should call your parents," Will says calmly.

"No!" Andrew yells.

"I should tell them what a filthy little sinning fa

The least I can do is help Julia figure out what happened.

For Kara.

But also for Andrew and Lily. And Josh.

The next morning, as soon as Dad leaves for the office, I hold Julia's card and stare at the phone. I can't help but think about that night at Deborah's in Zurich when I was such a desperate mess, yet she stayed so calm. She knew exactly what to do and who to call. She completely took control and steered me out of my nightmare, even when I thought things were hopeless, even when she hardly knew me. Deborah is exactly the kind of person I want to be.

I call Julia and give two stipulations for our next meeting:

1. It has to be at a restaurant several towns away
   from my house, closer to New Orleans.
2. Julia has to bring Josh.

My hand is still shaking when I hang up, but for the first time since I got home, I feel like I'm taking control. Even if I don't know exactly what I'm doing, I refuse to sit around hoping the tapes will somehow miraculously disappear while the people responsible for our abuse could be out there recruiting more people. Recording their deepest secrets. Using them to their benefit, no matter the emotional cost.

I'm not scared anymore—I'm furious.

\\\\//

They're waiting when I get there. The seafood dive is bustling with the local lunch crowd. Josh doesn't see me until I sit down across from him.

"Hi," he says. He blinks nervously, then quickly looks down at his lap. My heart aches with regret. The same person I fell for just a few months ago is right in front of me—close enough to touch. And he looks exactly the same. My head has to remind me about the lies—*his* lies—that led us here.

"You look good," I say in a cordial tone.

"Thanks." He smiles, but his eyes are hollow and sad, just like the last time I saw him on the train.

Julia opens the checkered cloth nestled in a basket in the middle of our table and pulls out a piece of freshly made bread. She butters it gingerly, seemingly oblivious to our awkwardness. "Let's get down to business," she says. "I've been a journalist for fifteen years, and I can tell you this story has the potential to blow this 'Kingdom' apart the minute the ink hits the page. All sources can be first names only to protect you and other victims."

Victims. I swallow a gulp of water, trying to stay composed.

Julia pauses and leans forward. "Here's the thing. I don't think your friend Kara drowned, and I don't think it was an accident."

Josh and I exchange glances, but neither one of us speaks. He doesn't seem nervous or fidgety. Just sad. It's almost a relief to hear someone say what I thought all along.

Julia looks at me. "As Josh and I already discussed, the only person who had the power to sign off on Kara's death as an accidental drowning without triggering a formal inquiry by the Italian authorities would be a parent."

"But her mother was never there," I say.

"Her father was," Josh says.

"What?" I ask. Then a sudden memory of Kara's voice: *My whole existence is a sin.*

Will was Kara's father? The room seems distorted and the ambient noise around me booms like someone is cranking the volume all the way up. I look at Julia. "Um, Julia? May I have a moment alone with Josh?" I ask politely.

"Sure," she says, quick to accommodate. "I need to check my messages anyway. I saw a pay phone in the lobby."

Josh's eyebrows furrow in thought as she stands up and walks out.

When she's a good distance away, I turn back to Josh. "Look. I know I set this up, but are you sure we want to do this?" I ask. A father and daughter are both dead. Everything about this situation—one Josh and I both were tangled in— suddenly feels dangerous.

Josh shifts in his chair and leans forward so he won't have to talk so loudly. "It's going to come out anyway. I just . . . I need to know what really happened. To her," he says.

"I do too, but there could be consequences. Retaliation for talking."

"We need to know the truth." His eyes are glossed with grief.

"What about the Sin Lists?" I watch him closely as I say it.

A look of panic shoots across his face. "What about them?"

I can't help myself. I want to know his version of the truth, so I play dumb. "Who has them?"

"I don't know. Ben never found them when we were in Italy. He was frantic. I heard the church blamed him when we got back, and he was marked and disconnected. Meredith went through every corner of the entire villa before I left, too. They're just gone."

"You don't think they had copies somewhere else?" I ask.

He shakes his head. "Think about it. How disorganized we were over there. Think of how many tens of thousands of members are in the Kingdom and how many people who confessed were recorded. If they'd had copies why tear the villa apart?"

"Do you think we should tell Julia about them?"

"*No,*" Josh says abruptly, practically jumping out of his chair. "We just want to know what happened to Kara. The Sin Lists have nothing to do with her."

I look at him again, this time suspiciously. "Is that why you were in my room that night? And why you met me in the train station?"

Josh puts his head in his hands. He talks quietly while pressing his fingers into his forehead. "Emily, you have no idea how sorry I am. About everything. I said things in those confessions I should have never discussed with *anyone*. Things about my family that would ruin their lives forever—especially my mom's, and I would never do that to her. I trusted Ben, and he destroyed my life."

I wince at Josh's words. I talked about things I'd never want anyone to hear. And I can't even think about Andrew's tape without crying. I should have never played it at all.

Josh is right. No one should hear any of the tapes.

Julia strolls back toward our table.

"So. Are we okay here?" She looks back and forth at us. "How about we order some food."

"Okay. But I think it's time I introduce you to someone this afternoon. I can't really talk about any of this without him."

"Who's that?"

"My dad," I say.

As we're leaving, I ask Julia if she could give us another minute alone. "I need to talk to Josh again. Privately," I say.

"No problem. I'll wait in my car until you're ready," she says.

Josh and I walk around the restaurant to a deck overlooking the marsh. A breeze rolls across the bayou, cutting through the sweltering humidity. Boats pass in the distance, leaving silence in their wake. I can hear people laughing from the tables behind us at the top of the steps.

I turn back to Josh. "I just want you to know I forgive you." I reach into my purse and hand him his tape.

As he reads the label, his face turns pale.

"Don't worry. I didn't listen to it," I say.

He studies my face.

"Honestly. I didn't," I say, looking straight into his eyes.

"Thank you," he says, gently touching my arm before slipping the tape into his pocket.

As I watch him walk away, my heart sinks.

I can tell he believed me. But I can also tell the tape was all he wanted.

Frustration with recovery. Always remember there is hope. Eventually, something will give way and your new normal will emerge. You may even discover a new path, or a higher purpose, as a direct result of your experience.

The Blank Tape

I try to pretend the other Sin List tapes don't exist.

I've been so busy hanging out with Alex that I almost let myself forget they're still hidden in my closet. Festering. It seems manageable until I come home to a quiet bedroom, so quiet I can almost hear the voices talking at the same time. Even though I couldn't bring myself to listen to the other tapes, I already know what's on them. The openness. The pleading. The pain. The fear and shame. The unspoken desire for the struggle to end.

But that's the thing. When you're in the struggle, there is no possible end—it's just a never-ending loop of unattainable demands. When you're living it, you can't see which way is up. And after you leave, it feels like you're lost, like someone led you into the depths of a labyrinth without a map, and then abandoned you to find your way out.

The shame is overwhelming, and not just because I feel like such an idiot for not seeing what was really happening.

Kara died. Her mother will never see her again. The list of possible things I could have done—stayed with Kara and the Americans or tried harder to get her to come back—haunts me every night when I wake up from the nightmares. I want to make it stop, but I'm scared of reaching out to the one person I'm most afraid I'll disappoint.

I'm terrified of telling Dad everything. Of what his reaction will be to the fact that I could be implicated. I can't even fathom how I would bring myself to hand over the Sin List tapes of other people. *Maybe I can fix it on my own.*

I open my closet and shuffle through the tapes. Every cassette is labeled with the initials matching the other interns, except Kara, whose tape was always missing. A few of Kara's music mix tapes are in the box, maybe in an attempt to mask the others. I dig through all of them again and notice a blank one.

I pull it out of the case. There's no label and it is rewound like new. Then I notice the plastic tabs at the top have been removed to protect it from being recorded over or erased. I place it into my Walkman, pull the headphones over my ears with a sense of dread, and press play.

Chills spread across my arms when I hear Kara's voice.

"You promised," Kara says.

"God has a plan for me."

"In California?"

"Stop asking questions about my wife, Kara. I knew better than to trust you to be a DP."

"Really? What were your other options? To have Shannon be mine and ask me about all of my sins so she could tell her family back in Boston? My entire existence is a sin and you know it," Kara says.

I remember hearing this conversation at the villa. A long sequence of static crackles through their silence.

"Then *I'll* tell her," Kara finally says.

"What?"

"I swear to God I'll tell her if you don't."

"*Kara*. Just stop."

"You. *Promised*. And now you're choosing them over us. My mother dedicated her life to the Kingdom even after what you did to her. She saved *your life* in Africa. I'll tell everyone about that, too, that you aren't a living miracle, you pathetic piece of shit."

Silence.

"Tell. Her. Or I'll do it for you."

The sound of a door slamming ends the conversation. I watch the tape reels spin all the way to the end, but there's nothing else to hear.

I slip the tape out, secure it in its case, and clasp it to my stomach. I rock back and forth until I find a way to stand up and go downstairs. I'm grasping the case so hard the plastic front cracks in my hand.

Dad is sitting at his desk looking at a document, his glasses pushed down to the tip of his nose. He looks tired and weary and engrossed in what he's reading.

"I need to talk to you," I say. I sit down on the worn leather chair across from his desk and fidget with the tape.

He looks up at me and glances at my hands. "What do you have there?" My dad has had years of experience knowing the exact moment when someone is ready to talk about something important. I know it's why he hasn't been pushing me these past few weeks. He can see it coming from a mile away.

Still, I hesitate.

"It's a tape. And I think it could explain more about what happened to Kara."

"And where did this tape come from?" He takes his reading glasses off and extends his arm. I place the tape in his hand.

"I thought it was a blank tape at first. I found it with Kara's mix tapes."

"Mix tapes?"

"Like music mixes with favorite songs. This one looked blank, but the tabs were pushed out so I listened—"

"Stop there," he says. He holds up a hand for me to stay quiet, places the tape on his desk, and looks at me in the same way he must look at his clients every day. "Emily, Deborah and I have been tracking down the many strings running in every direction from this case, and believe me when

I say it's a doozy. But the fact of the matter is that Kara's own parent was there and didn't question the conclusion of the authorities."

"I know," I say. I think about hearing Meredith and Ben in the office, about the needle by Kara's arm that was never mentioned by anyone else, about Kara's pale blue skin. I just want to make the memories and the nightmares stop.

"As an attorney and, more important, as your father, I would never advise you to do anything that would put you in harm's way. Think about it." His voice begins to rise with intensity. "Absolutely nothing on that tape would convince me to let you reopen an international case based on an item belonging to the victim—oh, *and* that you brought home before telling anyone else about it until just now."

He holds up the tape, his face reddening with anger. "As far as we're concerned, this *is* a blank tape." I flinch at the tone of his voice.

He looks at me again and softens. "Sweetie, nothing will bring her back. The authorities will sort it out, right or wrong. Either way, this *group* has been destroying lives for a long time, and our focus is on putting a stop to it. I promised Julia Jones I would stay in touch for her article, and I intend to keep that promise, but it has to be done in exactly the right way. One good journalist can be a lot more effective than a thousand lawyers."

This is all so easy for him. *Why didn't I call him in the first place?* Then the familiar wave of isolation hits me from all the times I needed him most and he wasn't there. Of all the times Patti called *for* him when he was too busy to do it himself. Even after the horrifying incident with Sadie, Dad's reaction was a dismissive relief when he found out she was sent home—the problem had fixed itself. He had no idea about the fear and loneliness I felt every single night in that very same dorm room.

"Look," he says. "I know how to fix this. Just let me do my job while you focus on getting better. You've been through enough." He stands up as a gesture that we should move out of his office and just walk right back into our regular lives.

But I can't bring myself to move. My chest tightens as I press my fingers into my forehead. "I've been 'through enough' because you haven't been there for me. Why do you think I wanted to go so far away for school? There was *nothing* for me here!"

His expression is blank, like he's staring at someone he doesn't even recognize. He slowly sits back down. "Sweetie, you begged to go to Boston. It tore my heart out to have you so far away from us. But Patti and I decided it was time to let you make your own decisions."

"Yeah, and you must be *so* proud," I sniff. "I made some really spectacular decisions, didn't I? And now everyone looks at me like I'm a stupid girl who fell for some obvious trick, when no one understands a damn thing. I never *joined* a cult. Those people were my *friends*. My *only* friends. And the sad thing is I still care about some of them." The tears are pouring now.

Dad's eyes furrow with concern. "Em, that's how they operate. They took advantage of you, and I'm so very sorry you had to go through this. Let me make this right. I will bring them down, but you have to let me protect you in the process."

I desperately want to accept his offer, to believe that he'll take care of me, and forget everything that happened. But I can't stop thinking about the other tapes I brought back and the pain they hold. Or what Meredith said to me after trying to steal my mother's necklace.

I'm terrified, but I know I have to ask him.

"When Mom died, did you question the conclusion?"

The entire room pulses with silence as the question hangs between us. Dad is frozen in shock. "Why in the world would you ask me that?"

"It's just that we never talked about it, you and I. And I—" I pause and look down at my lap. "I remember everything that happened that day." I have to whisper the last two words.

He clears his throat as if he's about to speak, but I cut him off.

"Someone in Italy said something to me. Something horrible. About her death not being an accident. Why would she say—"

A controlled anger crosses his face. "Let me tell you something about those *people*. They would say *anything*, sometimes even the most calculated and hurtful things imaginable, to keep you in. They did the same thing to so many others just to keep them from leaving. Their goal isn't the Bible, Emily. It's to tear members away from their families by turning you against us."

His voice is low, almost too low to hear. "Your mother was the most incredible and fearless woman I've even known, but she couldn't overcome a sudden shift in nature. No one could've survived that undertow. She always thought the warning flags were for other people, but that goes back to long before you were born."

He walks up to me and puts his arm on my shoulder, his eyes glossy with nostalgia. "You are so much like her. And I think the best thing you can do for all of us—including her—is to go out there and be a teenager again. Don't waste another precious minute of your life on things you can't change."

But even as we walk into the living room and sit with Patti in front of the television, pretending life is normal, all I can think about is how I *could* change things. How I could try to fix this entire situation, or at least do my part to help.

How could *anyone* possibly move on like everything is okay? Pretending nothing ever happened.

I have to do something.

Controlled Burn

My mother is at the end of a narrow winding road.

It's a beautiful place where Spanish moss hangs from ancient oak trees and the calm waters of Biloxi Bay sparkle in every direction. There's a bench beside her, and I used to sneak away to read books there when I was in high school. I never told anyone because I knew people would have thought it was odd. They wouldn't understand that it felt comforting just to be near her.

Today, I grip the old pillowcase I filled with the Sin List tapes and sit down on the bench. Every tape is inside, except Kara's "blank" one, which I sealed in a padded envelope with Julia's card on top.

"Please help me. I have no idea what to do," I say into the air.

I watch the water glisten as I wait for a feeling, for some sort of sign. I sit quietly for minutes. The breeze brushes against my face, but it feels just like it always does.

I finally get up and walk to the edge of the water. For me, water has always been a connection to my mother's brief existence. It's where we lost her, and to me, it's where she stayed. Over time, I came to believe she emanated everywhere in that living, glinting mass, watching over me from wherever I happened to be. I picture Kara and my mother way out in the Gulf—past the oil rigs, past the fishermen, beyond the crisscrossing traffic of boats, where no one could ever find them—gracefully threading through countless swells along the deep blue curve of the globe. The animated image makes me smile, but I'm not a little girl anymore. It's like the mermaid. This time I know it isn't real—it's just something to make me feel better about being grounded here in a world without them.

I stand there so long that the tapes become heavy. I switch them to my other hand. Turning away from the water, I walk back to my car and drive away.

The massive pre-bonfire structure looms against an electric horizon. Overlapping swaths of gold and orange and magenta glow like an otherworldly backdrop behind the tranquil blue bay. Summer's mom always told us there's a reason so many artists live here on the Gulf Coast. It's why she stayed. "Nature's inspiration is infinite," she'd always say.

I spot Summer on the beach. She's walking toward our friends, who are working on the bonfire. These are the people who've known me for years. The old me, at least. I fidget with the driver's-side handle, gathering the courage to open the door.

Then I see Alex approach Summer. She high-fives him as if mimicking a surferlike gesture for his benefit, and this makes me laugh. I watch her pull Alex into the group. Just beyond them, the pine-fringed stretch of Deer Island stands between the beach and the wide-open depths of the Gulf of Mexico.

Something like euphoria fills my heart: *I'm really home.*

I watch Alex and Summer work together to fuel the bonfire. As the flames begin flickering up into the sky, everyone disperses toward the shoreline. I grab the pillowcase in the passenger seat and open the door.

Everyone is shin-deep in the water, hanging out and drinking beer, but I walk toward the fire that crackles and snaps under the rising smoke.

I stop close enough to feel its roaring heat as pieces of wood collapse and shift, making the flames surge in unpredictable directions. I toss the knotted pillowcase into the middle and stare deep inside. I watch for a visible change in the color or intensity, but the bonfire consumes it with its steady burn as if nothing had ever been thrown into the flames.

EMILY X-

(continued)

The Kingdom fell in Florida, a place where the sprawling limbs of a live oak obscured the green Ford Taurus parked underneath. The vibration of cicadas had intensified into a morning song through the thick, damp heat. The car doors were closed shut, like the car had been abandoned for a stroll along the water, or an afternoon of fishing, or even a quick illegal exchange, none of which would have been uncommon on this out-of-the-way peninsula. Instead, a lifeless man was slumped forward against the steering wheel, vomit covering both his shirt and the inside of the windshield.

"He was supposed to be on his way to meet us here the day he was found. But he had been . . . *suffering* for a very long time." The recently widowed 40-year-old blonde, who officially goes by Meri now, sat with her bare feet underneath her legs on a white slip-covered couch. The curved wall of windows behind her framed a breathtaking view of the Pacific Ocean. She turned her head to stare at the never-ending sequence of distant waves rolling in, then wiped a tear from her eye with a perfectly manicured hand, before speaking.

When I gently brought up her late husband's miraculous survival in Africa and the reports from the snake dealer I interviewed in Florida, her eyes flickered a hint of defiance. "Will must have thought he was immune to sin. That he was invincible and could do just about anything he wanted. . . ." She twisted her long hair and placed it over her shoulder before lifting her chin. "But that's where he was wrong. The Bible teaches that *no one* is immune to sin, and following the specific steps to salvation as laid out by the Kingdom is the only way."

Her mouth tightened into a bitter smile. "I guess in the end, our poor Will found that out." Her chin quivered as she stood and walked to the glass wall, her white sundress swirling in the breeze of an open window. "We miss him every single day. And it's very difficult to lead this church without him, but I have to find a way to be strong," she said, wrapping her arms around her tiny waist, as if comforting herself, her large wedding ring reflecting the morning sun. "Nothing, and I mean *nothing*, is more important than this calling."

One student member in Boston adamantly insists the Kingdom is a positive force in her life. "A handful of bad apples sinning abroad cannot deter our mission to help young people find the Kingdom," Heather says, offering me a pamphlet. "Through our new leadership in Boston, we will show the world what we really are."

Many former interns, as the Kingdom calls them, disagree with Meri and Heather, saying the cult caused them to drop out of college. The lucky ones have the resources to check into deprogramming facilities to undo the brainwashing they were subjected to during their time in the Kingdom; others find support in a most unexpected place: each other.

"Other ex-members out there can be your greatest allies. It's just a matter of finding them," Andrew says. "Emily is the one who tracked me down. We talk almost every day now—it helps, you know. To make sense of it all, everything that happened to us."

As details of the deadly mission trip to Italy continue to come out, everyone—including those involved—are left questioning: How could this have happened? Some will say it was predatory manipulation. Others will say it was just students unprepared for the real world.

For Emily, things aren't so clear-cut. "I don't have an answer," says Emily. "They made me feel like I belonged, like my existence truly mattered. They made me feel loved. And for most of us, that's enough."

Author's Note

When I moved from a small town in the Bible Belt to New York City in my early twenties, I struggled to talk about the fundamentalist evangelical upbringing I left far behind. I grew up attending church three times per week; chapel and Bible courses were every weekday. We didn't have proms in high school because dancing was one of the many things strictly forbidden. Hell was *not* an abstract place. My post-college friends had questions—understandably so.

"So like the movie *Footloose*?" a few would eventually ask. *Yep. Pretty much.*

Then one said: "Oh, I've heard of that. It's a cult." *Whoa. Wait.*

Cult?

A controversial religious sect that flourished in the nineties was, in fact, an offshoot of the religion in which I was raised. Though my childhood church and the infamous sect shared similar names back then, each kept a wary distance from the other. I remember hearing words like "charismatic" and "multiplying ministries" whispered to describe something controversial happening somewhere else. When journalists began exposing their questionable practices, numerous ex-members came forward to describe the aggressive tactics and controlling behavior that accelerated congregation sizes and contribution numbers. But the movement spread like wildfire in the nineties, as recruiters began targeting college campuses, seeking out students who seemed lonely or out of place. Multiple universities had to ban these groups from their campuses—not for their purported beliefs, but for harassing students.

In 1997, *The Washington Post* reported a typical college student was "likely to be approached at least once by cult recruiters." Many students would never know they'd been approached, as cults frequently change their official campus names to benign titles to slip under the radar.

In my research for this book, I was shocked by how many campus cults have been operating since the nineties and are *still* thriving today. I read numerous heart-wrenching personal accounts by ex-members—brave individuals willing to publicly relive their nightmares so other survivors would know they aren't alone, and to warn potential victims. Each real-life story weighed on my heart. How could people willingly inflict damage on vulnerable students away from their families for the first time?

The more I studied multiple cults, the more I saw a clear answer.

Brainwashing isn't science fiction—it's very real. And it's extremely dangerous. A brainwashed individual can be coerced into believing—or doing—just about anything. Whether coming from a Bible-based cult or the NXIVM "sex cult" from recent headlines, the tactics are nearly identical. High-pressure groups are defined as "cults" by their manipulative and abusive behavior, regardless of which particular doctrine they claim to follow. As *Those Who Prey* shows, any doctrine can be twisted to fit any motive.

One thing I learned by discussing this book's subject matter with strangers and friends is that most people know of someone affected by a cult, and it's often kept secret. Survivors understandably can be reluctant to discuss their experiences for fear of stigmatization. Some worry people may think they weren't smart or savvy enough to recognize the signs. But in reality, this couldn't be further from the truth.

As the saying goes, no one "joins" a cult. Seeking a genuine connection can make anyone vulnerable to those trained to prey on others. Cults also pretend to be one thing—promising to change your life for the better—and they rarely show their true colors until you're in way too deep to easily walk away.

Finding a way through the dim labyrinth of fear and anxiety can seem impossible, but I hope Emily's journey in *Those Who Prey* will illuminate a path. Although the characters, situations, and cult in the book are purely fictional, the general recruiting tactics are realistic and still used by many cults today.

I wanted this book to show *how* this happens. How it could happen to *anyone*.

Escaping a repressive situation can be truly scary; however, unflinching strength and a deep capacity for empathy can be found on the other side.

If you or a loved one is struggling with cult trauma, or if you simply want to learn more about cults from a reliable resource, the International Cultic Studies Association is a solid starting point: icsahome.com.

Acknowledgments

Getting a book ready for publication requires more sets of eyes and hands than I ever imagined. I'd like to thank the following people who helped me get this manuscript ready to fly out into the world.

Shannon Hassan, my amazing agent who believed in this book from our first conversation—for her keen editorial eye and steady approach that led to my dream publisher. The entire team at Marsal Lyon Literary Agency.

Alex Borbolla, my brilliant editor, who gives the perfect insight with a touch of humor and lots of dog pics. Working with you is an absolute joy! Debra Sfetsios-Conover for designing such a compelling cover for this book. And Adams Carvalho, whose haunting cover image still makes me stare in awe. Thank you also to Clare McGlade, Tatyana Rosalia,

Crystal Velasquez, Chantal Gersch, and the sales and marketing team at Simon Teen. To the entire Atheneum family: I'm *so* incredibly proud to be part of your team!

It's difficult to pinpoint the moments that lead to a writing career as they are happening in real time. But when you look back, you can see it so clearly.

I'm incredibly grateful for the following:

Friends from the SoHo days at Jumbo Pictures: Watching all of you achieve your creative dreams over the years has been a huge source of inspiration to me. Ken Scarborough for the museum walks and bookish talks amid the crisscrossing streets and avenues that cracked open my creative brain. Al and Alysoun for the coolest adventures. Scott and Michelle Fellows for all the fried eggs!

The University of Mississippi Department of English—a place where I finally began to hear my voice and develop it on the page. Donna Ladd at *Jackson Free Press* for helping me learn to "shut up and write" while giving me a place to rave about books early on. Thank you also to all the magazine editors who supported my work over the years.

Women of Words, the Gulf Coast writing group who kept me going when a hectic life almost kept me from writing: Valerie Winn, Faith Garbin, Cynthia Tanner, Bev Blasingame. And Mary Ann O'Gorman, a kick-ass critique partner, dear friend, and fabulous fairy godmother.

Those who offered feedback and encouragement along the way: Matthew Pitt, Jordan Sanderson, Shelley Ingram,

Barbara Lee, Tara Skelton, Javier Gómez, and so many other colleagues and friends. Marc Poole for letting me sneak into his art history class, and Curtis Houston with Wild Woods Creative for the graphic design expertise.

The writing community, especially Liz Lawson, Tanya Guerrero, Laura Taylor Namey, and Eva V. Gibson for their specific advice and constant shout-outs. And Shannon Takaoka, debut pal and critique partner extraordinaire. The Roaring 20s and Class of 2K20 Books debut groups for the virtual camaraderie.

Kristen Brandt and the Mississippi Arts Commission for supporting this book's journey through the publication process. And the independent bookstores throughout our state for consistently lighting the way forward, even during the most uncertain times.

My mom and dad, who always encouraged me to follow my dreams, even when those dreams were far-flung and a bit far-fetched for a small-town girl from Arkansas.

Dr. Ann Brown, who called me into her office after reading my undergraduate essay to tell me I should consider a career in creative writing. I didn't fully process the suggestion at the time, but now I think about this a lot and never hesitate to tell my own undergraduate students the same thing every time I run across a piece of writing that lights a flame in my heart.

My brother Randy for being the best tour guide ever. Amy Pruett Hernandez, Emily Dwight, and friends who studied abroad with me—there's nothing better than a travel buddy with a Eurail pass, a passion for art, and a sense of adventure.

Anne Daniel and Kimberley King Clearwater, for the lifelong support system. All the friends and family members who encouraged me to stick with this path.

The readers of this story who may recognize similarities from their own personal journeys.